VARSITY PROPERTY

BWWM Dark Hockey Romance

LAGUNA GROVE VIPERS
BOOK III

JAMILA JASPER

ISBN: 979-8-3303-3677-7

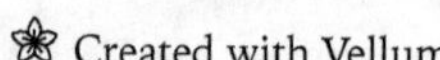 Created with Vellum

DESCRIPTION

You're serving your true purpose, Raven. Get used to it.
She agreed to help a friend and ended up here…
Contracted to Dustin Rathbone, a sociopathic campus
hockey player whose brute instincts make him want to use
her supple body *in every way*.
<u>**Dustin is fifteen times hotter than he is intelligent.**</u>
And Raven's a straight A student, consistently at the top
of the class.
Maybe there's a way for her to buy her freedom…

Disclaimer: Chapter #1 contains slight changes from the
preview chapter in Varsity House Pet, so don't skip it!

CONTENT AWARENESS

This is a dark romance with themes that some readers may find potentially triggering including mentions of violence, racism, foul language, mentions of sexual assault and other topics suitable for adult readers.

DUSTIN RATHBONE'S FUTURE PLANS FOR THE ACQUISITION OF HIS PERFECT WOMAN

DUSTIN

I'm broken. 6 years ago, I had to choose whether I would let the awful shit destroy me or whether I would claw my way out of that weak fucking mess and find myself again. I know who I am. Dustin Rathbone. Strength. That's what life is all about, separating the strong from the weak. I won't ever let someone make me feel weak again. I will never give up control to anyone again.

6 years ago, I chose strength. I chose the ice. Skating saved me when nothing else could. I chose my brothers over letting the pain snap me in pieces and I made it to a top tier hockey college. I'm living my dream and I'm finally at peace with what happened. Finally.

After high school, I found my real brothers— the Vipers— this perfect outlet for my outrage. I had healing to do. I found myself in punches and hard checks. I found women, each one more gorgeous than the last. In six years, nothing could change me. Nothing could give me purpose… until her.

I'll never forget the first time I saw her walking into the English department with a pair of thick black glasses and a stack of books cradled precariously in her grasp. Nerd. That was my first thought. My second thought was less of a thought and more of a physical reaction. Hard. She never knew I was watching.

She still doesn't know I'm watching — or how long I've been watching. I don't want to stop. I want to keep her. To own her. Soon.

I promised myself I wouldn't let it get this far. I promised myself I'd stop after finding her online, after the lies, the hiding, the secrets, the fake identities, the fishing for information I could use.

I promised myself I'd confess the truth. But I can't stop. I enjoy living in the shadows and I don't want to come out. It's safe in the shadows. It's where monsters like me belong. It's where we feel safe.

I surround myself with monsters — creatures like me — snakes, spiders, cockroaches, skinks. Creatures that were never meant to fit in. I can fake it well enough. I've practiced the facial expressions, the reactions I'm supposed to have. I've practiced emotions hundreds of times so that I can fit in, get chicks, make my friends think I'm normal. I know I'm far from normal.

I haven't really felt anything in six years — not since before I turned eighteen. I'm dead inside and the only thing that brings me any pleasure is causing someone else's pain. That's why I need to keep my distance from her. I know I'll only hurt her because I desperately want to hurt her. Letting her in to my fucked up life would destroy my angel.

Every day, I fight this urge to break her and every day I know I get closer to losing the battle.

I want her.

She's nothing like the women I used to try to fix my shit. She's not my hot thirty-year-old neighbor with her collection of XL dildos and a traveling husband. She's not a pair of drunken sorority chicks with low self-esteem. She's nothing like any of the bimbos I've used to salve my pain.

I'm losing control around her. I don't know what I'll do next. I just know that I've already gone too far and if I let myself take another step towards her, I'm going to fuck her up. I'm going to ruin her life.

Raven Rose.

After watching her read for an hour, I approach her window from my hiding spot. Fuck. I've already burned through two joints. I'm properly toasted and relaxed enough that all my inhibitions have vanished. It's easy to lose myself watching her. Now, I'm close enough to see her, close enough to feel my heart race as I watch, but hidden just enough that she can't see me watching. She'll never know.

I unlock my phone and message her from Brett's profile. Brett. She has no clue that Brett McClure doesn't exist — that it's me, hiding behind a profile, collecting her secrets and using them to my advantage. I don't know what compels me to be like this.

Brett: I'm still sorry I didn't show up. I was nervous.

She waits a few seconds before looking at her phone. I don't want to wait. I've been patient, damn it. I want her to do something. I want her to respond. Discomfort surges through me. She's only reading. Why can't she put down that book and pay attention to me?

Eventually, she can't ignore the powerful tug of her cellphone. None of us can, really.

Raven: You let me down again. I'm done, Brett.

Something catches in my throat. This is the third time she's tried to end our friendship. It's my fault. I keep chickening out. This time, my finger hovers over the keys, and I weigh my words. If I do this, I'll commit to setting my plan in motion. I'm great at planning. My plans helped

Cole land Kya Ambrose, the annoying mouthy feminist he got hooked on. My plans also helped my boy Jayce get Makeba, the tall chick from his physics class.

I can get Raven Rose... Even if she ignores me. Even if her friends want nothing to do with me. I want her, so I'll fucking have her. I just need patience.

Brett: I understand. I won't contact you again.

She blocks my account. Fuck. What was I thinking? I won't contact her again?

It's a fucking lie and I know it. Raven won't know that. I may leave Brett McClure behind, but I'm definitely contacting her again. I want her. Once she sets her phone down, she strips her hoodie off. My breath catches. She wasn't wearing anything under that hoodie. No bra. Her tits are gorgeous. I hope she doesn't walk over and close the blinds, ruining my fucking view.

If her roommate comes in, I'm going to lose it. Hopefully, her roommate Kya is back at the hockey house straddling my teammate. Lucky guy.

I want a woman of my own. I want her.

Raven... She turns away from the window to grab a t-shirt, denying me a view of her breasts. Her tits turn me on so much. I told my teammate Jayce Clutterbuck I was on the hunt, and I meant it. Raven's my prey and she doesn't even know it yet. I've toyed with her slowly. Teased her. I finally have all the information I need to seal the deal when I finally get my hands on her. I've spent a long time preparing for this.

Hunting women is like hunting anything else. You need patience. Raven turns around bare-breasted and I nearly cum in my pants. Her nipples are large and dark against her dark-copper skin. She glows. My cock tents my forest green Laguna Grove sweatpants and the urge to touch myself heightens. I just want her to touch her tits. Play with them a little. I want to put my tongue in places she'd never let me go. She doesn't have a clue what she does to me. She doesn't have a clue that she's broken my brain and pulled this out of me. My tongue teases my lower lip and I keep wishing she'll do something unexpected, like touch her tits or push her hands into her panties and play with herself for me. My cock wants to burst.

She slips into that t-shirt and my little show ends. Fuck.

She cracks open a book, and it's like the world vanishes to her. Seriously. I stand outside her window for 35 minutes before she gets up again, just watching the way she twirls those braids around her finger or how her tongue grazes her lower lip when she gets to a good part in her story. It's Friday night and she's just here... in her bed... reading. She fascinates me.

I don't think there are any chicks like this at Laguna Grove. When she returns to her bed, I notice she has something in her hand. What the fuck is that? I lean in, but I still can't make it out. I'll have to get closer to the window if I want to see, but that means I risk getting caught.

When has she ever caught me? I've done this as often as I could this semester. We're still in hockey preseason and there's nothing better to do than to hunt down the ones that got away. Raven. It's been a year since we first met – 377 days exactly. I've had other women in my bed since then – lots of other women. But there's one fantasy I can't get out of my head. Maybe it's how she looked that first night when she walked into Pesthouse with her friends. Young. Happy. Pure.

She reminds me I used to be innocent. She reminds me I used to be weak. I want to have her. I want to break that innocence. I don't even have a good reason. There's something about her that gets my cock going, that makes me want to climb through that fucking window and take the woman I've been watching for such a long time. She climbs into her bed and that book opens right back up.

Christ. Is she just going to read that thing all night? I don't know how she can stand it.

I can't help myself. I shuffle closer to the window. I know I'm taking it too far. I know what I'll do if I keep going with this fantasy. I know she doesn't lock her windows. My breath catches as I nearly trip. Luckily, I'm not that much of a stupid fuck. I lean against her window and... oh. She slides her hand holding that thing between her thighs and it's pretty obvious what it is. I'm so close to the window that my breath fogs up the glass. I don't even care that she might notice. That thing is a vibrator.

A fucking vibrator. She's reading a book and using a vibrator. This chick loves reading so much she's literally flicking the bean to words. I can't stop myself. My hand slides into my pants and grips my hard cock. Fuck. He feels even bigger than normal today. Her back arches slightly as she gets that thing in a delightful spot, and then she squirms. I can almost feel her pleasure as I watch through the window. Her body moves so fucking beautifully as she teases her cunt.

I barely stroke myself before I cum hard. Fuck. All she did was squirm in her bed with a piece of plastic between her legs and I lose control. I can't handle being near her. I'm too fucked up.

The worst part is, this isn't the first time this has happened. Not the vibrator thing. Sometimes it's just the way she holds her pencil while scribbling her homework. Sometimes it's those nerdy fucking glasses. I keep telling myself I'll stop doing this. I haven't had sex with a woman since July. I can't have sex with anyone else when I can stand here and touch myself thinking about her.

I'm broken.

I don't know how much longer I can stand this. I don't know how much longer I can go without feeling her skin beneath mine. If this is me holding back, I'm totally fucked when I let go with her. I'm going to break her too.

Maybe I have already broken her. I don't know. All I know is that I need to clean myself up and prepare for phase 2 of my plan, which doesn't involve cumming in my pants while staring at a woman through a piece of glass.

My plan involves cumming inside Raven.

RAVEN'S RECIPE FOR A PERFECT FRIDAY NIGHT

RAVEN

Are you the only one of your friends single on a Friday night? Welcome to the club. Sophomore year was supposed to be different, but for me, it's worse. Both my friends have boyfriends — hockey players who have a packed social calendar — and it's really awkward to be the fifth wheel. Three wheels make a tricycle, but five wheels are just awkward.

It's not like I don't enjoy my solitude. That's when I get to read, learn about myself, rub jojoba oil on my feet and dig into my self-care. Still, I expected sophomore year to be filled with the unexpected. I wanted drama... maybe even a flicker of romance.

The only "romance" in my life sits stacked on my desk in order of preference.

With these seventeen books from the college library stacked on my desk, I have a "to be read" list that grows faster than my natural hair in braids.

I curl up in bed with Kya's black cashmere hoodie on, pulling out my favorite vintage romance novel from the stack. The copy I have at home I got from a church sale, but the cover on this edition is perfect. It's one of those vintage water color covers you can't find anywhere anymore — not even at church sales.

The story is an absolutely filthy bodice ripper with a violent kidnapper, a white woman who loves to scream, and it's set in the Scottish moors. It's so good. I change into a t-shirt and climb into bed with "old faithful".

Romance novels are better than having a boyfriend, honestly. I just need to remember that when I feel all weird and sad.

I turn the page to my favorite part – of course, I've read this book like a hundred times – and as our dastardly protagonist rips our heroine's pantaloons off, my phone buzzes. Shit… it's Sydney. Off goes my vibrator. My home girl calls me once a week, but I thought she had canceled our phone call tonight. Damn. I shuffle in bed, searching for my buzzing phone.

Oh, well. My book can wait. Unlike an actual boyfriend, a book boyfriend can come back to life and make you cum whenever you need it.

I answer the phone and try to sound normal. "Hey, Syd."

Sydney doesn't notice my breathless tone, and she immediately launches into her sentence without a greeting.

"Raven! I can't believe I got you on the phone," Sydney says, gasping like she just ran a mile. "Don't you have a date tonight?"

Sydney knows I don't date.

"No."

Sydney laughs.

"I just got back from a crazy night. Let me tell you all about it."

"Okay."

I swing my legs back and forth as Sydney regales me with her exciting stories from the local state university in our town. She likes reminding me it's my fault I'm not hooking up in a basement somewhere because I go to school around a bunch of white kids. I've explained several times that Laguna Grove has the best English program in the country. It's a privilege to be here for my education.

"Anyway," Sydney says. "He takes me upstairs and his roommate is like... right there. So in the end, I guess I had no choice but to get with both of them. He didn't know, though. I hope he doesn't find out."

"Wait, you slept with his roommate too?"

"After I was done with him. Girl, college is a blast!"

My stomach tightens. I don't want to seem lame or anything, but I never want to hook up with two guys in one night, especially not roommates.

"Why are you so quiet?" Sydney says, sounding a little frustrated.

"It's nothing."

"You're judging me, aren't you?"

"No! I'm just... surprised. I thought you were all in with Khalil."

And she cheated on him. With his roommate.

"Okay, but his roommate had a big one. I mean... bigger than nine inches big."

"Wow."

"You're only acting like this because you're still a virgin," Sydney proclaims. "Just give it up already. Get one of those white guys to give it to you good."

"Sydney..."

Sydney sighs and seems to let it go. I don't want to 'just give it up already', but I don't want Sydney to think I'm judging her either.

"I'm just playing, girl. I know you're focused on your studies," she says.

I breathe a sigh of relief that she's letting this go on her own.

"Yeah. Thanks."

Sydney laughs. "Girl, you are such a prude. You just need a guy to fuck you good."

"Is that why you called?"

"No," Sydney says with a teasing tone. "I have valuable information for you."

"Oh. Great."

"It's about your pussy."

"Um…"

"Aunty Shanida had a dream about you."

I groan. Aunty Shanida is one of our church aunties who is always having a dream about who is going to find a man, or whose man will cheat on them, or who will never find a man, or whose man will have a baby by someone else. She claims her dreams are prophetic, but I just think she enjoys gossiping with everybody and that's how she gets the tea — pure trickery.

"Do I even want to know what the dream was about? And what my pussy has to do with it?"

I can't believe I'm saying those words out loud, but that's what being friends with Sydney is like. I've known her since we were kids going to church camp together. I don't know if she would get along with Kya and Makeba, but she's one of my oldest friends.

"We prayed on it," Sydney says. "Everybody in Bible study heard the news about what's coming for you…"

I grimace, grateful that Sydney can't see me. The last thing I want is a group of old women praying for my pussy. It's way too embarrassing, which means my mama probably had something to do with it.

I ask tentatively, even if I know the answer. "With my mama there?"

"The spirit took her," Sydney replies somberly. The spirit is always taking my mama and making her writhe on the floor of the church. I think it's because her sugar's low and she's in denial, but I keep that to myself since I don't particularly like being a grown woman dodging punches from my mama.

"Great. Now my mom is speaking in tongues because my romantic situation is that desperate. Doesn't she know how hard it is to find a decent guy on this campus? It's a tiny college in Cracker McCrackerville."

Sydney snickers at my comment about Laguna Grove, but she's too excited about this dream to rub in how much more fun she's having in college (thank goodness).

"Girl, let me tell you the dream," Sydney says. "It's a real prophecy. If you go out there this weekend, you're going to meet the chocolate king of your dreams."

Now this prophecy is starting to sound like something worth my damn time… Visions of a young Morris Chestnut dance in my head and my thighs throb.

"A chocolate king? Taller than six feet?"

I wander over to my window and notice there's something drawn on it. A heart in fog with two words. NICE CUNT. I try to wipe it off, but it's on the other side of the window. What the fuck?

"Sydney… hold on…"

"What's going on?"

"Nothing…"

I press my face against the window, but there's nobody out there. I close my blinds. It was probably some dumb prank. Kids at this school are gross.

"Sorry, Sydney. Continue."

"Oh, yes. And he's going to have a job, and a new Jaguar, and he's bald-headed with brown eyes."

"Bald-headed?! Sydney, I'm nineteen. I don't want a bald-headed man."

"Girl, he goes to church! Every Sunday…"

I don't even go to church every Sunday. Suddenly, this prophesied chocolate king is sounding like he's going to be a problem if he's going to try dragging my ass to church and away from my precious reading spot.

"Is he at least going to be fine as hell?"

"Yeah, girl! Like a young Tyrese… all chocolate and sexy… Ain't that exciting?"

"I don't think anyone like that even goes to Laguna Grove."

"Y'all got black men," Sydney says. "I know y'all do."

Yeah, and they all like white girls. None of them would even look twice at me. They think all black women are thirsty too. I asked Jarrod French for the homework assignment after I missed a creative writing class once, and he told me he wasn't interested in dating black women. Just like that. I would have never even considered dating his peanut-headed ass, anyway.

"Sure. We got black men. Maybe there's hope," I offer weakly, even if the situation is beyond hopeless.

"Act now, Raven. The prophecy is going to happen SOON, maybe even this weekend. That's why I called you."

"This weekend? Are you sure? I don't have any plans. I'm in sweatpants. It's Friday night."

"Then get out of sweatpants, girl, because –

"Hold on," I interrupt. "Sydney, someone's knocking on my door. Can I call you back?"

"Sure thing! Get all dolled up and go out somewhere. You'll meet him. I know it. Get laid, Raven. Get laid."

"I'll call you back."

I hang up, unclear if I'll really call Sydney back or not. I know she cares about my love life, but with all my romance novels and the flaky guys I talk to online, I have plenty of men to stimulate my imagination. At least the guys in romance novels aren't total disappointments.

I throw on a hoodie and open the front door to my bedroom, which turns out to be a complete mistake.

In front of my bedroom door, there's a note on the ground and a red rose. Weird. I pick up the rose and then the note, heading into the room I share with Kya. I shut the door behind me before reading the note.

Dear Raven,
I've been watching you & soon you'll be mine.
Secret Admirer

I throw my door open one last time and glance up and down the hallway again. After the incident last semester, our dorms are more secure than ever before. No one can get in here without their student ID, so whoever left this note attends Laguna Grove.

"Hello?"

There's no one there. Someone left the note, knocked on my door and then booked it. Weird. I shut my door again and return to giving the note another close examination. It's a little creepy for a note from a secret admirer. 'Soon you'll be mine' sounds like something you say right before you're about to kidnap someone. Creepy.

I text Kya and Makeba a picture of the note. I want to hear what my homegirls think about this one. It's not the first 'secret admirer' note I've received. Kya thinks it's a prank. Makeba thinks it's some guy in my poetry class. She's right – poetry guys do love writing and they can be romantic. But I don't know if these notes are romantic or threatening.

'Soon you'll be mine' feels threatening.

I walk back over to my window and open my blinds again to see if I notice anyone leaving the building. Someone smudged the heart out and drew something new over it. It's just one word, but it's enough to chill me.

Soon. Nausea knots my stomach. Who the hell is doing this?

✲ 3 ✲

A MAN WITH A PLAN

DUSTIN

"I need you to do me a favor, Cole."

I skate around Seabrook, digging my skates into the ice to turn as he launches a shot into the goal. He suspects me — as usual. I can work with that. It's easy to get people to do what you want as long as you understand them. Cole is easier to read than he thinks. He shoots again and swerves around me suspiciously, blond hair flowing from beneath his helmet.

"I hate when you ask me for favors," he groans. "What?"

His eyes are ice with a little crinkle around them. Kya's probably been getting on his ass about something or other, making him testy.

He won't take too kindly to me asking for too much. But I need him to do this for me, so I need to play it cool and act casual. I need to be the guy people think I am. Dangerous.

"I need to talk to Raven."

I watch him for the smallest hints of a change in his body language. Cole is the more transparent of my friends. He wears his emotions right on his sleeve, making him simple to manipulate when necessary. I don't enjoy manipulation, I'm not that much of a creep. Sometimes, manipulation simply better serves my purpose.

Will he do what I want, or do I need to up the ante?

"Kya's roommate? Why?" Cole raises his eyebrow and pulls his shoulders in. See what I said? He's fucking suspicious.

Worse than that, Cole asks too many fucking questions.

"You don't need to know that."

He bristles with frustration. I hit a corner shot and when the puck bounces back against the back of the net, I pass it to our team captain. One more semester and he's out of here. I'm going to miss that motherfucker when he's finally sucked into the world of professional hockey, far as fuck away from me and my bullshit. What the fuck will I get into without Cole to keep me in line?

"Okay," he answers reluctantly. "What do you want?"

I need to calm down and stop acting so fucking suspicious. It's normal to like a girl. Well, normal for normal people and a big fucking problem for me. If I act normal, Cole will let his guard down... eventually.

I clear my throat and answer him crisply and confidently. "Make sure Raven's at the party tonight."

"You don't need me for that," Cole says, working on a few stick tricks as he answers. "It's our first party back and my last first party. Kya's bringing her entire crew. 100% chance she'll be with them."

Cole. He's the heart of our team. He's half the fun in playing and he keeps us all on our toes. Out of all the friends I've made throughout my years playing hockey, Cole and Jayce are realer than anyone else. I need assurances, but this might be good enough. Fucking Cole... how am I going to get along without this motherfucker?

"We'll miss you when you leave, man."

My past may have broken me, but I'm not a liar. I can't imagine the team without Seabrook keeping us assholes on our toes. He's kept me from so many nights in jail, I've lost count. He's stopped me from punching Jayce's lights out and from torturing my conquests with tarantulas. Cole is the closest thing I have to a moral compass.

When he's gone, it'll be up to me to make sure our hockey team keeps winning games and bagging hotties and raising hell out here. But without him, who knows how far I'll take things.

"I'm heading to Boston this weekend for some pre-training. Not sure I'm going to make it through school the whole semester."

"Seriously, brah?"

Cole nods. "The dean thinks I can handle doing some classes online. I didn't want to fuck with the team's energy."

"I wish I knew earlier…"

My ears burn. I don't want to lose either of my best friends. It's bad enough they have girlfriends now and I always have to be the fifth fucking wheel.

It won't get better when Cole leaves, and it seems like he won't be here long. Shit. Who knows what the fuck I'll get into without Cole to keep me in line? No worries, raising hell at Laguna Grove is my specialty. I'll get into something…

"I'm only here to move Kya in and support the team. Training starts soon."

Cole skates around me and we toss the puck back and forth with sharp slaps for a few minutes. I'm too fucked up by the news to say anything. By the time the proper season starts, we'll need a new captain.

"Maybe there's a jersey with your name on it," Cole says with a grin. I half-smile back.

He knows I'm not pro-hockey material. I'm rich enough to make the team, that's not the problem. I have the family name and the family money and that can buy you the training you need to build any gaps in skills. The game isn't the problem, it's my character that's fucked up.

I won't stop drugs. I won't stop smoking weed. I love playing and I'm fucking good, but I don't have the dedication to look after anyone but myself. I'm in this for the chicks, the attention, the fights that give you the sickest adrenaline rush – and don't forget the fucking parties. The best part of hockey is the seedy underbelly, and I love being the monster under the bridge.

Cole knows that, but he doesn't stop trying to improve me and dig out some kind of hero beneath the surface. He's like a big brother that way, but Dustin Rathbone has never been the hero in anyone's story. I'm comfortable being the villain. Anything is better than being the victim.

"Going pro. Not sure it's for me. But who knows?" I answer, trying to sound like I'm letting his lecture sink in. Nothing gets into me anymore. Nothing. I know Cole cares about me, and a part of me cares about him. Another part of me would sell him out for an extra ounce. It's just the way I broke when I fell.

"I'll get her to the party. But don't do anything I wouldn't do, okay? Talk to her."

He knows I have a 'thing' for Raven because of a stupid drunken confession one night. He just doesn't know how far I've gone with my obsession and how far I plan to go after tonight.

I could laugh at Cole giving me advice about chicks. Talk to her? Whatever happened to 'put the whole dick in her'? He seriously needs to check himself.

He must have forgotten that I wrote the book on picking up hot Laguna Grove chicks. Get the whole dick in her. That was my line. How quickly even your friends forget your brilliant ideas. I don't need Cole's help with women. I know exactly what I need to do to keep Raven. I only need to lure her to my lair first.

"Don't worry, Cole. I'll talk to her like a normal guy."

Cole's golden eyebrow raises. "Not *like* a normal guy. Be a normal guy."

He knows me too fucking well, but he still can't read my mind. Thank goodness.

I smile. I know he notices that my eyes never match the upward curve of my lips, but he never acknowledges it.

"Got it, brah. Nothing to worry about."

He's worried, but he's too scared to push me. Everyone's too scared to push me. My teammate Jayce has a reputation for his temper, but my anger burns differently. My rage burns cold and eviscerates everything in its path. Every guy on the team has seen me lose it just once. I lost control. I can't afford to do that anymore. I don't want people learning what happened to me and how I lost the ability to feel anything – especially compassion.

I only care about getting what I want and making sure the people around me work towards my goals. If someone doesn't have a use in my life, I eliminate them. I forget about them. Cole always has his uses, but now he has the most important use to me: bringing me Raven.

He's the perfect lure for an unsuspecting sophomore, drunk with her sense of experience after surviving a year of college. Cole's the smiling blond reformed-asshole boyfriend. They'll never suspect anything if he makes it clear he wants Raven's presence. He's the good guy.

I promised her I would see her soon, didn't I? What kind of man goes back on a promise? Just thinking about that night gives me a semi. I went too far, but a part of me feels like I didn't go far enough. I won't make the mistake of denying myself a reward tonight.

With Cole's partial agreement to help me, I have six and a half hours to prepare the environment and documents I need for my plan. I need a prison and I need a trap. Six and a half hours and the girl belongs to me.

Tonight's party has a masquerade theme. My idea. No one suspects anything because I make it seem like Jayce Clutterbuck's idea. I'm the one who loves anonymity, secrecy and darkness – and tonight I need all three to secure my objective.

I love my best friend, but man, is it easy to plant ideas in his head. I'm on pins all day through classes. I forget to stop myself from staring a few times in my new philosophy class. It's a junior level course, but somehow Makeba Winston's in it and she squirms so much beneath my stare.

Her fear delights me, which only makes me stare harder to study every expression of discomfort. By the time our class ends, she scurries away with her head down, desperately avoiding my gaze.

I forget how staring makes me seem less human.

I've always scared the crap out of her and my staring just makes it worse. I want to stop, but I can't. Fear could have killed me, but I turned it into an aphrodisiac instead. That feels much better than the alternative.

I just hope Makeba doesn't warn Raven against coming tonight when I slip into my black suit and take minimal measures to disguise my identity. I'll have darkness on my side. It's not a real Pesthouse party without the throb of rave music and dungeon levels of darkness.

Under the red light in my bedroom that keeps my menagerie of pet reptiles in 'night mode', I take a while to find the mask. It's small and simple, but it's enough that I look like every other dick hockey player at Laguna Grove, both anonymous and invisible. Perfect.

I don't worry about Raven's mask or what she might wear. She won't ever be invisible to me, not even in a crowd.

I don't bother helping set up the party this time. I have too much to get done and not enough time to do it. It's feeding day for Ovie and I got him a guinea pig. My teammates and housemates hate when I feed Ovie large prey, but if he got more large prey, he wouldn't escape so much… would you Ovie? I run my fingers over his enclosure and open the latch. I open the box and tip the frightened creature into the cage.

Ovie doesn't move at first, but he stiffens with that predatory awareness of what just entered his oversized enclosure. *He's got his own dorm in there.* I shut the top and plant myself on the stool in front of his enclosure with a stiff drink in my hand.

I'll need plenty of whiskey to get through tonight without completely losing control. Despite the cages and enclosures, I keep my room pristine. I clean daily with harsh chemicals so there's minimal scent. I hate potent smells and filth. Even my cologne just smells clean. Raven will understand once she's here how I expect her to keep things once I have her.

The guinea pig squeaks its ass off like that's going to change its fate. *Squeak, squeak, you poor fucker.* He just drew the shit cards in life. That's how it works. It doesn't matter if you're a rich kid or a guinea pig. Shit just happens. You decide how to deal with whatever tries to break you. I polish off my flask and Ovie hasn't moved on the guinea pig.

If I didn't know any better, I would say he takes pleasure in the scent of terror emanating from the creature. He denies himself to make the pleasure greater. Is there any way Ovie's that smart? I don't know, but Ovie's getting pretty big. I don't know if a guinea pig will satisfy him much longer. I didn't think they were supposed to get this big... Weird.

I tap my fingers on the side of the glass as Ovie moves his head toward the creature. Wake up, Ovie. Time to eat…

Here we go. Not much time until his feeding response. More whiskey makes watching the messy scene better. I tip more liquor down my throat and guess the exact moment Ovie lunges.

3… 2… 1…

Pain. The animal squeaks in pain until its body stills and Ovie's gullet forces itself open. There's something cathartic about watching him feed and watching him take another animal's life. It feels fucking great.

Jayce: Get downstairs, you sick fuck. Party's on.

Fucking Jayce. He's right. The party's on, and I have other responsibilities to attend to now. Tomorrow, I feed Big Sexy and Pastrnak, my tarantulas. But Ovie's feeding night is always my favorite. Good night, Ovie. I double check the latch on the cage when I leave my bedroom, my heart throbbing with anticipation. I can't wait another minute longer than necessary to have her.

I like the loud throbbing party speakers and a good fucking bass line. It's so loud that I can't hear myself think and I fucking love it. Creeps prefer any conditions that make it easy to remain invisible. I don't have to worry about anyone noticing me at a Pesthouse party if I want to blend in. Every guy on the hockey team stands over six feet tall, so I can look like Barkov, Foote, or anyone else. Chicks might find me in a crowd under normal conditions, but with my mask, I can lurk around the edges and avoid detection from every damn lacrosse or field hockey biddy who wants a shot.

I don't want anything shallow and temporary anymore. If Cole did his job, Raven should be here soon with her band of sophomore chicks. I won't have to lurk in the shadows or wait for her to wander into my bedroom looking for the bathroom. I won't deny myself the satisfaction of the hunt.

Men love the chase, hockey players need it. Something about the game we love hardens our wiring that way. The woman I want is always the one who runs away – and no one ran faster than Raven Rose the first night we met.

I just need to stay away from Kya and Makeba. Raven's friends have better instincts than anyone and even if they don't know what I'm planning, they're the only chicks who eye me with suspicion instead of awe. My charms never worked the way I intended on Makeba and Kya... Well, she's just impossible.

I don't have Cole or Jayce's magic over them. I don't need to win them over – I only need to avoid them.

Raven's my prize tonight, and I'll get my hands on her... soon.

I get Cole to pump the keg and pour me a red cup of foamy, shitty beer. It's gone in a few seconds. Tastes like water. I'll need a hell of a lot more alcohol in me if I'm going to pull this off. I'll need to be numb when she fights back, so I can keep a cool head and numb out when she scratches me or tries to poke my eyes out. Weed would help but that would give me away in a second. I hate to admit I have a reputation, but with weed, I definitely do.

After half an hour of pretending to give a shit about Katie Casanova's lacrosse bruises, I smell Raven's perfume. I know every perfume in her collection. She wears Yves St. Laurent Opium to school because it makes her feel grown up. On the weekends, she wears Clinique Happy because my sweet Raven thinks positive vibes will help her find her dream man. Tonight, she wears her party perfume. Gucci Bloom. I smell her the way Ovie smells fear on his prey.

I turn my head as far as it can go to catch my first glimpse of her. My body responds immediately, my shoulders tightening and my cock sprouting a semi. Fuck, she looks perfect.

She isn't afraid of anything tonight. I can tell from her sexy black high heels, the cute knots in her long braids, and that fucking dress. The thought of any other man seeing her in that dress besides me makes me want to run over to her and unceremoniously drag her upstairs like a caveman.

She struts over to the bar with her friends chattering excitedly and then she uses her impressive new height to reach her arm over the crowd of freshmen to get beer for her friends. She laughs at something Makeba says, highlighting the gorgeous dimple in her copper cheek. Everything about her awakens my cock.

I sneak around the kitchen out of her view so I can keep watching behind the Pesthouse kitchen island. Her handmade gold mask has large pink feathers around the eyes, the same pink as the silk pink dress that hugs her curves. She probably isn't wearing a bra under that thing. Raven weighs approximately 165 lbs with curves in all the right places. Her braids graze her waist, and that silk dress moves with her in a way that makes my cock stiffen instantly. This is the last time I watch her without touching her.

She doesn't know how much it kills me not to be close to her. I spend so much time watching her, it's like a part of me forgets we're not together and she's barely aware of my existence. Her best friends make their opinions about my reputation clear. I'm a creep, a player, a bastard, a dick, a douche bag. I've heard these insults straight from Kya's eternally moving mouth. The rumors make Raven ignore me. I hate that she doesn't see me.

Most women on this campus can't ignore me, or they wouldn't dare. It's the eyes, some say. Others report the best part of me hangs between my legs. I don't know how Raven acts like I'm invisible. She sucks my breath away without knowing it, and I can't fucking stand it. She won't talk to me because of her friends. She won't look at me. I have to hide in the shadows when I deserve to have her in my bed.

I need to separate her from the herd. That dumbass Canadian sophomore Logan Hargreaves stumbles past me just when I need him. I grip his forearm before he can lunge for the fridge and take out that stupid fucking leftover poutine I already ate earlier.

"Hey. You know Raven Rose?"

I tighten my wrap on his forearm. I can smell how fucking drunk he is, which means he'll be good for what I need. I know everyone in Raven's classes, so if this little shit lies about knowing her to me, I'll arrange a meeting with Big Sexy that he won't forget.

"Y-yes."

Perfect. Drunk and slurring, Logan smells like he's thrown up twice. His shirt has a mysterious dark stain on it and there's a little dab of white powder beneath his right nostril. Fucking degenerate. He probably won't remember this in the morning, which suits me well.

"Get Raven alone in this hallway. Ten minutes or I'll kick your ass."

"Yeah. Whatever man."

He attempts to yank his arm away, but finds the task impossible. He's still a kid with a lot of growing to do on the team. I can take him in a second and even piss drunk. He knows that.

"Don't fuck with me, Hargreaves. Do what I say."

Logan pulls his forearm from my tight grip, but I can tell I scared the shit out of him, which means he'll obey. Good. It's always better to have someone do your dirty work for you. Write that down, because it's great fucking advice.

Now I need to wait ten minutes and establish a half-assed alibi in case her friends come looking on Saturday morning and they need to sift through the drunken memories of a hundred party guests to solve the case of the missing hot chick.

I slide onto the dancefloor and make myself the center of attention – mask off.

"Let's get this party started, Pesthouse!"

Cheers. Louder music.

"Tonight, we're going to fuck shit up! Here's to another year of wrecking shit on this fucking campus. Can I get a wooooooo!"

I obviously get a "wooooooo!" I work the room with precise timing and encourage everyone to get stinking, fucking drunk. I take shots with a group of freshman girls who all write their phone numbers on the white collar of my Brooks Brothers dress shirt. I throw a "guest shot" in a round of Beirut happening at our pong table, and I make sure anyone who can get in my way doesn't get the chance.

Cole has Kya pressed against the wall in one corner with his hands on her waist and his tongue down her throat. He's distracted. Perfect. Jayce and Makeba snuck away upstairs the second I stood on the table. Jayce can't keep his hands off her and I give him shit for it, sure, but I can't blame him. My friends aren't broken the way I am. They can handle women and relationships, but I can't do a normal relationship. I need things done my way. Maybe it's a Rathbone family trait, maybe it's my fucked up past, but it doesn't matter.

When I get my hands on Raven, I'm done searching for another woman. Once you have a good one, all you need to do is make sure you don't let her go. I've found the perfect woman. Now where the fuck is she? Hargreaves shows up three minutes after our agreed upon time, his arm linked with Raven's like he's the one who owns her. I didn't tell him to bang her, I told him to bring her. Rage courses under my collar and I loosen my tie so I can think. I'm sober enough to avoid punching his lights out... for now.

Neither of them can see me as they giggle and walk down the hallway. Raven's heels click loudly on the floor, the awkward but sexy steps of a woman who doesn't normally wear high heels, but who wants to look fucking hot. I like that she saves her effort for special occasions, making her silk pink dress that barely covers her thick, curvy thighs a rare treat.

Those copper thighs have tempted me for way too long.

"What do you want, Logan?" she whispers. She touches him. I want to break his fucking back for letting her touch him. I have to keep my long-term aims in mind, so I struggle, but I keep my fucking cool. For now.

I hear the current of fear in her voice, but there's desire too. Are you fucking kidding me? Raven has the hots for Hargreaves? I could kill that fucking Canadian with my bare hands. Fuck his dontcha know ass accent and his slick tongue.

"I wanted to do this," he murmurs. *No.*

The motherfucker leans forward and kisses her. He kisses her. My ears burn and blood rushes to my face. I'm not cool or in control when I emerge. I told him to lure her here, not try to get his dick in her. I spring out of my hiding spot, startling Raven and startling that idiot Hargreaves even more.

"Get the fuck off her."

Raven flinches and turns to look at me, wrinkling her nose because she can't recognize me. She smells like champagne and it's a sweet fucking smell. My voice catches and I can't give Hargreaves the dressing down I want to give him.

This isn't part of the plan. She isn't supposed to hear my voice, but in the dark and with my mask on, she can't tell who I am. Not yet. My heart races as I step closer to them. Logan drops her waist and clears his throat.

"I did what you asked," he says. "Now hand over the coke."

When did I promise this Canadian fuck any coke?

"Get out of here before I cut your dick in half and saute it. Move."

I step between them so Raven has little chance at escape. The last thing I need is to have her running away and screaming her head off.

"Wait, what's going on?" she says. Yeah, she's definitely tipsy. Good.

"Sorry," Logan mutters.

"Leave," I snarl, grabbing her forearm before she can run off. She whips around to look at me and takes her mask off.

"Which one of the creeps are you?"

Fuck. She doesn't recognize me. My voice catches. I could tell her I'm Brett. I could confess now and probably make my life ten times harder. At least I wouldn't have to lie to her. I can't bring myself to tell her the truth. I didn't prepare for the truth. I prepared to acquire the woman I want for the night. I reach into my kit for what I need.

"You don't need to worry about that, kitten."

With Hargreaves gone and stinking drunk, no witnesses remain. I press the rag to Raven's face and clamp it over her mouth for ten seconds, counting backwards as my hand balances on her hip precariously. Her soft stomach spills between my fingertips and as her eyes flutter shut, I pull her body against my chest, accidentally hiking up her silk dress a few inches. I smooth her dress as I count backwards.

4... 3... 2... 1...

Raven loses control of her legs first, falling limp in my grasp. Her body weight presses against mine and my cock stiffens instantly. Success in the hunt.

I effortlessly lift her off the ground, pulling her arm around my shoulder. If I want to get her into my bedroom with no one noticing, I'll have to head out the normally locked back door and take her up the fire escape. Light work. This is easier than having her struggle. She's 165-lbs by how her body feels against my chest, and I hold every pound of her body close to me.

Don't worry, kitten. I'll take great care of you.

A HOCKEY PLAYER'S BEDROOM

RAVEN

I smell wet dirt and bleach. The last thing I remember is standing in a hallway with Logan. He's cute, preppy, blond. Not my type and there's no spark, but he's in a couple classes with me and cute enough to kiss. I don't know why he asked me to kiss him, but I was all alone at a hockey party and had a few drinks in me, so kissing a tall, blond hockey boy with a wealthy family in England seemed like a good idea.

I don't know how I found out about the wealthy family. Probably the drunken rambling before he kissed me. Then the kiss just happened, and it wasn't anything like the kisses in the books I read.

I knew what he was going to ask from the way he looked at me, but now... it must have all been some trick.

I remember Logan kissing me, and then… it's all black. No memories. The blank space in my mind is like a gut punch. I hate feeling like I don't have a toehold on my reality. My stomach tightens. He drugged me. I can't imagine Logan Hargreaves drugging me and dragging me upstairs to his bedroom, but that has to explain everything.

I've heard his poetry in our freshman seminar together, so honestly, I never saw it coming. All he writes is sad stuff about not fitting in as a British boy in Canada. He's a little dopey, and he smokes too much weed, but he's goofy and fun, not the type to roofie someone.

How could I be so wrong about him?

As I slowly come to my senses, more information about my environment filters in, and reality replaces my hazy notions about Logan. Smell comes first and then I can taste. I can taste the chemical I inhaled on my tongue. My stomach lurches as I absorb some more of the bitterness and struggle to remain conscious. As the burning sensation spreads down my esophagus, I cough loudly and thrust myself out of unconsciousness.

Blindfold. I'm wearing a blindfold and I'm sitting up. Okay, that's better than waking up tied to a bed, but I don't know what I'm doing here or why Logan Hargreaves would drug me and drag me upstairs to his bedroom.

My voice feels scratchy, and like if I scream, nothing will come out. Screaming probably wouldn't help, anyway. If Logan thought screaming would help, he would have gagged me. I need to keep my mind sharp and stay 100% clear.

My heart refuses to settle and beats faster the more I awaken to my situation.

"Hello?"

Footsteps. I hear footsteps and I smell really strong cologne. It's not bad cologne, just strong enough that I know it's expensive. The cologne smells like cool pine and bergamot, but it's covering up the dirt and bleach, which means the wearer must be close. I don't want to sound scared.

"I can hear you," I say, trying to sound strong. Instead, my voice sounds hoarse from whatever chemical I just inhaled a mouthful of. I cough loudly, almost missing the smooth silky voice responding to me from the dark.

"I know."

That's not Logan Hargreaves' distinct Canadian accent. My stomach flips again when I realize that makes my kidnapping situation worse than I expected. I blink and flutter my eyes, straining to see through the black cloth wrapped around my face, but obviously, I can't make anything out. I need to listen and try to match that syrupy New England accent to a person. Whoever this is has a deeper voice than most men I know. But I know it. I just can't put my finger on who the damned voice belongs to. Not yet. I have to get him talking.

I know who drugged and kidnapped me. I just need to think about who I know who could do something like this.

If B.J. weren't in prison, he would be my first guess. Also, the voice sounds nothing like B.J.'s high-pitched and simpering whine. That's all behind us now. B.J.'s behind bars and, according to our sophomore dean, the administration has taken extra measures to make sure Laguna Grove College is safer than before.

At least this narrows down my options for suspects. With campus security strict throughout the night, whoever did this has to be a student.

"Who is this?"

"Really, Raven Rose?" he draws out my full name, teasing the alliteration with his tone. "You don't recognize my voice?"

He sounds frustrated and maybe even… angry? I hear his footsteps as he shuffles across the room again and I run through my list of people these footsteps could belong to. Big. Whoever he is must be enormous because his footsteps are heavy, and he walks with a purpose, but other than that, I can't identify him. I need more clues. I need to see his face. I wriggle again and then freeze.

My captor's hand touches my face. I notice how rough his hand is and how the touch sends this shiver running straight through me. My throat constricts more than before and I crease my thighs together, hating the way my carnation pink dress rides up my thighs. If he hadn't tied my hands, I would smooth the dress down and keep my legs covered.

The voice definitely belongs to a man. It's deep, but soft and he talks slowly, like he isn't in a hurry and like he's never been in a hurry. Most people in the Northeast talk like they're getting charged by the minute. I miss the slow-talking, smooth-talking Southern way, but this voice almost reminds me of the place I used to call home.

I don't know how long I was out, but I can hear music downstairs, so there's still a party going on. I must still be in Pesthouse, which means I'm in a hockey player's bedroom. No wonder he didn't gag my mouth. I could scream as loudly as I wanted to, but no one would hear me. And the hockey players party until sunrise, so I'm stuck without a chance of screaming for help for the rest of the night.

After a summer being the fifth wheel to my friends' relationships, I think I would recognize either Jayce or Cole – the only known kidnappers of Pesthouse. Unless…

My captor's hand travels over my jawline and a shiver runs down my spine. His touch is firm. Controlling. A name pops into my head. I know exactly who the hand belongs to. It could have only ever been him, right?

I should have recognized that cologne. He wore it on the first night I met him. I don't know why the hell I remember that, but I just do.

"Dustin."

Every detail smacks into me at once and something resembling a memory flashes in my head, causing a surge of nausea to wrack through my body. Dustin. He had to be the one wearing the mask. Dustin drugged me. My throat tightens, preparing to emit a pointless scream, but the wiser part of my brain overrides that impulse to struggle by screaming. No one downstairs will hear me, and I don't know what Dustin wants.

Whatever Dustin wants, I also need to know why he needs me for it. If I can just solve that mystery, I can get out of here. No screaming. No drama. I can talk my way out of this. I'm an English major, right? I just need to put my wits to use.

"Finally," Dustin sighs, his hand falling from my face and then resting on my shoulder. He touches me like we're close, his palm curving around my shoulder and nearly squeezing, but not quite. His possessive hold provokes a strange response in my body. My heart races and my thighs squeeze together. I try to wriggle free again. His calloused hands from rough years of athleticism run over my bare shoulder like he's savoring the experience. I feel like I'm his prey and he's teasing me before the kill.

"What are you doing? I already know who you are, so you can take my blindfold off."

"Aren't you going to shriek in fear?" he asks, again in that molasses voice. "Aren't you going to squirm and beg for mercy? Give me a little entertainment?"

Dustin hints at his motives. Pleasure. Kya and Makeba both warned me he was sick in the head. I didn't guess that he was this sick, but I probably could have guessed that given everything I know about Dustin Rathbone. His terrible reputation precedes him, and maybe it's wrong to judge him because of rumors, but what if the rumors are true?

I wriggle against the binds again, but nothing works. He tied some pretty damn good knots.

Last year, we met at a party, and he seemed like a smooth talker. I'm not immune to his looks. He has short, slightly wavy, light brown hair that spreads into a sexy hockey flow beneath his helmet and his eyes could pierce through a sheet of metal. Half of our campus calls him "the guy with the eyes". It's unfortunate the perfect 6'4" package comes with the Dustin Rathbone attitude.

He's a smooth talker when it suits him, and otherwise, he's cruel. Everyone who tangles with Dustin runs away like their life depends on it. He's had more women in his bed than nearly all the guys in Pesthouse and those women won't talk about him, but they won't talk to him either. Something bad happens in Dustin's bedroom whenever he's alone with a woman.

He's going to do something horrible to me.

His eyes may be gorgeous, but he has no soul behind them. Everyone jokes about his soulless eyes, but I stared into them the first night I met him. His eyes made my voice catch in my throat that first night, and not just because of Dustin's hotness, but because of the darkness I saw behind them.

I had to force myself to run away from him a year ago. He's hot, but too much trouble and too dangerous. When you stare into those crystal eyes, you can see that he's dead inside. But I'm not staring into his eyes. I'm staring into a sea of black and despite my efforts to keep calm, I'm internally freaking out. I just don't want Dustin to know that. I need to improve my chances of survival by scanning my brain for any ideas from a book I've read.

If he senses my terror, he wins. If I allow him to derive pleasure from my pain, he wins – and he probably won't let me go. I need to make this boring for him. I need to secure my freedom.

"I have no desire to entertain you. Now take my blindfold off."

His ready agreement surprises me.

"Fine. But I put the blindfold on for your sake, kitten."

This time, it's harder to hold back my vomit. Kitten? I read romance novels, so I've heard it all when it comes to bad pet names. Honeybear. Girl. Pocket. Schmoopie. Poopsie. Muffin. But 'kitten' takes the cake.

"Don't call me kitten."

He takes two steps forward.

"I do what I want... kitten."

Air whooshes past my face as Dustin extends his arm over me and behind my head to untie the blindfold. I wriggle my hands a bit to feel what he used to secure my hands and feet. Soft ropes. Not the type of stuff you would normally have lying around. He planned this. My blindfold falls away and Dustin steps back. I don't remember seeing him at the party and seeing him for the first time stimulates an annoying reaction. He looks great in a suit.

I don't think I've seen Dustin wearing anything except hockey gear and sweatpants. He doesn't need to attempt to keep his bedroom populated with willing women. That begs the question of why he drugged me and why he brought me here. Dustin doesn't need to choke a woman with chemicals to get her in his bedroom – not with those eyes or with that chiseled body. Ugh. Why does my brain do this?

My already racing heart quickens, and my throat constricts with a ticklish choking sensation. Dustin's bedroom is a house of horrors and a part of me regrets allowing my eyes to settle upon the tanks and enclosures that line Dustin's large bedroom. He keeps so many bizarre animals that my eyes don't know which one to focus on first.

When Makeba described this place, she made it seem like surviving Dustin's reptile den was a piece of cake. Clearly, Makeba has a high tolerance for creepy crawlies because my desire to give in to my gag reflex heightens. He has tarantulas, cockroaches, a variety of lizards and then that horrifying snake. I notice blood and fur in the snake's enclosure and nearly lose the small amount of beer and champagne in my stomach. My mouth fills with spit and the chemical on my tongue tastes stronger. My head swims and my eyes refuse to focus on anything in Dustin's creep den.

"Shit…" Dustin whispers, running his hand over my cheek again, lifting my head and forcing my eyes to meet his. "Don't go out on me again. Here…"

He picks a bottle off his desk and I try to wriggle and thrash my head as he puts the bottle under my nose and then forces my head still. I shake my head and make desperate attempts not to breathe, but I can't avoid breathing for long. I gasp and a sharp smell hits my nostrils. Damn.

"Smelling salts. Goodbye nausea," he says, one firm hand still on my cheek. "Feel better, kitten?"

The smelling salts replace my nausea with a coughing fit and there are tears in my eyes from coughing by the time I can breathe enough to answer Dustin's question.

"Do I look better?" I snap.

His voice remains perfectly calm.

"You always look gorgeous. Especially now. I love Kya's dress on you."

Every warning I've heard about Dustin Rathbone rushes into my head. *He's crazy. He's not all the way there. He has a few screws loose. He has secrets. Dark secrets.*

My eyes flash to his, and I immediately regret giving him the dignity of eye contact. In the red light, both our eyes reflect a uniform color. Without the hypnotic color of Dustin's eyes, I can only see and feel the darkness emanating from him. But my fear subsides as I stare into his eyes. I don't believe he's going to hurt me. Maybe that's stupid, considering my circumstances, but Dustin has another purpose here.

"Does this really seem like the time for compliments?"

He runs his finger along the inside of his collar, loosening his tie slightly. His neck is so thick and muscular.

"Sorry," Dustin says. "I find you... difficult."

His gaze bores into me.

"Clearly you didn't find tying me up and dragging me up to your room difficult. What do you want, Dustin?"

Questioning him activates my fight-or-flight response because I'm pushing against a man who can fight like an animal. Adrenaline surges as I stare at him, considering his potential response. I find Dustin nearly impossible to read, but I don't want to make him angry. Dustin is larger and ten times more terrifying than either Jayce or Cole. I've watched him play hockey countless times. He shows no mercy to any of his opponents. Jayce finds himself in the penalty box more than the other players, but I've watched Dustin break ribs and noses without flinching. Violence comes easily to him and, unlike Jayce, Dustin Rathbone never loses control. He calculates all his moves, and he probably calculated this one.

He touches his chin and then drops his hand, staring at me the entire time.

"I want you to belong to me."

I don't expect Dustin to say that. Why would he say that?

"Um…"

Before I can ask him to clarify, Dustin forges ahead with all the bold, delusional confidence of a Laguna Grove hockey star.

"You, Raven Rose, will sign a contract and agree to become my property for the rest of the academic school year." He smirks again and then drops the smirk, gazing at me with those creepy eyes.

Okay, I said Dustin had a few screws loose, but clearly I underestimated the number of screws loose.

"Why on earth would I agree to that?" I ask, wriggling my wrists again, in case Dustin did a shitty job of securing me to the chair. No such luck. He secured my binds so damn tightly. He bound my legs too, so there's no kicking him, no defense except my words.

"Remember the sick fuck from last semester? The gun nut?"

I cannot see the relevance of bringing up B.J. Satterfield. My ex-friend pulled out a semi-automatic rifle in the freshman girl's dorm and changed our low-key private college forever. I don't want to think about B.J. He's in prison, exactly where he belongs.

"Yes."

My response is as flat as I can muster. Dustin gains pleasure from rattling me, and I won't give him that pleasure now.

"Before his minor incident, I arranged with your friend and he gave me some information about you. I think you'll want to keep that precious information to yourself, especially at a school like this."

I roll my eyes. Haven't the hockey boys tried this before? Blackmail won't work on me. It doesn't matter what dumb fake ass secret B.J. sold Dustin.

"I don't have any secrets, Dustin. Nothing you say to blackmail me can convince me to stay here and act as your property. I don't know what could possess you to ask a fellow college student such a thing."

Dustin smirks. I've never seen him smile quite like this before, but his eyes remain still and dead as his lips curl in the cruelest expression I've seen him muster. My fear response finally kicks into overdrive. Maybe I've underestimated Dustin.

"Everyone has secrets, kitten. Even you."

Then there's silence. I suppose I'm searching my memory for any potential secrets he could refer to. I'm just not the person Dustin thinks I am. I don't know what the hell B.J.'s dumb ass told him, but I'm too boring to have any juicy ass secrets.

Kya and Makeba have secrets. They're the fun ones with the loud personalities. I'm the quiet friend who everyone else overlooks. I read books. I get my homework done. I attend classes. I hang out with my friends. Unlike Kya, I don't have a stash of erotic stories and unlike Makeba, I've never found myself on the wrong end of a few tequila shots making drunken videos.

Dustin can't possibly have any dirt on me. I just don't have any dirt.

"I don't," I tell him forcefully.

I know myself. I don't have any secrets. I suppose he could just make shit up. He's Dustin Rathbone. Anyone would believe him.

"Do you want to risk that?"

Dustin's little smirk returns, like he knows something I don't. I won't fall for his cocky hockey dude attitude. This has to be a bluff — he has nothing.

"Yes. Now untie me."

"That won't happen until you sign my agreement."

This time, his smirk turns into a full-blown grin. Fuck that stupid grin. I'm done playing Dustin's stupid ass game.

"Are you missing the part where you don't have any dirt on me? I won't sign a stupid contract. I can't even sign a contract with my hands tied."

He shifts his weight to his other foot. Dustin hasn't blinked in several minutes, which would normally scare me, but if Dustin wanted to hurt me, he would have done it and I don't think he would have hesitated. My brain stops pumping adrenaline through me. He might be a freak, but… I think I'm safe for now.

This dumb contract is probably just another dumb hockey player scam and once I figure out what he wants, I'll sign his dumb contract and leave this bedroom.

"You're going to sign the contract," Dustin says calmly. Then he stuffs his hands into his pockets and stares at me for an uncomfortably long time.

When he finally talks, he doesn't sound like he's any closer to letting me go. "I'll let you think about it. I need to feed Big Sexy."

That's not the snake's name. Everyone knows about Dustin's snake and its escape habits.

For once, that freaking snake is in its enclosure and for once, there seems to be a somewhat secure latch keeping the uncomfortably enormous snake from orchestrating an escape.

But Big Sexy? I can't even imagine which of his nasty pets he would have named "Big Sexy". I watch him turn to the various cages and enclosures, stopping in front of a tiny glass cage holding an enormous spider and then a spider that's somehow even bigger than the first. I think they're tarantulas, but they look bigger than any nasty and hairy spider I've ever seen. Ew…

One of these fucking spiders is definitely pregnant. Holy shit.

"Dustin, seriously. What do you want? I won't be your property, but maybe we can strike a deal or something. You know… a sane proposition?"

He doesn't turn to face me. He reaches into a box and pulls out three mealworms. I gag and force myself to look away. Dustin appears blind to my distress. I hear him pop the lid off the cage and then I hear the unfortunate sound of three meal worms plopping against the bottom. Don't throw up. Don't throw up.

"I don't appreciate the insinuation that I'm crazy, kitten."

I tighten my voice, still desperate to prove that I fear nothing, especially not Dustin Rathbone's little tarantula stunts.

"Prove your sanity then."

Dustin smirks and I squeeze my eyes shut as the tarantula lunges at the mealworm he drops into the cage. Oh, God… no. Why did God make some animals so damned nasty? And why the fuck can't I look away from this greedy feeding? My stomach churns, forcing my gaze elsewhere.

I can either look at Dustin or his pets, so my gaze finally snaps to him. His brows soften and Dustin lowers his voice. Ah, there it is — his dirt.

"You're broke, Raven. You're dirt poor. Your parents don't have two pennies to rub together and you're their only hope. You're a first generation college student and you will graduate from this expensive shit hole with $247,237.89 in student loans."

I hate that he stuns me into silence.

"I don't know why you majored in English," Dustin continues. "You're not likely to make enough money to pay that off. And that semester abroad in Italy you want to take next year? Unlikely without more debt."

What the fuck? What the actual fuck? Dustin knows too much about me and I don't know if I believe he got all this information from B.J. I want to call Dustin a liar, but I'm too stunned because he knows the exact amount of student loans I need. There's no way he can know that without... I don't even know what.

"How dare you call me poor!"

Why does my pride have to crop up at the worst times? I should stay on my toes and keep thinking about a way to escape Dustin's clutches, not fall for his stupid ploys to get under my skin. I also need to find out how he got this information about me. It isn't really a 'secret', but when you go to a school where everyone has at least two $1,000 Canada Goose jackets, you keep your scholarships, grants and pending student loans to yourself.

You're dirt poor. His words make my skin crawl, but not because he's wrong. I just hate the way he puts it and I hate the way I feel ashamed of something that isn't my fault. I wrestle harder against my arm binds again and feel some slight, encouraging give. That doesn't mean I'll escape, but at least my wriggling makes progress against Dustin's stupidly tight knots.

"I don't mean to upset you, kitten."

"I'm not upset."

I sound obviously upset. Fuck.

"Sorry, but it's true. You don't have any money and I just turned twenty-one this summer."

Since when is Dustin's birthday relevant to my life? He's probably a damned Gemini. My Instagram witchy queen always warns us against these Gemini men. Then again, his room organization makes him seem like a Virgo... Too bad this is the wrong time to give a shit about evil ass Dustin's star chart.

"Happy fucking Birthday, Dustin. Now untie me and stay out of my damn business."

He raises an eyebrow and that cocky ass smirk returns.

"I like your fight." What an annoying attempt at a 'compliment'.

I glare at him with all the ferocity I can muster. My glowering has absolutely no effect on Dustin's demeanor. He loosens his tie a bit more and approaches my chair. How can Satan's right-hand man look this fucking good? Dustin crouches so we're at eye level together and he blows wisps of his wavy hair out of his face.

"Now that I'm twenty-one, I have a trust fund, kitten. Millions. If you sign my contract, I'll pay your tuition, get rid of your loans, and I'll send you to Italy for your junior year. We can help each other."

He runs his tongue over his lips and puts his hand on my bare thigh. My thighs squeeze together and I want to kick my legs out, but Dustin's palm keeps me still. I don't know what kind of help Dustin wants from me, but my instincts warn me against giving him an inch.

Bad things happen in this bedroom. So why can't I remember to keep my guard up?

"I won't sign a contract with absolutely no proof that you mean what you say. Dustin, I get it. You're creepy and you want to scare me. Mission accomplished. Now let me go, and ditch the damn contract."

He rubs my thigh gently, causing the strangest sensation to shoot through me. Rage? Anger? Something else? A lump fills my throat.

"I am nowhere close to being finished with you, kitten."

He walks over to his desk, unsurprisingly bare. I don't think I've ever seen Dustin holding a book of any kind and apparently, he doesn't even see the merit in keeping his college textbooks on his desk. He carries a stack of five printed pages over to me.

"I'll untie your hands so you can read this."

The papers are cold when they land on my thighs. Thankfully, Dustin's room isn't very chilly, although it certainly has its flaws. The tarantulas lift their legs against the side of their cage, celebrating their recent feast, and my nausea heightens again. I need to stop looking at these gross spiders. Big Sexy looks even more gargantuan rearing up on its hind legs. Disgusting.

I glance down at the page in front of me. I can't believe this is Dustin's idea of a sane proposition. The title on the page jumps out at me. Varsity Property. The words on the page blur together. Shit. I need to focus. Dustin rounds the chair and works to untie my hands. Relief floods me, but I can't exactly escape without my legs. My hands are free and I grab the papers, rolling them up. As Dustin stands, I whack his head hard. He doesn't give the big bad reaction that I expect.

"Ouch. What was that for?"

Despite his exclamation, he doesn't sound hurt, or even remotely bothered by my retaliation.

"I'm not signing this. I don't want to be your sex slave and I don't want to feed any of your pets while you're at hockey practice. I'm not signing a document that makes me your property."

He puts his hands in his pockets.

"You're not thinking clearly, Raven."

"I don't need a guy who lives with a bunch of reptiles to tell me how to think."

Dustin smirks, because he seems to find all of my protests amusing.

"Tarantulas aren't reptiles. Want to meet one?"

I obviously know that tarantulas aren't reptiles. But I don't feel the need to identify accurately all the creatures in Dustin's man cave.

"No, Dustin. I don't want to meet your tarantula. And I'm not signing this."

"Let me paint a picture, Raven. You leave Laguna Grove, you get a decent job, $45,000 a year, give or take, but your student loan payments are going to eat into that. You won't escape poverty. You won't help your parents. You're going to serve drinks in a shitty bar just to pay rent in an overpriced city until you give up and…"

Silence settles for too long. I hate that I'm curious how Dustin's 'story of my life' ends.

"And what?"

"You get depressed and you kill yourself."

Silence again.

"That is really fucking dark, Dustin."

Dustin shrugs. "The worst part is you'll probably die a virgin."

I wish I could reach far enough to kick him in the damn nuts.

"Money isn't everything," I snap. How the hell does Dustin know I'm a virgin? He probably assumes I'm so uncool that no guy would sleep with me. Ugh. Awkward. Dustin's rubbing motion turns to gentle squeezing.

"You're right. It isn't everything," He says. "But your mom has type 2 diabetes, and it costs a lot to manage. Your dad isn't in great health either. They're good people, Raven. If you sign this contract, you won't be a burden to anyone anymore. You can help them the way you want to. You can be the perfect daughter you want to be."

How the fuck does Dustin know all this stuff? I want time to think, but I won't get it while I'm his captive. He's right about money, though. I don't want to show him he's struck a nerve. Everyone knows Dustin Rathbone is ridiculously rich, but I didn't have a clue that he was "pay off student loans" rich. I didn't know he had more money than any crazy ass hockey player should have access to.

I want to clap back, but he's right about my loans and my job prospects. I love reading and writing, but there isn't much money in my passions unless I get really lucky.

I keep telling my parents I'll figure it out, but to be honest, I don't have a serious plan. Everyone in my life kept telling me I was smart, and I had to go to college, but no one told me how I was supposed to do everything else. Nobody told me how much debt I would take out to get this college degree.

"I need proof that you're not messing with me."

Dustin snickers. "Oh, I'm messing with you. But not about money. You want some proof? I'll give you fifty-thousand dollars in cash. Aside from the deal. Just a little upfront payment."

I scoff. "Okay, Dustin."

He walks over to his desk drawer as I flip one page of his contract. As Dustin opens the drawer, the cash practically jumps out. Bound wads of cash fall onto his chair and onto the floor of Dustin's dim bedroom.

Holy shit. That's a lot of money. It's more money than I've ever seen in my life. Dustin grabs one stack, spreading the sudsy cloth scent of the cash throughout his bedroom.

"See this? One thousand."

He throws it at my feet. Then another.

"Two thousand."

This is more money than I make in two months at my on-campus job. Holy shit. I am totally failing at holding my cool internally. I want to reach down and snatch those hundreds off the ground.

"What's your point, Dustin?"

"I'm not done counting."

"You won't stand here and count out $50,000."

I'm not stupid. Dustin might have a lot of cash, but he won't just hand over $50,000. He's not serious. Even if Dustin isn't joking about this, surely there's a better option for getting colossal sums of money than signing a contract and becoming Dustin Rathbone's property.

He might even keep me in a cage like he does with that big ass snake…

I don't even want to consider that option. If there's any part of Dustin Rathbone that's serious about this, then he knows that $50,000 on its own would be a game changer. I could take that money and run… anywhere.

But… what about the rest? Is Dustin's crazy ass for real here? Offering to pay off my tuition is a lot of money.

I planned on taking out loans and busting my ass to get the best job possible. I took the loans, I'll have the elite education, I have to make it work, right? A part of me knows he's right. Unlike Dustin and the other rich kids here, I can't afford that ten year pay cut to build my skills. I have debt to pay, so I'll have to take the first job I get and strike out on my own…

Dustin makes an interesting proposition. What if I had zero college debt? Like, none. Black women are the demographic in America most affected by student loan debt. I'm not complaining our anything, but it's a reality that I can't ignore.

I can't even imagine living like the other kids at Laguna Grove, never wondering where my next dollar is coming from, traveling across the world, making choices based on what I want and not just what I can afford. I can't lie to myself. I'm tempted. The only black woman I know with that type of privilege is my best friend, Kya. Most of us don't have professional athlete dads. Most black women in my position can't afford to turn down that amount of money. Dustin notices my contemplative silence and I hate that I have a tell.

He grabs the contract and taps the stack of papers against my thigh. Every time he touches my thigh, I flinch. I feel… strange.

"Consider it a good faith offer," he says. "If you sign the contract, you take the cash and I promise, if you fulfill your end of the agreement, you'll get the rest."

"Give me those papers."

Dustin smirks, but he releases his grip on the papers, allowing me a chance to read his stupid contract. Judging by the font choice and formatting, he put far too much effort into the contract.

❧ 5 ☙

PROPERTY AGREEMENT
BETWEEN RAVEN ROSE & DUSTIN RATHBONE

RAVEN

"**Y**ou put a lot of effort into this, huh," I grumble, running my fingers over the raised font on the thick white paper.

"Read," he commands.

I throw him a glare to let him know I don't appreciate his little comment, but I keep reading the document.

For the duration of the semester, the signee, Raven Rose agrees to become the full property of the honorable Dustin Rathbone.

"Honorable? Seriously?"

"You'll soon learn that I'm a man of my word."

"I still wouldn't go with honorable."

"Can you just keep reading?" he says through gritted teeth.

As the property of Dustin Rathbone, the signee Raven Rose agrees to a variety of tasks related to the maintenance and upkeep of Dustin Rathbone's lifestyle in exchange for care, honesty, loyalty and financial compensation.

"You call living in a dark bedroom with a bunch of lizards a lifestyle?"

He struggles to suppress a flash of anger as I struggle to suppress a smirk. It's a little easy getting under Dustin's skin. Maybe I can annoy him into letting me go before he forces me to sign his dumb contract. Then again… *money.*

The scent of the money surrounding me wafts into my nostrils, overwhelming me with reality. The most practical thing to do is *take the money.* So far, all he's asked for are a 'variety of tasks'. How hard can that be to complete?

"Aren't you even the slightest bit terrified of what I'm going to do to you if you don't comply?"

I glance up from the stack of papers and look Dustin right in the eye.

"No."

Then I keep reading without waiting for a response or reaction from him, but my tongue feels heavy in my mouth.

Dustin expects his new property to service his daily needs including daily breakfast of oatmeal, freshly squeezed orange juice and a side of yogurt with blueberries.

Dustin requires a nightly deep tissue massage to aid his recovery from practice.

Dustin requires daily sexual release which Raven Rose must provide with an orifice of her choice.

My stomach turns.

"What the fuck is wrong with you?"

He leans over my shoulder to re-read his own words, forcing me to inhale the scent of his cologne. His body warms my shoulders from his closeness and I squirm in my seat again as he speaks.

"What did I do wrong?" Dustin replies with that aggravating smirk plastered on his arrogant ass face. He knows exactly what he did.

"An *orifice* of her choice?"

Just repeating his words out loud messes with my head. *Sex.* This is about sex? Dustin Rathbone doesn't need me for sex. He doesn't 'need' any particular woman since there are always several options begging for him. I've never seen Dustin at a Pesthouse party without eventually having a girl on his arm – usually one of the lacrosse or field hockey girls.

"Your little friend Kya would hate that, wouldn't she?"

"Shut up, Dustin."

He bristles, but he doesn't reply.

Any woman in her right mind, not just Kya, would find herself utterly repulsed by Dustin Rathbone's contract and everything he represents. He's *that* guy on campus that treats women like objects. He thinks he's better than everyone because he's an athlete. He picks on the weak – just like he's doing to me.

Once you get past his hot old school prep appearance... he doesn't bother hiding the truth about who he is. He revels in his awful reputation, like those regency novel rakes, but worse.

. . .

I kiss my teeth and continue reading the "Daily Tasks" section of Dustin's demented contract.

Dustin requires his room cleaned daily with a mixture of all purpose cleaners and bleach as well as daily laundering of his clothing and sheets.

Dustin requires assistance with his homework before hockey practice daily.

"Seriously? You want to pay someone to do your homework? You pay tens of thousands of dollars in tuition just to have someone else do the work? Make that make sense."

His voice drops and turns stern. "Raven…"

"Let me guess, another threat? I'm still reading, so you can't kill me yet or drop a spider on my ass or whatever."

"I wouldn't put Big Sexy on your ass."

I roll my eyes. Naturally that's the part of the conversation he pays any attention to.

"So you named that ugly fat ass thing Big Sexy?"

Shit. I bite my lip. My mama always told me my big mouth

would get me into trouble one day. I can't help it. I love reading and writing — sometimes the words just fall out.

"Yes, that's Big Sexy," he says, his voice barely rising above a whisper. "And *he* isn't a fat ass thing. He's a tarantula and he's special."

"*He* is pregnant."

Is Dustin stupid? That spider is like ten times bigger than the other one. I've read enough books and watched enough documentaries to know that female spiders are much bigger than the males. Everyone who can Google knows that.

Hell, "Big Sexy" might actually be an accurate name for the knocked up spider running around the cage. Clearly another spider found her sexy.

"He's male, Raven. Male spiders can't get pregnant."

If Dustin wants to live in denial, so be it. I try not to gag as the definitely pregnant spider drags its ass across the glass enclosure. My ancestors are screaming in my ear to run away from the white devil and his beasts from hell, but my curiosity has other plans for me and keeps my eyes glued to the page.

I'm dead fucking broke. My ancestors wouldn't want me to be broke, right?

Dustin's daily massages after hockey practice must be performed in sexy outfits of his choosing. Dustin will provide an additional budget for upkeep.

Dustin expects his property to reside in his bedroom where she will read, complete her homework and enjoy her recreational time.

Dustin expects the signee to participate in daily calisthenics with him for both of their physical fitness.

Dustin agrees to please his property and commit to daily tasks for her improved happiness and well-being.

"That last one's suspicious," I say, pointing to the penultimate daily task on Dustin's contract.

"Don't you want to be happy?"

Coming from Dustin, that's obviously a trick question.

"I don't need you messing with me to be happy."

"Right. All you need is a cup of chocolate and a good romance novel, preferably a pretty nasty one."

How the hell does Dustin know that? Sure, we've met, but it's not like we're friends. I swear I've written those exact words on my blog. There's no way Dustin found my blog – it's mostly fiction writing based on my life, but not interesting enough for Dustin to latch onto. Maybe he's just good at reading people.

"You're wrong," I say. "I also need peace and quiet."

Dustin might be able to provide $50,000, but he definitely can't shut up long enough for me to binge an entire romance novel in his presence. No man is that perfect.

"I can be quiet," he reassures me.

He says everything in that frustratingly ominous tone of voice. I hate how that stupid voice makes me squirm and feel all funny between my thighs.

The signee, Raven, must submit to one of Dustin's dark urges daily until she satisfies him.

"Dustin. This is way too open-ended to agree to."

One of his dark urges? How many dark urges does he have? My gaze flashes quickly to Dustin, but he's doing that staring thing again, giving me an idea about his dark urges. *They're too dark for me to handle, probably.* Again, my ancestors beg me to flee, but I silence all the sane voices in my head.

"This would go a lot faster if you stop interrupting and read the entire contract," Dustin says.

The wads of cash lying at my feet are the only reason I don't respond with another sassy quip. I have to think this through with a clear head, so instead of coming up with comebacks, I need to consider how this could impact my fate.

He's offering a lot of money – more money than I could ever imagine. I know he can back it up too. I've heard what other Laguna Grove kids talk about – second houses in Aspen, trips to St. Thomas, private jets and yachts, everything a poor kid can only dream about. I wanted to go to my dream school to better myself for the future, but staring down the barrel of my student loans always makes me wonder if I made the right choice.

I keep trying to tell myself that I'm not considering Dustin's offer and I'm just buying time until I escape. I hate that I think the entire dumb contract isn't that bad. Except for the dark urges thing. That part could get real…

But maybe Dustin's just a dumb rich kid with too much money to burn and I can make him breakfast and tidy his room for a quarter million bucks. Maybe he doesn't know that maids and cleaners don't even make a fifth of that. I know that for sure – my mama cleaned houses for years when we lived in Georgia. We scraped by every penny we had and wasted nothing. I can't even imagine having enough money to give away $50k.

Dustin's right. I need to keep reading. Maybe he'll say something so atrocious, I'll walk away from the most tempting offer of a lifetime. *Would sex with Dustin really be that bad?*

I force myself to keep reading.

Dustin requires weekly feeding for all his pets, which will be the signee's responsibility.

Dustin requires weekly deep cleaning of all cages and enclosures, including his own.

"Did you call your own bedroom an enclosure?"

"Read, Raven…"

Dustin requires his property's weekly appearance at Pesthouse party events dressed in outfits of Dustin's choosing — a different outfit each week.

Dustin requires weekly tutoring in his weakest subjects.

"Are you crazy?"

"Yes. Keep reading."

Damn. I at least expected him to argue about the crazy thing. He wants me to act now, but I still need time to think before I do something crazy and sign this. *All he wants is sex. I can do that. I may not be experienced, but I can learn… and then all that money will be mine.*

Dustin will provide monthly assessments on the signee's performance.

Dustin requires assistance with the management and budgeting of his monthly allowance.

At least the monthly tasks seem easy. Wait, no. That's not how I need to think about this. I need to say 'no'. I can't let Dustin trap me in a sex contract that also involves putting my hands in the cages of his weird lizards. One of them keeps looking at me and it has a blue tongue. That can't be natural, right?

The signee may petition Dustin Rathbone for any amendments to the contract.

Dustin requires access to personal information about Raven including lists of all her friends and enemies.

"Why do you need to know that?"

"Your enemies are very important to me."

"That doesn't answer the question, Dustin."

Upon completion of the contract, one academic year, Dustin will release Raven from all her obligations to him and submit a payment to the agreed upon amount of $250,000. Dustin will additionally provide Raven with a stipend for her trip to Italy amounting to the total of her plane ticket, accommodations and a budget for shopping and entertainment.

"That's more than my student loans," I blurt out once I finish reading, hating the words for escaping from my lips and making it sound like there's a chance I'll sign Dustin's stupid contract. My heart races as I squeeze it tightly and suppress my urge to make my problems go away. Sex, a little cleaning, and keeping Dustin's grades at a C average ought to be manageable. *Raven, no!!!*

I have to get out of this without succumbing to the incredible temptation of $250,000 — plus the $50,000 stacked all around me. And that trip to Italy...I knew it was a mistake to spend so many weekends scrolling through my cousin Lisa's pictures from the Amalfi Coast, but Italy is a total dream. It's the perfect place to fall in love. As long as you don't mess with the mafia, Italy is *perfect*.

If I spend one stupid year as Dustin's "property", I can earn my true freedom — forever.

Romance novels give me strength to resist this crazy ass white boy…

I know what my friends would tell me. Kya would use her hair dryer to mount an attack against Dustin. Makeba would tell me to sign the deal and scam him out of even more money. And as for Sydney…

Get laid. She definitely wouldn't approve of Dustin, though.

Where the hell is that bald-headed and religious chocolate king my homegirl promised?

All my friends would handle this so differently. But what would Raven Rose do? This is my choice. It doesn't matter who thinks I'm crazy or who thinks Dustin is several beers short of a six-pack. It's my decision.

"Do you have any amendments to the contract?" Dustin ventures, placing his hands back into his pockets. He's acting like I've already agreed to sign his stupid document. *He knows me better than I want to admit.*

"Yes," I tell him. "You do your own homework, and I'll help."

"Fine."

He bristles at that request.

"And as for the sex stuff…"

"Non-negotiable."

"Then why did you ask if I wanted to negotiate?"

"I wanted to be nice."

"You realize by faking it… you weren't nice."

"Yes."

I roll my eyes. How the hell will I tolerate spending every day answering to this white man?

I have to play it cool. I don't want to seem desperate and jump on Dustin's offer of endless money and a trip to Italy. I scrunch up my face and re-read every word, specifically reviewing the worst parts of the deal to remind myself the dark side of my fate if I press the pen to paper and become Dustin Rathbone's property.

He *has* to know how creepy that sounds to a black woman, right? Maybe that's where he was going with those 'dark urges'. I shudder. Dustin has everything when it comes to looks, but how hot do you have to be to cancel out racism?

Just because he wants to sleep with me doesn't mean he's not racist. What's he going to do when he realizes that my boobs look different from the girls he's used to. I have brown nipples and darker skin between my legs, and tightly coiled hair… and all those *differences* that scare white guys away. He'll want to break the contract once he realizes I'm not some sex-pot lacrosse chick. What about my money then?

"Don't you have hordes of women to take care of the sex stuff? Why don't we stick to the reptiles?"

The disappointment on his face demonstrates that I've missed the point. *Sex. He really wants the sex part.*

Dustin's brow furrows and then he forces his face to relax. He never relinquishes control of how he presents himself. If I couldn't read his emotions in those tiny expressions, I could get lost wondering what he wants from me or what he's going to do next.

Dustin taps his foot twice and then buries his frustration, returning to that reptilian cool. His voice is smooth and slow, reminding me that he's always in absolute control. At least that's what he wants me to think.

"I want you."

"Why?" I snap at him.

The money smell makes thinking rationally difficult and Dustin's cologne makes it even harder.

"Because, Raven. We're the perfect match. I have something you need and you have something that I need."

We're the furthest thing from a perfect match.

"I don't want to agree to this." My protest sounds so damn weak, but the slightest protest proves more than enough to disturb Dustin's sensibilities.

He moves his jaw back and forth, then conceals the rage.

"Can you really afford to turn down $50,000, kitten?"

I hate that he calls me kitten.

He has no intention of negotiating, does he? He offers me a chance to review the contract so I know what I'm getting into, but Dustin's ruthless, stubborn and beyond proud of that reputation.

I've gone to countless hockey games with my friends and I've seen how Dustin Rathbone handles himself on the ice. He doesn't just have killer instincts — he listens to them.

"Yes. I don't want to submit to whatever degrading sexual fantasies you have. I'm not that type of girl."

Maybe I'll scare him off by playing up the prude thing. I'm not sexually experienced, but I'm not a prude. I just want to wait for the right guy. Until then, I'm preparing myself for my future guy with lots of reading on the subject.

That future guy isn't going to be Dustin Rathbone. He's down for sex and hookups, not making love the way I want to my first time.

"I know," Dustin replies calmly. "You've never had sex. But... I bet you look hot when you cum."

His tongue darts over his lips after his comment. My cheeks grow hot and my lips freeze half-open as words hesitate to spill out. I've never had sex, and I've definitely never had a guy say something like that to my face. *I bet you look hot when you cum.*

Holy shit. I assumed Dustin wants to have sex with me as some kind of power play. Everyone knows how the hockey players talk about the black athletes on campus. They fear them, they think they're better than them, and the idea of conquering 'forbidden fruit' appeals to them.

Maybe he wants this for another reason. *I bet you look hot when you cum.* My cheeks feel flushed and an answer takes forever to spill out. I'm such a damn dork sometimes.

"How do you know I've never had sex?" I stammer eventually.

"I know you."

I don't like his answer. Again, it's far too ominous. I don't like *several* things about Dustin's personality or that messy sexual contract. He probably doesn't have to worry about emotional entanglement, but I don't want to end up in a situation that gives me Stockholm Syndrome or nothing.

He wants me to be his property… and he wonders what I look like when I cum.

Are your first sexual experiences supposed to be this weird and confusing? Maybe it's because I'm a late-bloomer. Sydney had sex at church camp when we were sixteen. She's never met a guy offering her hundreds of thousands of dollars for sex. I waited around too long and now, only the freaks want a twenty-year-old virgin.

The smell of money overpowers the smell of wet earth in his room and even overpowers the smell of Dustin's cologne. He's giving me an additional $50,000 — just to give him a chance. That must count in his favor, right? *No, Raven! Don't do it…*

I don't know how I ended up in this situation with Dustin, where he's offering the only thing that could tempt me. Without loans, I can take care of my parents instead of chasing bills. I can follow my dreams… *I can go to Italy.*

"My friends are going to kill me if I sign this," I mutter as my last ditch attempt of guilt-tripping myself out of signing the contract.

"Don't tell them."

"What the hell am I supposed to tell them? You want me to sleep here every night."

They'll definitely notice if I spend all my nights in Pesthouse.

"I thought you were creative, Raven. Use one of those *books*," he sneers. "Make up a story…"

I roll my eyes. I shouldn't expect any better from Dustin than sneering at books. His nightmares probably include having to read anything longer than a text message.

Men seem to revel in sitting around telling lies. Clearly, he's one of those men. I can't just lie to my friends. They'll see through me sooner or later. Despite how close I am to signing the contract and sealing my fate, I can't help but attempt to dig out some weak attempt at a moral high ground.

"I'm not lying to my friends for you."

"Correct. You're lying for well over $300,000. What's the big deal? Just tell them… *I'm your boyfriend.*"

Now I want to get out of this chair and smack Dustin across the face. He can't seriously expect my friends to believe that two weeks into our sophomore year, I spontaneously started dating Dustin Rathbone. Not only would they never buy the story, they would lose their freaking minds. *Dustin's a creep. He's hurt my friends. He's not boyfriend material – not even fake boyfriend material.*

"Are you on drugs?" I snap.

"Five shots of whiskey, a couple beers, two edibles and half a Xanax."

Great, so he's crazy *and* drugged up. Just what I need.

"I'm not lying to my friends."

"Fine. Tell them that you're my slave. My property."

He regroups when he catches my mean glare. "Come on, Raven. We'll be having sex every single day… Just *lie.* Call me your boyfriend. How will anyone find out the truth?"

Has Dustin lost his mind? I can't run around telling people that he's my boyfriend. No one at Laguna Grove would believe that. Dustin's reputation with women is sordid and unfortunately, it's true. The first night I met him he ended up in bed with three different girls on the field hockey team.

"The truth always comes out," I reply. I don't know why my answer sounds so weak. The truth came out about B.J. Even my financial situation must have found its way into the public discourse if Dustin Rathbone can pull up the exact numbers of my student loan.

Dustin gives me an uneasy look.

"What does that mean?"

"No one will believe you're the boyfriend type."

Ha. He finally looks offended.

"Why might that be?"

"Try not sleeping with the entire school if you want anyone to believe that you suddenly turned monogamous."

"You don't know what you're talking about, kitten," he says, resuming his calm.

Then he hands me a pen.

"You'll need that to sign."

He's so fucking sure of himself. I hate that. My cheeks burn as I take the pen from him. I don't know why I'm holding the pen and my hand hovers above the contract. Maybe the money smell hypnotizes me, but my fate swirls out of my control.

"I'm not signing this."

I click the pen open. *Fuck.* What the hell am I doing?

"I expect you down here bright and early to review your assignment," Dustin says. "I'm a generous master. I'll give you one more night of freedom."

I bite my lower lip and refuse to look at him. *Just think of the money, Raven. The money will make it all worth it.*

The tip of my pen presses against the page and I take a deep breath before I sign my life over to Dustin.

6

VICTORY & PATIENCE

DUSTIN

I keep the contract folded under my pillow and set her free for the night so she can stash her loot. $50,000. I spent that on her like it was fucking nothing…

I'd do it again too. She's worth every fucking penny.

Once she handles my finances, I'll have a much easier time moving all my cash around. See? That's why I love capitalism. Outsourcing.

The party downstairs winds down to a dull throb of music, a couple games of 'Ruit and loud, lip-smacking hookups going down against every wall. Barkov and Kane secure their last-minute conquests for the night. Girls hot off molly and liquor will go home with pretty much anyone. I don't mind numbing out when I go at it, but I need the chick to be awake, you know?

Raven. My prize arrives in my bed tomorrow. She doesn't know how much my generous night of freedom hurts me. Waiting another minute hurts. I know I have to let her go tonight and prove to her that I'm a good guy. I won't have to keep that mask up for long. Once I get her in my bed, she'll learn pretty fucking quick that I'm the furthest thing from a good guy.

Fuck. I'm so into her. I need to smoke to take the edge off things and I scour the party for anyone interested in taking a few shots or playing pong again.

I don't need to troll the dance floor searching for desperate chicks to pick up at the last minute anymore. It's liberating to know I have the woman I want securely under my control. See, that's where Jayce and Cole fucked up. You don't need to threaten someone to get your way — you just have to find out what they want and give it to them. I prefer contracts and negotiations to brute force. Of course, brute force is sometimes necessary.

She'll melt like butter in my hands, I know it. I have exactly what I want from Raven – and I'll have more of her. Before she leaves, I slip an earring from her ear and stick it in my pocket. I can't help but take a trophy. I have several of them, but this one is my favorite.

If she doesn't come back because of the contract, she'll come back for her gold. I offer to help her haul the $50,000 to her bedroom, but she declines my offer and sticks it into my hockey bag instead, promising that she doesn't need my help. I can't believe she plans to walk the half mile back to the sophomore dorms toting cash all by herself. It's so hot when she does crazy shit just to push me away from her.

I follow her anyway in the truck to make sure she gets home safely and she doesn't even notice my truck. Raven, Raven, Raven... If I wasn't there to look after her, who knows what kind of creeps could find her out there walking all alone? Who knows what they would do to her.

The morning of my first perfect day, I eagerly expect her arrival, and I start my day with my usual routine. I clean the cages and enclosures, taking special care to inspect Big Sexy. Raven's suspicions rouse my concerns. I'm not ready to be a father.

The tarantula's stomach has been round lately. But I know my animals. This is a case of overeating, not pregnancy. Jayce is a shitty pet sitter, and he probably gave Big Sexy a few too many crickets... right boy?

Raven doesn't know my house pets better than I do. Fuck.

I drop to the ground and pump out a couple hundred pushups. That's when Ovie wakes up. He loves pushups. Ovie moves his head when I move in the morning, expecting more than I'm willing to give since he just had food yesterday. Not now, boy.

Once I clean everything, I continue my daily calisthenics and send a text to dad before heading down to the ice for a quick and dirty practice skate with Jayce. Dad's been busy lately, which I don't mind. When he checks how I've been spending my allowance, he's going to flip.

Thankfully, I have Raven to fix that for me soon.

I'm early to the ice, but Jayce has clearly been here for a while. He skates around lazily without me, but he hasn't been here alone long. I smell Makeba's perfume when I meet him in the bleachers. She probably just snuck off. Jayce doesn't seem as peaceful as he should for a morning skate. What's twisting his balls today? Since the summer, Jayce's skin darkened to a deep tan and blond streaks his hair. I don't enjoy spending too much time outdoors, especially not in the sun.

"What were you up to last night?" He asks.

Is it my guilt, or does Jayce's question sound like an accusation? I smile – the easiest deflection. It works on nearly anyone.

"I had a great time."

His next question sounds even harsher than the first. What's going on with this guy?

"Did you hurt anyone?"

Define hurt? See, Jayce and I probably have very different definitions of the word hurt and it wouldn't do either of us any good if I answered his question based on confusing information.

"No."

Jayce presses me, which might make me nervous under other circumstances, but I already worked out our cover story. Hopefully Raven sticks to the plan instead of running her mouth…

"Really? You didn't kidnap anyone?"

"If you have something to say, brah. Say it."

Jayce grunts and skates onto the ice first with our three pucks for some shooting practice. I wouldn't mind skating and sprints, but Jayce prefers starting with stick skills, especially since the summer.

He insists on shooting practice ever since his summer coach recommended he differentiate himself as a defenseman by playing more like a forward. Jayce makes a great defenseman. His conventionally attractive face makes people underestimate him. He wants me to underestimate him now and I know my best friend wants me to slip up.

If I expose Raven's secret to her friends, she'll kill me and I'll lose everything I want. After a few sick corner shots, Jayce picks up his conversation where he left off.

"So. You haven't been hanging with any of Makeba's friends, right?"

"Define hanging?"

Smirk. Hook shot. That distracts him.

"A goalie would have nabbed that."

"Bullshit."

He shoots. Misses. I shoot. I miss. We skate around and get our shit together for a few more minutes.

"Bullshit," Jayce repeats. "Yeah. I'm calling bullshit."

I need to get Jayce off my back about this one.

"Do I need your permission to flirt with chicks now?"

Jayce picks his skates into the ice until he stops. Great. Now he's going to 'get real' with me and clearly, he has some ideas about me that I'll need to correct. Just stay calm, Dustin.

"Hargreaves said you drugged someone."

I don't want a lecture from Jayce about my methods. And as for that snitch, Logan. After hockey season, I'll consider giving his arm just the tiniest fracture for revenge…

"You're listening to Logan Hargreaves now? Kid does more Xanax than a real housewife of wherever."

Jayce refuses to give up. He's the only guy on the team who can push me and get answers. He's better at detecting my bullshit than Cole, unfortunately.

"It's a simple question, Dustin," Jayce presses, skating around me in slow, deliberate circles.

"All you need to know is that I have a girlfriend now."

Jayce picks the ice so hard he nearly falls over. Luckily, my braindead best friend comes to a dead stop and only stumbles before catching his balance. Jayce's shit-eating grin tells me he doesn't believe me for a second.

"No you don't."

"Yes. I do."

Ye of little faith…

"No, you don't. You don't do girlfriends, Dustin."

"Normally, I do other people's girlfriends. This time, I've met someone, and she's special to me."

Jayce snickers. "You are full of it."

He never notices how uneasy his questions make me, or how he plays right into my hand. There's a reason we're best friends. Jayce lets me carry my shit quietly, questioning nothing and accepting everything. I don't like the inquisition, but I need to stay focused if I want him off my back about Raven.

I relax and tease the puck down the ice before tucking it into the corner of the net and letting it bounce across to Jayce.

I snort. "That's what you get for accusing me of a crime."

"Kidnapping isn't a crime," Jayce shoots back. Isn't his step-dad a judge?

He might want to check the facts with his dick of a step-dad or with his smart ass girlfriend. I pass again and Jayce misses the shot. We both chase for the puck and he gets there first.

"You smoke too much," Jayce says. "You could get faster if you quit."

"Now you sound like Cole."

Jayce groans. "Stop. I'm not like Cole. I'm still a dirty little shit."

Yeah, right. Makeba has him whipped and tamed. He doesn't fight like he used to.

"Oh yeah, prove it."

I check Jayce hard on the chest. I enjoy bringing the fight out of him. A dirty hit, a thump on the back. Anything that teases the demon out of him brings me peace. I love my best friend, but he's wild when the rage hits him. I envy him for letting out that part of himself. I have to keep my rage a secret…

Jayce's fist flies towards my face. I hit him where it hurt and he's punishing me. I duck and push him against the boards. We fight and rough house for a few minutes until we're both sweating and neither relinquishing the upper hand. Then Jayce pushes me off him and skates backwards, squinting into the bleachers at a short, curvy figure approaching.

"Is that Raven?"

It's definitely her. Fuck.

"Who?"

"Don't fuck with me, Dustin. You know Raven. Kya's freshman roommate."

Shit. She's early. I thought I'd have a second to get Jayce off my case before explaining to him. Isn't she a sophomore yet? She's supposed to know to show up late to things now that she's all grown up. Raven doesn't care that we're staring at her. We both seem to escape her recognition entirely. Raven cozies herself in the bleachers, pulls a book out of her bag and flips it open. Just like that, I'm invisible.

She doesn't know how much she pisses me off.

Jayce skates up to me and grabs the back of his neck with hands like a lobster claw.

"Dustin. What the fuck is going on?"

That stern dad-voice works a lot better when it's coming from Cole.

"I told you... I have a girlfriend."

"Raven Fucking Rose?" he snarls.

Why the fuck is he talking to me like I'm a bad kid? Jayce needs to chill out. Didn't I tell him she was the hot one? It's natural that I'm making my move...

"Problem?"

"Yeah, I have a problem."

Shit. He's serious. Jayce's wild anger I find enjoyable. His righteous anger reddens the tips of his ears and makes him stammer like an idiotic baboon. Even if that sounds funny, this won't be pleasant in the slightest.

"What's the problem? She's a cute girl."

"Are you fucking kidding me, Dustin?"

"I thought you said I needed to try some black pussy?"

Jayce frowns, searching his memory for something that he definitely never said.

"No. No, I never said that."

I can distract him long enough to change his memory of the situation or to think of a better way out of the bullshit.

"Are you sure?"

He never said that. But reality shifts, doesn't it? Whoever believes in their reality more can make it true. I run my tongue over my lips. With helmets off and tempers flaring, Jayce could land an immense blow to my head if I say the wrong thing. But I know if I say anything at all, it'll probably be all wrong.

"Dude, she's my girlfriend's best friend. I know what sick shit you're into. I don't want you messing with her. Makeba will lose her shit."

Jayce doesn't know 35% of the sick shit I'm into.

"I don't need your permission to pull."

Jayce pulls up inches away from me, rage bubbling beneath the surface.

"It's not about that, man. I care about Makeba. I don't want you hurting her or her friends, got it?"

"Whatever, brah."

Jayce might rile me up, but exploding in front of Raven won't serve me. It doesn't matter what Jayce or anyone else thinks, we have an arrangement. She belongs to me.

Jayce recognizes anger. I don't know how he stays cool now, but he has a superior hold on his anger than he had last year. I could have pushed him over the edge by now a year ago. This isn't the Jayce I remember from before the summer.

"She's a good person. She stayed at our place all summer. She's looking for something real, Dustin. She's a friend."

Why does this fucker talk like I'm going to slice and dice her? I have control of myself and my urges might be dark, even a little twisted... but I could never injure or harm Raven Rose.

Jayce is just like Cole, utterly lost in his sappy bullshit. Neither of those fuckers understand what's going on here. They can't possibly understand how it feels to watch a girl so long and fight every temptation to touch her. Keeping cool keeps my advantage. I can't let him get under my skin.

"She's a nice chick," Jayce says. "She's looking for something real."

Finally, a place to break the tension and get my best friend off my back.

"Who's realer than me, brah?" I smirk, breaking the ice and teasing open the tension around Jayce Clutterbuck.

We exchange glances and say his name at the same time. "DMX."

That breaks the tension between us and we keep skating until I zoom around the rink and hear a tap on the glass. It's Raven pointing to her watch. Jayce distracted me from her presence in the stands.

What the hell, kitten? I race to the rink door while Jayce picks up the pucks, a smirk plastered on his face. I don't know what that smirk means, but I hope he keeps his mouth shut. The empty rink becomes our tiny bubble once I approach her, and it's just the two of us.

She doesn't know how much it fucks with my head to stand so close to her. I could reach out and touch her right now. I could succumb to all my fantasies and take her perfect, curvy body against mine. I keep my voice as steady as possible. Raven's braids sit in a high bun on top of her head, highlighting her apple cheeks and round face. She's so fucking hot.

"What do you want, kitten?"

My voice catches, but she doesn't notice. Thank fuck. I hate she can make my voice weak and I especially hate that she can make me forget about the rest of the world.

"Calling me kitten wasn't in the contract. Come on, it's time to go. I've been searching for you everywhere."

Her tone lights a fire in me.

"You're my property," I whisper. "I give the orders around here."

"Fine. Be late to class then, but I'm sticking to the contract and looking after your upkeep. A part of your lifestyle involves attending class, right?"

I scowl. I see she read the contract through again – entirely sober. I wonder if she regrets signing it. It's like she knows I'll take any loophole I find if she leaves one. I wonder if I'm underestimating her.

There's a heavy pout on her lips and her eyes are all beaded together like a woodchuck. Yeah, she's pissed.

"I'm coming," I tell her. "I just need to change."

"Good. You smell bad."

"Do I?"

I sniff my pits but there's too much sweat on my face and I just inhale liquid sweat. Fuck.

"Take a shower," she commands, holding her nose and wrinkling her watery eyes.

"See you at the lockers then."

"Dustin!"

I swivel around and skate back over to Jayce, ignoring her repeating my name. I can cross the ice much faster to head to the lockers. Jayce unfortunately watches our entire interaction and his dumb, yet still suspicious expression returns.

"Girlfriend, huh?"

"Yup."

"She's already pissed at you. For no reason."

Jayce thinks he's Nancy fucking Drew. I don't need him screwing up my plans.

"Yup."

"You guys bone yet?"

"Nope."

Jayce snickers. "I don't know what the fuck you're up to, man."

He doesn't need to figure it out. The last thing I need is a lecture on morality from Jayce and Cole, or worse, any of Raven's friends interfering with our contract. I have her list of friends and enemies, so I know exactly who to look out for.

Neither do I, brah. Instead of answering Jayce, I grin. We shower and I meet Raven in the hall. I wish she came into the locker room so I could get her out of these clothes. She dresses up for class and she looks fucking great, like a sexy librarian. She even clutches that book in her hands, intentionally hiding the title. It's probably one of her dirty novels.

Jayce goes the other direction to pick Makeba up from her new horseback riding class. I'm alone with Raven again and losing my mind with observing details about her.

I can't handle being near her and keep everything going according to plan. I can't help my desires and I can't help wanting to take what I want.

Raven sits on the bench outside the locker room with that damned distracting book on her lap and she doesn't look up at me until I clear my throat.

"Didn't notice you there." She slams the book shut. Why do I suddenly feel like she's the one in control here? I need to change that. Fast.

"How much time until my class?"

I know she'll pass my first little test. Raven is very detail oriented.

"Fifteen minutes."

Damn. She's pretty good already. I guess it helps that we have the same class this morning.

"Perfect. Come."

"Dustin, my book!"

That damn book can fall into a puddle of water for all I care. I drag her into the locker room as she desperately uses her free hand to stuff it into her bag.

"Let go of me! What the hell are you doing?"

We're out of the hallway, away from my bedroom, away from everything and anyone that could stop this from happening. I grab Raven's cheeks and I kiss her. I didn't expect to find myself overpowered by my desire like this.

I promised myself I would wait and give her the perfect kiss according to her conversations with 'Brett McClure', the alter-ego I used to talk to her. I know exactly what she wants a kiss with a lover to feel like and fuck, she had such a way with words when she described it.

My words are simpler. Raven wants a soft, romantic kiss from a guy who really cares. Man, she fucking loves feelings. My fingers spread her braids apart and I push her against the tiled locker room wall, letting my lips tease hers apart. She's the first black girl I've ever kissed and I love how her lips feel.

She starts off resistant. First, her plump lips offer only gentle resistance. She presses her hands against my chest, offering more. I grip her tightly, because she belongs to me and I want her now. I can't wait a minute longer to have Raven's lips and even if our first kiss surprises her, I don't want to stop. She struggles to pull away after I grasp her harder. Then she pushes me. I can't move away from her. I stop kissing her for a moment to breathe.

"I'm not letting you go," I murmur. No. She doesn't get to push me away.

She presses her palms against my chest, but offers no resistance as I bend my head to taste her lips again. She yields to my lips and I stumble backwards with her curvy body in my grasp. I slam Raven back against the locker room wall and pull away for a breath. Her eyes dart around me in search of an avenue for escape. I'm not letting her get away from me. No fucking way.

"Don't pull away, kitten. It's just a kiss."

Her eyes are so fucking scared, but Raven has nothing to fear from me. When I decide I want a woman, I'm all in —

and I'm all in with Raven Rose. By the time our contract ends, she won't want to leave me. I'll make sure of that.

Just the best fucking kiss of my life. I press my lips to hers again and she makes a soft unwilling whimper as my tongue slides into her mouth. I've only been alive so I could reach this moment. I tug on her lower lip with my teeth and then suck on her full, sexy lips until I need another breath of air. I keep my hands in her hair and gaze at her face, imbibing the surprise, the humiliation and the arousal gushing through her.

Fuck. She loved it.

All she can muster up is one weak-willed word.

"Why?"

I run my fingers across her cheek. More. I want more from her and if I don't stop, I'll take it.

"We don't have time for more," I whisper. "Thanks for sticking to the contract, kitten. Let's get to class."

If I don't stop myself, I'll fuck her here against the wall and I need to stick to my plan. Raven Rose is too damned tempting. I screw up, I lose her. I know how this works. But fuck, watching her walk away from me hurts. I want to pin her ass to the wall and take her. Ravish her.

Patience, Dustin. She belongs to you already. All you need to do is keep her close.

7

CONFRONTATION

RAVEN

top thinking about the kiss. Stop thinking about the kiss. I repeat the phrase like a mantra and miss all the helpful critiques from my creative writing class. It doesn't help that Dustin's in my class and he's sitting across from me, staring. He stares all the time with those large, terrifying blue eyes, unlike everyone else's.

Women at this college have entire freaking group chats dedicated to discussing Dustin's eyes. They're that gorgeous. I drop my gaze whenever I make the mistake of accidentally staring back. It doesn't matter if those eyes are hypnotic. He's the white devil…

We sit around this large rectangular table with everyone in our discussion section and talk about each other's essays. It's one of these fancy liberal arts things that my friends back home make fun of me for — especially Sydney. She doesn't see the point in going to classes if it interrupts her party schedule. I don't care if she thinks I'm a nerd... I love this stuff. I love getting feedback on my writing and helping other people tease out their inner scholar.

Kya and Makeba understand my nerdy tendencies the way friends back home never could. We might have a small black girl crew, but at least we're handling our business and getting that education.

With Dustin's money, I can even take writing seriously someday — not just running a stupid secret fiction blog. Unfortunately, that means surviving Dustin Rathbone's 'dark urges' for an entire year, unless I can think of a better way out of this damned situation. I wet my lips and glance up at Dustin.

He hasn't blinked or dropped his gaze from me for a second. When I look up at him, he smirks, then drops his smile and keeps staring. He's just like those snakes of his, barely blinking. He runs his hand over the fresh sprinkling of stubble on his chin and then mouths something to me I can't quite make out, but it's definitely dirty. I drop my gaze again. One year, Raven. You only have to survive one year.

Today, that year feels like an eternity away. If one stupid kiss can get me this hooked on Dustin, can I spend a year in his service without developing... feelings? Ugh. Just thinking about having feelings for Dustin

I don't know why he doesn't sit next to me when we walk in together, when I already know he told Jayce we were dating because my phone has been buzzing off the hook with texts from my friends.

Fuck. They're going to stage an intervention and if they question me, I'll crack. I'll crack and I'll lose all the money I need to pay my student loans and go all the way to Italy. Hell, I still don't know what I'm going to do with that $50,000. I have some ideas.

Dustin runs his tongue over his lips, still staring. I glance down at my notebook when I feel a foot on top of mine beneath the table. He smirks. I attempt to tug my foot away when he presses down harder. He mouths one word to me across the table. "Mine."

Why is he so damned possessive? I struggle to believe I'm not just another in a long line of conquests. Considering how the hockey boys talk, it's probably some weird racial domination thing. I don't know why it doesn't feel that way, or why he has dropped none of his normal cringe-worthy Dustin Rathbone comments on race…

Mine. He means that damned word, doesn't he? He made me sign a contract. He kissed me like he didn't want to let go of me. Just like that, I'm thinking about that stupid kiss again and losing myself in the sensation of his lips against mine. I had this idea that white boys had thin lips and his kiss would be all teeth, or awkward because of his rough stubble, or his ashy pale skin. But Dustin takes care of himself and he wasn't all teeth and his lips were far from thin and dry.

Why am I thinking about this kiss like I enjoyed it? Dustin isn't my type of guy. I like guys like Jamie Fraser from Outlander – fictional, traditional, and unattainable. I hate that I catch myself glancing at Dustin a few times, staring at his smirk or getting lost gazing at his curls. His hair gets all fluffy and curly when it dries, making him look cute instead of dangerous.

Dustin's stupid, annoying face distracts me so much that I miss our section teaching assistant Nancy, calling on me to comment on Jaleda's essay. It's just a kiss. He shouldn't have a hold on me like that. Like everyone else, Jaleda has spent the first part of the semester writing a lot about coping with the shooting that happened in our dorm. She writes each new assignment about her roommate's death. The noise. The blood. The gunshots. The smell. Different details stuck out to each of us.

I spent most of the summer waking up in cold sweats, sure I heard B.J.'s boots outside my bedroom. It wasn't until I visited Jayce and Makeba that my dreams subsided and I felt like myself again. Dustin would come over from time to time back then, but we never spoke. He was just always out of reach... silent, forbidden, foreboding.

I'm sure Jaleda's essay was deep and powerful, especially since she lost her roommate, but... I wasn't listening thanks to stupid Dustin.

Dustin slides his foot under the table and presses his toes on mine, keeping his sneakers powerfully planted on my shoes, so I stammer some embarrassing answer that earns me a glare from Nancy, who can obviously tell that I'm bullshitting. I take pride in being an excellent student and I don't need Dustin's annoying ass making me look bad.

Shit. I glare at Dustin the rest of class, but he only seems to enjoy that I'm looking at him, so I force myself to look away and make a list of ways I can sabotage his stupid ass when I get back to his bedroom.

I cross my list out when I remember how much money he's offering. He might annoy the hell out of me, but people have done so much worse for so much less money. I signed the contract, now I have to go through with this. I write the dollar amount in my notebook three times, pushing the part where I have to have sex with him out of my head.

I'm not exactly looking forward to being Dustin's 'sexual release'. He agrees that it's part of the deal to please me, but he's an athlete. According to Kya, athletes commit 71% of campus rapes. Predators don't care about making the situation good for the woman.

I don't have the experience to know if a guy who kisses like that can be bad in bed. I doubt it. If I have to believe what's in the romance novels... No... I can't let myself think about Dustin being good in bed. I'm doing a job. That's it. No emotions. No desires. Just... a job.

There are certainly uglier men to lose my virginity to... much uglier men. Dustin might be a dick, but I can't deny that he's fucking hot. He's shirtless liquor ad in Times Square levels of hot. Yummy... but so damned wrong.

After class, I help Dustin with an inordinate amount of homework in the library before I hurry to lunch with my friends, where I expect the tribunal to await me. He drops his creep bullshit for a minute to get his homework done, and a part of me wonders if he's trying to impress me with his efforts. Hm. He should apply his efforts to 'impress' our English teacher since he got a C+ on his last essay for ending it with 'honestly, I'm done here and going to smoke some weed'.

I've been dodging text messages all day, and I don't think Dustin's stupid idea to lie to my best friends will actually work. They'll never believe that we're dating. I don't even think Jayce bought Dustin's stupid story, and Jayce isn't exactly the brightest bulb. Makeba convinced him there was an amusement park beneath Manhattan last summer and he believed it for three weeks.

When I get to lunch, what I face already looks worse than the tribunal. Seriously? If my friends didn't already spot me, I would have snuck over to the far side of the dining hall with my newest mafia romance and hunkered down for a fictional crazy adventure instead of a real one.

See, a normal, not-so-stressful tribunal might involve Makeba and Kya testing my spirit to see how I caught the white devil. This is worse because they brought Cole and Jayce to our lunch table and they both look tribunal levels of serious. Is Cole even supposed to be here right now? We're not too far away from Boston, I guess, but I don't think the fact that I'm 'dating' Dustin Rathbone required

Cole to take a special trip. They look ready to snatch my wig. Great. Thank you, Dustin…

I mumble a greeting and ignore the bewildered expressions on Kya and Makeba's faces. Jayce rubs Makeba's shoulder lovingly as Cole greedily wolfs down some of the tofu on Kya's plate. I don't know how Kya eats that stuff.

I glance down sheepishly and set *Sweet Savage Flame,* my latest vintage read, on the table.

Cole speaks first, which surprises me, since Kya looks like she can't hold herself back.

"I came up from Boston for this emergency, Raven. We're here to discuss… recent events with you."

Recent events? Kya's dramatic streak just might have rubbed off on her boyfriend.

Why are they all so serious? Okay, they all think I'm dating Dustin Rathbone and admittedly, that's insane. But still…

Kya touches Cole's forearm. "Babe, don't mansplain."

"How did I mansplain?"

"I just had a feeling it was mansplaining," Kya says, shrugging and shoveling some tofu dipped in balsamic vinegar into her mouth.

Cole rolls his eyes and sips Kya's sugar-bomb of a coffee order, probably just to put something nasty in his mouth that would keep him quiet. It's best not to get Kya started on one of her hot topics and Cole knows his ass could sit there bickering with her all day long.

Makeba picks up the slack.

"We have to be honest here," Makeba says bluntly. "We all saw this coming."

"Yeah. Well. It gets worse," Jayce says. "I wasn't going to say anything but—"

Makeba interrupts him. "Then you probably shouldn't say it."

"Can I finish?"

"Okay, just make sure it's not racist first."

Jayce shoots Makeba a glare, but she only shrugs and eats a French fry off his plate. Jayce leans forward, pushing the plate over to Makeba so she can devour the rest of his serving, and he turns to me. Jayce has a handsome face, but I disagree with nearly everyone else at Laguna Grove. He's much more terrifying than Dustin.

"Dustin used a fake profile to catfish you. I know you're probably in love with him already, because he has that effect on women, but... he's been catfishing you since last year."

"Since last year?!" Makeba says. "Seriously, Jayce? And you tell us now?"

Jayce tilts his head with a dopey expression on his handsome face. "Babe, I forgot."

In love with Dustin? Why the hell would Jayce even suggest that? Too many pucks to the head, probably. Dustin might be a catfish and he might be a great one, but love? L-O-V-E love? No way. Not me.

Dustin isn't exactly the type of guy you fall in love with. Oh my God. They actually think I have some type of emotional attachment to Dustin. I guess that's our lie, right? We're fake dating and I'd better sell it.

Wait… hold up. Catfishing me?

"What are you talking about? Catfishing me how?"

"Yeah, what are you talking about?" Makeba presses. "Since this is the first damn time I'm hearing of this with your accomplice ass."

Jayce tosses his long brown hair out of his face. "I didn't think it was important anymore."

Makeba smacks his forearm. "Jayce, explain!"

"Dustin has all these different profiles, and I know he has one he uses to talk to Raven."

As if this white boy inclusive tribunal couldn't get any worse. "All those profiles". Holy shit.

"Which damn profile?" Kya snaps to attention. "Give us the name, Jayce. We already beat down one white boy. What's another?"

Cole puts his hand on Kya's forearm. "Babe, relax."

"Who's not relaxed?" Kya says, throwing a hard elbow into Cole's chest to toss his arm off her.

"It's Chet, maybe? Or Brent? Trent? Something like that."

"You mean Brett?!" Kya, Makeba and I blurt out at once. I regret eating anything for lunch because my stomach pulls a Simone Biles and I'm about to waste my food credits by upchucking all over the dining hall floor.

Dustin's a fucking liar.

"Yes," Jayce nods. "That sounds about right."

"You know, I think that name sounds familiar..." Cole agrees, taking another sip of Kya's coffee and making another face.

Dustin pretended to be Brett McClure. The guy I fell in love with online. The guy I lied to my friends about. The guy I thought I had a future with, if only he would show his face. I told Brett everything, and he confided in me, too. He wasn't a monster like Dustin. He was a sweet guy who had a tough life with a father who didn't care about him and a mother, so hopped up on Xanax that she barely knew her own name.

None of that was real.

When Brett didn't show for our third meetup, and after a few weeks of texting over the summer, I blocked him. I had to let go of my fantasy man and accept reality: I was going to die a virgin.

Well, at least I won't die a virgin. But my dream guy is a monster, a liar and a creep.

If he pretended to be Brett, he probably pretended to be the other guys I talked to during my online-dating-getting-over-Brett phase. I never saw Mike's face. Or Jason's. Coming to think about it, I don't even know if their profiles are still active. My chest tightens. He tricked me. Dustin planned this for a long time and he fucking tricked me.

I can't meet anyone's gaze. Did Kya and Makeba have to ensure my utter humiliation by having their boyfriends here? I'm a total embarrassment.

My best friends' boyfriends are also there to witness this public humiliation, making everything ten times worse. Cole and Jayce are cool people. They probably don't even spend enough time on the internet to get catfished because they're so busy partying. Fucking Dustin... I swear, I'm going to kill him.

I had no reason to suspect Dustin Rathbone would hide behind a screen, faking an identity for months to talk to me. Holy fuck.

Everything I told Brett flashes in front of me. I trusted Brett. That's how Dustin got his 'dirt' on me. My own care-less mouth. But now, my friends think this is an even wilder betrayal. They think Dustin tricked me into dating him. But he didn't. He's doing something much worse... I think. I actually don't have a single clue why he's doing this.

"I'm going to kill him."

Cole nods appreciatively, which surprises me. "He's crazy, Raven. Listen, I love him like a brother. I would die for Dustin Rathbone this minute, but he is certifiably insane. I'm sorry, that's just the truth."

"But you let his crazy ass lock me up in a truck?" Kya grumbles.

"He went rogue," Cole said, shrugging. "He's crazy, but... I don't know. Maybe there's a part of him that's a hopeless romantic. Do you want to take that chance?"

I'm glad that Makeba interrupts Cole before I can answer, because I need time to think about that.

"Firmly disagree!" Makeba chimes in. "Raven, I'm sorry, but I've been through it with these crazy ass white boys. It's Dustin... I can still feel the spider hairs on my stomach."

Jayce shrugs. "I mean... if she likes him, she likes him."

"But we know he lied to her," Makeba explains. "He's toxic, Jayce."

Jayce shrugs again. "Maybe he lied for a good cause."

Cole shoots him a warning look. He doesn't want to get into deep shit with his girlfriend just because Jayce is too dumb to keep his mouth shut.

"And what damn good cause might there be to lie?" Makeba says.

Luckily, Kya finally looks up from slurping up the last drops of her coffee and chimes in before Makeba and Jayce can argue.

"It's the physical thing, isn't it?" Kya says. "I get that. I vibe with that. I've been there."

Cole struggles not to smirk and turns bright red.

Kya continues, "But sweetie, he catfished you. He's the one who ditched you all those times and messed with your heart. I can't let him waltz into your life and ruin you."

He's a liar.

"I won't let him ruin me. We're just…"

I'm beyond tempted to spill the nature of our arrangement and get it out of the way. If they don't think I'm falling in love with Dustin, maybe we can stop having this conversation and I can go find Dustin Rathbone's ass and kick it myself.

"You are a hopeless romantic," Kya says. "He could take advantage of that."

"He probably already has," Makeba says. "He's been getting in your head online, girl."

Makeba has a point there. I spent so many days dissecting texts from "Brett" and trying to decode this mystery guy's behavior. I imagined him walking up to me randomly in public and finally introducing himself. I imagined him as tall, slightly tanned, and covered in tattoos. Dustin doesn't have too many tattoos, but he has a few. He definitely looks better than I thought Brett might.

Makeba knows how I felt about Brett. *Brett doesn't exist.* She doesn't have to worry, but my heart still races.

I get their point. Dustin's different. I agree with them that Dustin's different. This news about Brett puts everything he's doing to me in an entirely different light. But this is about keeping my dignity and keeping this a secret, so my friends don't worry about me. Dustin might be crazy, but... I can handle his type of crazy. Dustin's Brett? That means I know him too. I don't believe he faked everything. Those conversations were too real. He might have what he needs, but so do I. Plus, I have the most poignant counter-argument ever for my friends.

"Do I need to remind y'all that both of you kept crazy ass white boys?"

Jayce and Cole exchange glances, but they don't dare speak up. They respect and love their girlfriends' too much to argue that they went about seducing them in the correct way. What the hell makes Dustin Rathbone so different from Cole and Jayce?

"Honey, Dustin's different," Kya says. "He lied to you and used the internet to seduce you in secret. He has a kidnapping kit in his truck. He keeps predatory reptiles as pets. He's different."

Right. The whole catfishing thing. I bite my lip because I really don't want to talk about my awkward internet activities with guys at this school who are actually popular.

And seduce me? What the hell is Kya talking about? Cole puts his arm over her shoulder as she sighs with worry. Shit. Right. They think I'm dating Dustin. Considering the look of horror on my face, I'm probably selling it well enough. It's not like the news about Dustin being Brett hasn't shocked me too.

I have too many things to juggle at once here. First, I need to get them off my back about the dating thing. I'll handle Dustin's little lie later or save the information for my convenience. I just need to get out of this tribunal and focus on why I'm dealing with Dustin at all: money. I want the cash, right?

"Well, guess I fucked up," I say. "How can Dustin be Brett?"

That's not the answer my friends will expect, right?

Cole leans forward. "Raven, I'm serious. You're one of Kya's closest friends and I have to warn you that Dustin has…a sick mind."

"Somehow even sicker than Cole's," Jayce adds.

"Sicker than Jayce," Cole repeats.

"Sicker than Cole."

"Sicker than Jayce."

"Can you two shut it?" Kya snaps. "Raven, we know you're a hopeless romantic looking for the one, but we just want to make sure it's a guy who treats you right and doesn't lie to you."

She has a fair point there. A part of me doesn't want to believe that Brett and Dustin are even the same guy. But Jayce seems sure.

"Listen, you can confront him about it," Jayce says. "If he wants to be a decent boyfriend, he'll tell the truth."

"And I'll be on campus until tomorrow morning," Cole says. "So if anything goes wrong, I'll kick his ass."

"You're going to kick his ass?" Kya asks. "How? He's like the one guy at this school twice your size."

And he's a great kisser. I don't know why the stupid thought pops into my head. I haven't told my friends about the kiss this morning and this definitely isn't the time to tell them that my fake-boyfriend Dustin Rathbone kisses like he's read my romance novels. His lips were so soft and even if he urgently pulled me into a locker room and practically smashed his face into mine, the actual contact between our lips was so perfectly gentle. Damn.

I'm sure my cheeks are flush when I calm my friends down and finally get to eating some of that lunch. Dustin is Brett. That means he knows so much more about me than I could have ever thought possible. I exposed myself to Brett and even if I acted like he meant nothing to me and our conversations were just online, I fell hard for the guy behind the screen. I kept giving him chances to meet me and this past summer, my friends know I tried to break my addiction to talking to him.

He's not real. That's what I spent all summer convincing myself, and when we finally got back to school, I worked up the courage to block Brett McClure, the perfectly imperfect guy who listened to me pour my heart out every day for a year. My chest tightens once lunch finishes and I feel worse, not better, that I temporarily kept my secret.

I scuttle off to my afternoon poetry seminar, a mercifully Dustin-free class where I can hopefully spend the next hour and fifteen minutes thinking about anything else but his lips and his lies. He wants more from me than my servitude. I don't know why, but I'll have to confront him eventually.

After class, I worry Dustin will get pissed at how long I take to get to Pesthouse to begin my 'servitude' before practice. I don't know when I'll have time to confront him, but I don't want to hesitate.

I don't need to worry about Dustin, apparently. I say goodbye to Logan in the doorway of our poetry seminar before I feel a hand clamp down on my wrist the second I leave.

"Good afternoon, Raven."

Dustin is so damn bold. He pulls me aside and presses me against the wall right outside my classroom, kissing me like I belong to him. My back slams against the wall and I make a frustrated grunt as Dustin runs his hands over my hips and kisses me deeper, pushing his hips into mine after a few moments.

When his tongue parts my lips, I sink my fingers into his hair, acting purely on instinct because there's no way kissing him makes any damn sense. It's like I can't remember that I'm angry with him for lying. *He's Brett. He's the guy.*

Dustin doesn't seem to care that everyone else in my class is right there, not to mention all the people at our school walking down the hallways to get to their classes who probably don't want to be assaulted by hockey boy PDA.

But his lips…

He grabs my cheeks possessively and kisses me until he turns red. When he pulls away, his gaze seems different.

"Come," he growls. "It's time to fulfill the most important part of your contract."

❅ 8 ❅

TAKING MY PROPERTY

DUSTIN

I shouldn't have kissed her in the hallway. That's not part of our agreement, but I can't help myself. *She's so fucking hot.* Her lips. Her body. I've never had much strength to resist her. Now that I feel safe out of the shadows, I'm getting reckless. I can't have her here, even if she makes my cock so hard it nearly rips my jeans.

I drag her down the hallway all the way outside to where I park my truck before she yanks her hand away from me. I fucked up, I guess. Too bad that thanks to our contract, she can't run away. All she can do is offer her weak protest. I know she liked the kiss. The way she parted her lips and arched her body towards me gave it all away.

"What the hell was that for?"

"What the hell was what for?"

"Don't play games, Dustin."

Her resistance bugs the shit out of me. She wasn't putting up much of a fight when I pressed my lips against hers. I can't let her push me away now. I try to regain my grasp on her and she smacks me. Fuck. When did she get this petulant? I thought she was supposed to be making this easy.

"I kissed you because you belong to me. You signed a contract, remember?"

"You didn't mention kissing me outside my English class in the contract," she hisses.

What the fuck is with that pissed off look on her face? She doesn't have a right to act all angry. I fucking own her. That means I can do what I want – including kiss her in the hallway. See, this is why I never get into it with women. They don't understand contracts and deals, or things of that nature.

"What's gotten into you, Raven? You knew what you were signing up for."

She still doesn't budge. Her angry face contorts into a more bitter rage.

"What's gotten into me? Are you out of your freaking mind, Dustin?"

Maybe I am out of my mind. What's it to her? And what's the point of staying in my right mind anyway? I have to keep my cool around her. I wet my lips and keep gazing at her, hoping my sternness bends her to comply. She must obey me.

"Get in the truck, Raven."

She meets my commands with further disobedience. I know I shouldn't let her get under my skin.

"I'm not getting in the truck until you tell me what you're hiding from me."

Does the word 'contract' mean nothing to her? I swear…

"If you don't get in the truck right now, I swear to God, I'm–"

"I know your white ass ain't threatening me. That wasn't in the contract either."

My white ass? Where the hell does she come off talking to me like this, damn it.

"Raven, get in the fucking car."

She plants her feet firmly and gives me a glare that says "I'm not doing shit". I search for a good place to grab her when she flings another accusation in my direction.

"You're a liar, Dustin. I signed a contract with a liar." She claps between each word. Every. Single. Word. It's the most dramatic outburst I've ever seen in my life. Can't she see how red my face and ears get? Can't she tell how much she's pissing me the fuck off?

Women… What is it with women? I love them, don't get me wrong, but sometimes I don't understand why they have to talk so much and argue so much. Everything here would be much easier for Raven if she just listened to me. If she obeyed...

I repeat myself, since apparently that's what I've got to do to get her to listen to me. "Get in the car."

"No!"

"Do you want your—

"I already have fifty-thousand dollars, which is more than I had last week. So if you want to play this, we can play."

How does she do this? How does she get the upper hand so quickly? Don't worry, kitten. You won't have the upper hand for long... Fuck. I need to give her something quickly and make her think she has a chance at winning. She doesn't have a chance in hell, but she doesn't need to know that.

"What lie are you referring to, kitten?"

She scowls when I call her kitten. It's my small way of reminding her who's in charge, but she'll get to experience a much bigger reminder soon.

"Brett McClure!" she yells, pushing me so hard that I nearly fall against the truck.

Fuck. Someone opened their big mouth. Brett McClure. What a man. What a myth. What a legend. I don't regret that brief experiment. Hasn't she ever heard not to trust strangers you meet on the internet?

The best place for me to get information about Raven was Raven. I did what any man would do. I lied to her, then slowly earned her trust and gained as much information about her as possible so I could follow her and lure her into my contract, then get her to fall in love with me. How else does Raven think people get married? I'm not into cupcakes and fairies and being so fucking boring the chick wants to kill you when she has what she wants – usually a kid or a ring or some combination of the two.

Unfortunately, if my kitten knows I'm Brett, I can't lie my way out of this because of the source. I covered my tracks well enough to avoid discovery. I wonder which of my fucking friends I'll have to kill for spilling my secret.

"What do you want to know about that?"

What's the point of lying to her now? I don't want to lie to Raven anymore. I have her, and when you finally get the girl of your dreams in your clutches, you don't lie or cheat or fuck around. You do everything in your power to never let her go.

"You won't even have the decency to deny it." Her voice drips with disappointment. Why the fuck does she sound so surprised? She knows the truth, doesn't she?

See what I mean about women? First, she calls me a liar, snarling like a Doberman as she does it, but I tell her the truth and she looks at me like I'm less than dirt. Does she want a pretty lie or the ugly truth? Which one will keep her...

"You wanted honesty, didn't you, kitten? Now get in the fucking truck."

"Bastard," she hisses, rushing around to the other side of the truck.

She glares when I get there first and hold the door open for her. Raven tosses her bag in and hops into the truck. A wave of relief rushes me. She could have run off right then or worse, broken our contract. That would totally ruin my plan. I get in the truck on my side, shut the door and click the lock, just in case she tries to make a break for it.

My plan already appears to be in shambles and if I don't act like I'm in control, Raven will weasel her way away from me. There's no fucking way in hell I can let that happen. I need her tonight. I've needed her for a long time and damn it, I've waited long enough and I've gone through enough trouble.

I make a mental note to slit the throat of whichever idiot ratted me out. Fuck, I won't do that. It was probably Clutterbuck anyway. Fucking asshole. After all the shit I did to help him get his girl… the least he could do is help me get mine. Can't blame him, though. He's an idiot. If it weren't for me, he would have failed physics last year after he stopped copying off Makeba's homework.

Raven folds her arms for a minute in the truck and the second I start the ignition, what does she do? If you guessed making friendly conversation, you would be wrong. She pulls out another fucking book. It's a different book from the one she had this morning. I glance at the title. *A Highlander Never Surrenders.* Where the fuck does she find this shit?

How many books can one fucking chick read, anyway? I run my fingers through my hair, trying to play it cool and obviously distract her from that stupid fucking book with my sexy hair. Raven is totally immune to charms that would have worked on any other chick. She doesn't look up from that book.

"You can't ignore me, kitten."

"Like hell I can," she grumbles and pretends she's talking to the book. I swerve hard on purpose and her tattered church-sale paperback flies across the truck.

"Dustin, what the fuck!"

"Aren't we going to talk?"

"About what?"

"Whatever boyfriends and girlfriends talk about?"

"First, I am your property according to that damned contract. And we have nothing to talk about, Brett McClure. You know all my damn business with your lying ass."

She's still upset about that? I thought when we stepped into the truck it would be like a reset. What the fuck is wrong with Raven? Why is she so goddamned difficult to please?

"What the hell did I lie about?"

"Is your damn name Brett McClure? Are you a wholesome farm boy from Massachusetts with the word 'Redneck' tattooed on his forearm? Do any of these words describe your rich, white, preppy ass?"

She's really mad. Great. That's going to make getting her into bed way harder. Pinning down Raven has already been a huge fucking project. This will only make it worse.

"Not exactly…"

"Not at all, Dustin. You're a demented rich kid with more money than he knows what to do with. Why the hell are you even doing any of this? Tell me the truth. For once in your damn life, tell me the truth."

Women confuse the shit out of me when they ask complicated questions and make complicated requests. Who defines the damn truth?

"You're asking a liar for the truth?"

She apparently regains custody of her book, because Raven hits me hard on the side of the head with it. Fuck.

"Ouch! What was that for?"

"Your moral character."

My cheek and temples hurt from the fierce hit. Doesn't she care I could drive us off the road? Luckily, we only have a couple minutes left before we get to Pesthouse. If it weren't for all these fucking stop signs, I would already have her in my bed.

"I don't have any moral character, Raven. You'll find that out soon."

She glares at me.

"What's the point of trying to scare me, Dustin? I signed your contract. You can drop the crazy ass bullshit."

I don't know how she has this effect on me, really. I want to scare her because I can't. I want to have her, because she won't let me. I want to own her because I know her heart will belong to a hundred thousand fictional men before it ever belongs to me. She has this hold on me that makes my skin burn and my cock hard. It's the desire to pursue a strong woman, a primal urge to pin her beneath me and conquer the impossible — a woman who doesn't wish for conquest.

"You're not scared, so what does it matter?"

She huffs and sticks her nose back in that book. Not on my watch.

"Your lips are soft, kitten. I can't wait to taste them again."

She keeps reading, but I sense my words unnerve her. She has no idea what I have planned for her when she gets back to my bedroom, and I know she must have a million thoughts racing around that pretty head of hers.

She doesn't reply, but I keep going.

"When we fuck, you're going to love it."

She flips through the next five pages urgently. She couldn't have possibly read that quickly. She's pretending to ignore me and doing a miserable job at it. Maybe she could hide her feelings better if she stopped squirming in the passenger seat of my truck.

"I can't wait to put my tongue in your pussy. Then your ass. Maybe I'll put my tongue in your–"

"What else would be left?" she grumbles. "Now, can you be quiet? I'm reading."

She gets me so fucking hard and so fucking angry.

I park in my spot behind Pesthouse, pulling obnoxiously close to Logan Hargreaves' Benz. I still haven't forgiven that asshole for putting his hands on Raven like he had the right to kiss her. Raven slams her book shut the second the truck stops and then she's all business. No more yelling at me about the Brett situation, just a stiff voice.

"I'm going to get your room clean before I submit to whatever evil shit you have planned for me."

I lean over and press my nose into her neck, causing her to freeze uncomfortably in the seat and move those delicious brown thighs again. It's so cruel that I have to wait to take her upstairs to have her when she smells and looks so fucking good now. Even her fucking scowl looks good. She rakes her fingers through my hair to push my head away from her. I kiss her neck and chuckle.

"Why so harsh, cupcake?"

"A nickname worse than 'kitten'. Congratulations."

Right now, she's acting like neither a kitten nor a cupcake–maybe a Trinidad Scorpion Pepper. A kitten would purr and rub itself against my feet. A cupcake would melt in my mouth instead of giving me mouth.

"Get out of the car."

She surprises me by giving no resistance to my instruction. She hops out of the truck with her bag slung over her shoulder and she finally tucks that book away. My shoulders relax. The kinky highlander in her dumb book has nothing on what she's about to experience tonight. If she can handle it. Unfortunately, I let my guard down too long and a sassy lecture erupts from Raven's lips.

"Thanks for telling everyone we're dating, by the way," she snaps. "That totally made day one of this disaster easier."

"I don't appreciate sarcasm."

"Avoiding sarcasm wasn't in the contract."

"What are you, a lawyer?"

"Maybe someday," Raven says. "I'd love to lock your crazy ass up for something."

She trots off to the door without waiting for me. I swear, I am still so irrelevant to her life... That will all change after tonight, obviously, but Raven wears my patience thin. She makes me impossibly hard and impossibly obsessed. Fuck, I want her so badly.

I catch up to her inside and her body visibly tenses at the chaos in the hockey house.

"Don't you guys ever clean up here? It smells like beer, vomit, and a dead sorority girl."

She gives me a suspicious glance as if I'm the dude who killed the sorority girl her imagination concocted.

"Upstairs to my den of iniquity, kitten. No beer there."

She rolls her eyes and stomps up the stairs as I follow until she gets to my hall and then my bedroom. She waits for me outside the door. Shit... I need to get her something. I reach into my pocket for a spare key and take her hand, slamming the key in it.

"You'll need that later."

Before she can protest, I push the door open and usher Raven Rose inside. My heart jumps into my throat. One year of anticipation. One entire year. And I'll finally have her in my bedroom all to myself. She doesn't know how many nights I dreamed about this perfect occasion. She doesn't know how much it hurt to not have her in my bed, to watch from the shadows and know that I could never touch her without ruining her.

I'm going to ruin her. But at least I'll compensate her well for the ruin. That has to make up for my selfishness, right? I turn the red lights off and illuminate my bedroom with my small standing lamp. Raven's chest shudders and she sticks her hands into her pockets, glancing around nervously at the cages and enclosures around my room.

Big Sexy hasn't moved in a while. He's been acting funny lately. Ovie's too busy digesting to move.

"Where do you expect me to sleep in here?" Raven asks softly. She always talks less harshly when we're alone. I love her sweet voice and I love seeing a side of her that the outside world doesn't get to see. Half the team calls her and her friends the 'loud black chicks'. Raven isn't loud. She loves reading and curling up alone. She's quiet. Maybe even... I dunno... cute?

"Book bag under the desk," I say. "We're sharing a bed."

"We have a lot of homework to get through before you even think about sharing a bed with me or anybody else."

Homework? Has Raven lost it? I brought her up here to do anything except homework. Obviously. I thought I made myself pretty fucking clear in the truck. We're here to fuck. Period. We've been waiting for this for a long fucking time, too. Did that kiss in the hallway mean nothing to her?

"I don't have time for homework. We only have an hour before I have practice. I need your cunt."

She raises an unimpressed eyebrow.

"That's plenty of time to get into your philosophy reading. You also have a small response paper due for your litera-ture class."

My cheeks burn. She's serious. She's standing in a bedroom with one of the most physically attractive men she's ever seen in her life (just being honest) and all she can think about is response papers. Words. Books. What's next? Reading while she gives me a blowjob? I have to resist her – even if she's just carrying out my fucking contract. I didn't make a priority list but I'm wicked sure that sex is the highest priority on the fucking list.

"It's not enough time," I muster up, soothing my nerves by sticking my hands in my pockets.

"It isn't? What do you propose we do instead? Clean pet cages?"

If I didn't know any better, I would guess that Raven Rose has never had a sexual thought or urge in her life. But I've watched her cum. I kissed her and felt her kissing back. She has sexual thoughts… they're just deeply repressed in that responsible college girl persona.

"No. There are other parts of the contract I require you to fulfill."

She doesn't need more suggestibility than that, but her body tenses as if the reminder fills her with horror.

"You don't need an hour for that," she protests weakly, but I notice her voice drop and her arms cross in front of her. Other people betray themselves so easily that it's no wonder they find it easy to betray one another. I can read every emotion on her face in the confrontation and I know if I keep quiet blue eyes on her, she will eventually crack. She's only human.

"What's wrong, kitten? I didn't make you pick up that

pen. You knew what I wanted. You signed up for my cock."

"I just don't understand why you need that. Can't you just… you know… Take care of it later?"

"I prefer fresh cunt."

Raven wrinkles her nose. Whatever. I'm not falling for her prissy bullshit. Raven needs to cum just like anyone else. She doesn't know how many times watching her squirm in her dorm room bed has made me cum. It's time for the real thing. Tonight.

"You stalked me, Dustin."

Stalked her? I am tired of her running from me. And I'm definitely tired of her running her mouth.

"I didn't."

"You pretended to be a different person. Don't deny it."

I close the distance between us. I expect her to back away and corner herself against a wall, or one of the enclosures. Raven's not like any woman I've ever met. She's fierce, and she refuses to budge.

"I pretended to be Brett. Yes. You caught me."

"And you planned this entire thing pretty damn well."

"Yes."

"But you won't tell me what you really want from me."

I made it pretty clear what I wanted from her in the car. Raven is the disobedient one.

"Right now, I want you naked."

"Is that really how this works for you? You order women to get naked and they obey?"

"Usually," I reply. "I can see I'll have to be different with you."

"Different?"

"Yes. Different."

I put one hand on her hips and then another. When she relaxes in my grasp, I squeeze her hips tightly.

"Listen, Raven. You will take your fucking clothes off right now. And if I don't like how fast you strip, I'm going to spank you on the ass until you turn red."

Her nostrils flare, and the mixture of rage and disbelief contorts her features.

"You wouldn't dare," she breathes.

"Clothes off. Now."

She glares at me defiantly. I drop my hands from her hips and take a step back to observe her. She isn't stick thin, which I like. Her curves don't sit the 'right' way, either. She has a soft upper body, a small but cute ass. Average tits. But she glows, even if she's nothing like the chicks you see at fashion shows or Boston cocktail parties. She fascinates me because she's different. After years and years of the same old thing, a man craves different women, different shapes, different attitudes. Different races.

I want to watch her undress and reveal the parts of her I yearn to experience up close. I want Raven to reveal her body to me slowly and purposefully so I can finally enjoy what I yearned for the past year and know that she showed me what I could have easily taken. I want my fucking patience to pay off.

"Tick tock, kitten."

She scrambles out of her hoodie first. Underneath it, she wears a navy blue long-sleeved t-shirt from some church camp. She doesn't rush to get the shirt off. That will be marks off for time. I can't contain myself once she loses the shirt. Raven covers up her gorgeous body most of the time, so to see her in nothing but a bra drives me wild. The hot pink satin lifts her copper-colored breasts into the perfect display of large, desirable cleavage. My cock wants to escape.

"Jeans off," I rasp. I don't mean for my voice to sound so old and desperate, but fuck, she's taking too long to get those clothes off.

It doesn't matter. I plan on spanking her anyway for making me wait a year to get her into bed.

"It takes a while to get the jeans over my thighs, you know," she mumbles. I sense she feels shy and even if I want to go to her, I need to exercise my patience. I'll have plenty of time to handle her when I swing her over my lap and punish her for my enjoyment.

Her thumb slips the button out of the hole and she exhales with relief as her stomach spills out of her jeans and she struggles to get them over her hips. Watching her soft body roll and move as she slips them over her hips nearly makes me cum in my pants. Why the fuck have I always had this thing for her? What about her full-figured body makes me harder than steel?

Her hot pink underwear matches her bra, but contains a tiny heart-shaped pattern on it. So fucking cute. So fucking innocent. Her arms cross over her body.

"Happy?"

She shoots the word at me with all the toughness she can muster. She's utterly vulnerable right now. I haven't shed an inch of clothing and I've kept my eyes on her as she strips before me, showing parts of herself that she's never intentionally shown to another man.

"No," I whisper. "I'm not happy, kitten."

She struggles to hide her disappointment, but she's incapable of hiding her fear. Her nakedness forces reality to settle in. I mean what I say and I'm going to do exactly what I promised her I would do.

"I took my clothes off."

"You're wearing a bra and underwear, kitten."

"I mustered up an ounce of dignity. You can see everything you want. Not that it's inspiring or anything…"

Fuck. The thought never occurred to me until her awkward words spill out. She's never done this before and she's experiencing something that I have never experienced, really. I've definitely never experienced it since the situation 6 years ago. She's insecure. She doesn't think her body is good enough.

"I like what I see, kitten."

Her eyes flash back to mine.

"I need to see more," I tell her before she can say something to impede what I want. "Underwear off. Bra off. Now."

"What about that spanking you threatened?"

I bite my lower lip to keep from outwardly celebrating the fact that I'll get to palm her smooth reddish-brown bottom with a rough hand. There's no escaping the spanking. I just wanted to give her hope.

"Clothes off."

This will be much easier if we stay focused and task-oriented. She starts with her bra — an interesting choice. Her breasts were always my favorite to watch through her window. She sometimes touched them and cupped them, pushing them together to simulate how they would look in a pushup bra or sexy dress. She undoes the clasp behind her bra and her breasts sway into view once the fabric hits the floor.

My cock surges. The drive to take her heightens, and my heart races as I desperately conceal my hardness. I don't want to scare her... yet.

"Panties off."

"I was getting to it..." she mumbles. "Impatient ass."

She drops her underwear and oh my fucking God. I bite my lip so hard it bleeds. I don't even bother licking the blood off my lip because my jaw parts slightly. My staring unnerves her. Raven drops her gaze.

"Stop looking at me like that."

"Like what?"

"Like I'm... a freak?"

I chuckle, even if I don't mean to dismiss her. "You are not a freak. I like everything I see."

"This was your plan, wasn't it?" she answers in a voice that sounds nearly defeated. "You just want to toy with me and humiliate me."

"No. I want to fuck you. And I'm going to do that. But first, Raven... we have a problem."

"What problem?"

"You took way too long to undress and now I'm going to spank you." I run my finger over her lips and feel her resistance and her rage wrapped up in the splendor of her naked humiliation.

"I won't let you hit me."

I grin. It's in the contract. She must submit to my dark urges, and I consider this one of them. My cock tents in my pants eagerly.

"I don't want to punish you, Raven. But… you broke the rules."

"I'm not letting your crazy white ass spank me," she sneers.

Her facial expressions convey her fury and her disgust, but Raven can't hide the truth from me. I know her too well. I've been watching her way too long.

"Yes, you will," I whisper. "Because it's going to get me hard feeling you squirm. That's a part of your duty, Raven. Satisfying me."

I'm already hard. But she doesn't need to know the effect she has on me until it's the right time. She will fulfill her contract, even with that sexy quivering lower lip. My kitten doesn't know how far I'll go yet and finally, she shows signs of cracking that hard ass exterior and exposing herself.

"Stop," she says forcefully. Even now, when she's so close to the edge, she fights back. I like her spicy spirit.

"No," I answer tersely. "You gave up control when you signed that contract. This doesn't stop until you get me off. Understand?"

She glares at me, but she nods.

"I know you're a virgin," I whisper. "But thankfully, virgins can still get spanked."

I walk over to my bed and sit. She stares at my lap, disbelieving. She can probably see how hard I am by now, but she's still going to listen. Raven will obey me — I'll make her.

"Bend over my lap. Now."

"Dustin…"

There's that mouth again.

"It'll be over faster if you listen, kitten. Now give me your ass."

9

MY PUSSY LIES

RAVEN

My hands clench into resistant fists as every fiber of my logical brain begs me to defy Dustin's orders. I feel my first flicker of genuine regret at signing that stupid contract. I promised to fulfill Dustin's dark desires and become the outlet for his daily sexual release. What's worse, my friends think we're dating. Everyone probably knows thanks to Dustin's big ass mouth.

"I—

"Our contract, kitten," he says smoothly.

It's unfair how perfectly sexy Dustin's voice sounds. He's evil. Everything about him is evil. He's too hot and what's worse, he knows how hot he is. He knows exactly what effect he has on the average woman and he knows he can have any woman on this campus he wants.

I need to stop thinking about Dustin and what he wants and the machinations of his twisted white boy mind. I'm going to get the bag. Isn't that what Gucci Mane would want me to do? If I'm at the point where I'm looking to Gucci Mane for answers, I must be lost in the sauce, as he would say.

I take a hesitant step forward. The corner of Dustin's lips crinkle victoriously. He pats his lap seductively.

"Come, kitten."

His eyes haven't left my body once. They roam ruthlessly over every inch of the flesh I've kept covered. His tongue darts over his lips as I take another step forward. Those intense blue eyes never leave me.

"Good girl."

I fucking hate what those two words do to me and how they make me want to get to Dustin's lap even faster. My logical side feels compelled to resist him, but there's a force deeper than logic propelling me to obey his command. Money. I keep telling myself I'm only doing this for the money.

That makes accepting my position here easier. I squeeze my eyes shut, like blinding myself to reality will change what I'm doing. I'm a strong, independent woman who doesn't need a man... but I submit myself now to the twisted desires of a white hockey player. I've finally gone to the dark side. If it were anyone other than Dustin Rathbone, Makeba and Kya would be proud, not disappointed. He doesn't have a kind bone in his body and he's going to prove that to me now with open palms against my ass. I don't want him to know I'm scared.

When I finally get close enough to bend over, Dustin's hand clamps around my forearm.

"I don't want you running off."

He knows I won't run. He has to know that. First, I'm naked. Second, where would I go? He promised me money, and he already gave me $50,000 to ensure my compliance with all his twisted desires. I'm here, aren't I? I don't have anywhere to run.

Dustin Rathbone has me right where he wants me. His muscular legs provide a bench for me to lie on and I approach his solid form as slowly as possible without defying him. Dustin awaits my arrival patiently and stares at my body as I ease closer. I bend over his lap, my breasts pressing into the thick musculature of his thighs as his hands run over my back like he's petting a cat.

I keep my eyes shut.

"Are you scared, kitten?" He whispers. His voice sounds like molasses and sweet tea. He doesn't get to have a voice that sexy.

I know he gets off on fear. I lie through my fucking teeth.

"No."

He chuckles and finally runs his hand over my butt. Dustin isn't gentle as he touches me. I'm his property, his possession, and he doesn't care to treat me like anything more than that as his hands forcefully rove my bare skin.

I've never had a man touch me like this before and I have nothing to compare his touch to. I feel surges of sensation through every part of me he touches and a strange growing desire for him. He gropes my ass and then spreads my cheeks apart. The hottest guy at Laguna Grove has me naked over his lap and he's examining me like he's about to eat me. I gasp as he spreads me wide and runs an exploratory finger over my creases.

"Couldn't help myself," he whispers, without sounding the least bit apologetic.

All women comply with Dustin's demands, and I'm just another one. I have to remember that before I get caught up in how it feels to have an attractive man running his hands appreciatively over my body. I have to remember this is just a rich boy's game — nothing more.

He lets my ass cheeks go and then jiggles them together. Is he going to start his sick mission to spank me, or what? I just want to get his torture over with.

I adjust my body on my lap as he continues to grope my ass, and then I feel something lurch beneath me. *Not just something, Raven.*

Oh God. It's big. *No. It's fucking enormous.* What the hell!? It feels like Dustin has another leg between his thighs and it's thicker than a yucca root. Saliva pools in my mouth and my heart feels like I just ran up seven flights of stairs with Freddie Krueger behind me. I can't be this close to it.

I can't *possibly* feel it touching my stomach as Dustin derives some sick pleasure from having me bent over his lap.

"Dustin…"

His name emerges as a desperate gasp and at that moment, when I finally realize the size of Dustin's dick, his hand lands on my ass with the sharpest smack I've ever felt in my life. You know how black parents threaten to knock you into the next week? Dustin delivers on that promise and I cry out in genuine anguish. My ass. Holy fuck. He just hit my ass really damn hard. My scream dries out my vocal cords in one swift exhalation. I'm already so raw… and something tells me Dustin is just getting started.

What the hell have I gotten my crazy self into? Will I really let him do this for some cash? Then again… who wouldn't take a little spanking for a quarter million dollars? I try to rationalize what's happening to me, but Dustin follows up on the pain by leaning in and whispering into my ear.

"I was going easy on you, kitten," he says. What the fuck? This crazy ass white man thinks that counts as going easy? Oh, hell no. That pushes me out of my fantasy. I can't sit here and let him turn my ass sixty shades of purple for a little money. Especially not if he can hit me harder…

Money be damned. I'm not letting this man whoop me all night. My fight-or-flight kicks in and I pick flight first. A morsel of sanity rushes me as I make an escape attempt. I lurch forward as I attempt to squirm away, but Dustin Rathbone's much bigger and stronger.

He holds me firmly against his thighs (and against the giant thing protruding between them). I can't believe my fight makes him even harder. When Dustin mentioned sick sexual desires, I had no idea how far he could take it.

No. I can't endure another slap. If fleeing won't work, I'll have to fight. I lean forward and sink my teeth into Dustin's leg. He sucks in air sharply and responds by spanking my ass again. The second slap is harder than the first and I scream so loud that I obviously let go of his leg.

"Fuck!" I yell, losing myself in the pain. My ass still stings from the first slap and both my cheeks feel like they're on fire. Dustin's warm hand touches my bare ass again and I flinch, even if this touch is far gentler.

"Don't bite me again, kitten."

He doesn't sound angry this time, but his voice drips with warning. If I fuck with him again, he won't just spank me into next Tuesday. No. He'll spank me into the next decade. Against my will, the pain forces tears to gush out of my eyes. I inhale slowly, forcing my body to stop crying, forcing myself to show some strength even while at Dustin's cruel mercy.

"I love your ass," he whispers. "And you'll have something to remember me by tomorrow when you can't sit down."

He strokes my hair lovingly, as if he isn't hurting me, as if the contrast between his painful slaps and his soft words ought to stir something in me. My voice trembles as I try to say something in protest, but no words come out.

"Three more," he whispers. "See? I'm going easy on you."

He removes his hand from my ass and I flinch again before I feel a warm trickle down my thighs. What is that? I attempt to turn around, but I can't because of how Dustin holds me against his thighs. But he runs his fingers over my inner thighs, taking the trickle into his hands and then chuckling.

"Fuck, you're soaked."

Huh?

I hear him sucking on his finger behind me, but when I wriggle again, his grasp tightens.

"Your pussy likes getting spanked," he says. "And I like your pussy."

"Dustin— OW!"

He smacks me again.

"Sorry, kitten. I'm getting impatient. It's hard to focus with your cunt juicing all over my leg."

I squeeze my eyes shut again as humiliation courses through me. What the fuck is my body doing right now? My nipples are stiff and ache as I press them into Dustin's legs and the trickle down my thighs turns into a gush. I've read dozens of books with sex and making love and none of them mention getting wet after receiving the most painful spanking of your life.

I grip Dustin's leg and I swear the next smack hurts less. Maybe somewhere in that lizard brain of his, there's a lick of empathy for me. My ass still jiggles and stings, my pussy still juices down my thighs, but the searing pain subsides quickly and I finally stop my stupid ass crying.

"One more, kitten."

I open my mouth to protest, and Dustin delivers his final smack against my ass. This one is big, so big that his 'third leg' jumps and hits my abdomen, nearly knocking the wind out of me after Dustin already went and slapped me. Right when he finishes, he releases me from his tight grasp and even if I escape his ass and run away, I'm frozen from the experience and holy fuck, my ass hurts.

Immobilized on Dustin's leg, I'm still at his mercy and he may have finished spanking me, but his inspection of my body remains unfinished. He spreads my ass and thighs apart and then swipes his finger along my pussy. A jolt of energy surges through me and I flinch so hard that I literally fall off his lap.

"Ouch!" I cry out as I hit the ground. My elbow slams into the floor and then my ass and I see stars as my freshly spanked ass contacts the hardwood floors in Dustin's bedroom. He peers over his thighs at my awkward, nakedly splayed body on the floor of his bedroom. Dustin grins.

"Sorry."

His annoying ass grin doesn't fall away with his apology. Trifling ass white boy.

"You don't look sorry."

"Isn't that what people say, though?"

"Whatever."

Dustin extends a hand to help me up. I stare at his hand like he's holding a rotten fish. He doesn't expect me to trust those invasive, slapping hands, does he?

"Come on," he says. "You took that well."

"Shut up."

"Why?" he says. "I got you wet, didn't I? You're welcome for the foreplay."

"Foreplay? You call beating the shit out of me foreplay?"

"Take my hand, kitten."

I'm so awkwardly laid out on the ground and I have little choice, so I take his hand and Dustin rises along with me, gazing down at me. Fuck, he towers over me and now that he has completely humiliated me, my usual smart ass comments fade from my mind. I'm just biting my lower lip to keep from saying something dumb that will make him hit my ass again.

"You're going to bruise," he says gently.

"Great."

His cheeks darken. "I've never done this with a woman before, Raven."

I ignore the strange flutter in my chest when he says that. I don't have any right to feel like there's something special going on between me and Dustin. I know what type of guy he is. He can have any woman in his bed and he often does, and none of these women look like me. And apparently he doesn't knock them into the next week. Why does he treat me differently?

"If I hadn't signed a contract, I would have bitten through your leg," I blurt out, hating how freaking defensive I sound. I don't want Dustin to think he can get under my skin. It's bad enough that he's halfway to getting in my pants.

"I believe that," he whispers. "But your body can't help responding, can it? You're wet."

"My pussy lies."

Dustin chuckles. "You're funny, kitten. But your cunt doesn't lie. We both know that. There's a part of you that wants exactly what I'm offering and if you didn't want it, no amount of money in the world could keep you here."

"You don't know me."

Dustin smirks. "Don't I? I'm Brett, remember. I know everything about you."

My cheeks burn with shame again. I don't know how I allowed myself to forget Dustin's most violating act yet. He impersonated someone and befriended me. I told Brett my secrets, spilled my heart out to him, and considered him an actual friend.

Maybe it seemed risky to Kya and Makeba, hell, even to Sydney, but the guy behind the screen was sweet, kind and attentive. He listened to my problems and gave me excellent advice when I needed it. Dustin violated me with his little mind game, and I didn't deserve that.

I shove him, and he doesn't move obviously, because Dustin's too big to be shoved, not to mention he avoids shoves from men twice my size regularly. His solid chest refuses to budge beneath my hefty push. He catches my hands against his chest, that annoying fucking smirk still plastered on his face.

"You got me really hard, kitten. I need to cum now."

See? Any time I get it in my head to have any type of feelings for Dustin Rathbone, I remember that he's arrogant, demanding and cruel.

"I understand," I mutter, turning my gaze away from those crazy blue eyes.

"Okay. But you should cum first."

My gaze flickers back to him.

"That wasn't in the contract," I blurt out awkwardly. I don't even know why my stupid ass says that. Dustin laughs — no more evil smirking, apparently I genuinely amuse him. My brow furrows and I roll my eyes as he gleans entertainment from me.

"I don't need a contract to do what's right. Now get on the bed."

"I'm not putting my ass on anything." I don't think I can sit for a week.

Dustin reaches around and grabs my ass hard, pulling me against him and sending searing pain through me again. I yelp in pain and he only keeps grabbing my ass. What the fuck is his problem? I wince and squirm, and Dustin keeps gripping me, refusing to acknowledge my obvious signs of pain.

"I'll hold your ass off the bed," he whispers. "And then I'll eat your pussy until you forget how hard I hit you. Okay?"

I nod, because there's no way out of this. Fuck. What the hell did I get into?

"What do you like?" he whispers. "Tongue? Fingers? Both? Toys? All three?"

I feel dizzy, like I'm reading one of those consent forms they handed out to us during our freshman seminar. How are there so many options? I've never been in this situation before. I know what I like when I'm on my own, but I can't ask Dustin to do that.

"I... I'm really inexperienced, Dustin. I don't know."

He touches my cheek gently. It's almost romantic. I feel so small looking up at him, but his hand on my cheek also makes me feel warm and half-relieved.

"I know you touch yourself," he whispers. "So show me what you like. Get on the bed and make yourself cum, then I'll do the same."

My throat tightens and my heart goes bungee jumping. I can't do that. I can't lie there and touch myself in front of Dustin. I've never done anything like that before and I don't even know Dustin like that to show me the more intimate parts of my life.

"I…"

"Do I need to threaten another spanking, kitten?"

I know he's teasing, but just in case, I decide not to give him another opportunity to knock me into the 2100s. My cheeks are still flushed and my emotions are impossible to control. I don't want to have this conversation with a guy like Dustin, who has more sexual experience than all my book boyfriends combined.

"I take a long time," I mutter awkwardly. Unlike women in romance novels, the sight of a dick doesn't send me into otherworldly pleasure. I need to warm up and then I need to keep myself going for a while and then I need to push myself over the edge. Dustin betrays no signs of impatience. He shrugs.

"I've got nowhere better to be than right between your legs, kitten."

"Can you call me something else?" I grumble.

"No."

His hands move slowly from my ass back to my hips. Thankfully, because of all the reptiles, Dustin keeps his room warm. I try to tune out the enclosures with various lizards, bugs, and snakes.

That doesn't explain my nipples, but I can't expect everything to be perfect. My body responds too well to Dustin, and as much as I loathe that vulnerability, he draws me in with this bizarre magnetism. Is this just what life is like when you're a super attractive white guy?

I swerve around him and Dustin moves with me, his body oddly in sync with mine. I lie on his bed, slowly, and he cups my ass as he gets on his knees. His hands are easier on my ass than the cotton on his bed would be, so I relax into his grasp.

"Wow," Dustin whispers. "I've never seen a black chick's pussy."

Naturally, he has to spoil the moment by whispering something totally awkward and possibly racially insensitive.

"Dustin…"

"Okay, do it."

"Your face is really close…"

"I'm watching," he whispers, kissing the tops of my thighs. "Now touch yourself, kitten."

I can't believe I'm going to do this. My juices are already dry on the surface of my thighs from the spanking, but

I'm still all squishy at the apex of my thighs. I close my eyes, which makes focusing on the sensations between my legs easier. Normally, I use a romance novel to get me going. This time, I close my eyes and allow any images my heart desires to flood through my mind.

His dick is enormous. Fuck. I hate that my mind wanders there. I've never seen it and I can't even imagine how it looks. They all have different shapes, you know. Large heads, small heads, thick cocks, thin cocks, long ones, short ones, and I can't imagine what Dustin's looks like just from feeling it, but I can imagine the sensation of something so large sliding between my legs.

I've never put anything up there. I always wanted to save myself for a boyfriend or some dream guy I conjured up from the pages of a book. I wonder if Dustin's size would make it feel better or worse? Probably better. My fantasies form coherent images in my head. Kissing. Touching. Hot skin pressed together.

My hands travel to my mound. I rub my outer lips with both fingers. Dustin exhales slowly, his warm breath coating my mound and sending me wild. No… I can't think about Dustin. My fingers slide between my lips and holy shit, I'm wet.

No romance novel, no sexy, erotic scene. Nothing from my imagination has ever made me this wet before. Heat courses through me and I rub circles around my clit, letting the wetness make it even easier for me to massage my clit. I start slowly and half expect Dustin to stop me impatiently, but he's quiet and all I can feel is his warm breath on my mound as I close my eyes and touch myself.

After several minutes, I feel awakened. Each rubbing sensation between my legs makes me squirm, and I let go of worrying what Dustin thinks and just touch myself and allow myself the pleasure. As for my imagination… I know what he looks like shirtless. I can imagine his solid form pressing against me and that third leg of his pressing between my thighs.

Pressure builds in my core as I imagine Dustin's cock, trying to picture the color and the shape and then the sensation of him sliding inside me. I suck in a sharp breath as I feel myself getting close. I've never brought myself this close to orgasm this fast before.

"Don't stop," Dustin murmurs, kissing the top of my thighs as I rub myself. "You're close, kitten."

His kisses push me over the edge. Before I'm ready, I feel the mother of all orgasms crashing into me. I thrash in Dustin's grasp, my ass lifting from his palms as my hips swivel and meet my fingers. I bury two fingers inside myself as I finish, and then sink my palms back into Dustin's grasp, whimpering in pleasure. I've never done anything like this. I've never let a man see anything this intimate.

I keep my eyes closed because as warm pleasure surges, hot shame follows and I can't help but feel like I've done something wrong. This type of display is for boyfriends — not Dustin. He's the hot, unattainable and psychopathic hockey player I know I should stay away from. Staying away from bad boys like Dustin should be easy. He's not like Cole or Jayce, with a heart of gold beneath his harsh exterior.

Before I can say something or use my feet to push him away, he kisses the top of my thighs again.

"That was fucking hot," he whispers. "What were you thinking about?"

My throat tightens again. Great. I should have known he would ask that question. I want to give a generic answer like Noah Centineo or Timothy Chalamet or something, but I know he won't believe me. The guys who get me going walk between the pages of obscure bodice rippers, not on the silver screen. Dustin knows that because he's Brett. I don't even remember how much he really knows about me, but I know it's too much.

"I was... just... blank mind."

The corners of his lips turn up into that devious smile.

"That's a fucking lie."

"I..."

He leans forward with his obnoxiously fierce, icy gaze freezing me in place. "Tell the truth, Raven."

He uses my name instead of 'kitten', that annoying ass nickname that makes the back of my neck feel funny. I don't know what the hell compels me to tell Dustin Rathbone the truth. Maybe it's the orgasm, maybe it's the vulnerability of touching myself in front of him while he cupped my ass in his firm hands.

"I imagined… your dick."

I bite my lip afterwards as if I can retroactively stop the dumb ass words from leaving my mouth. Dustin licks the top of my thigh next instead of kissing it. He doesn't smirk or chuckle this time.

"Good," he whispers. "You'll get my dick soon enough, kitten. Now spread your legs."

That's it? He watches me cum and now he thinks he knows what to do? My logical instincts force me to press my thighs together, but Dustin won't take no for an answer after all this. He sighs as if he doesn't really expect me to listen, but my obedience isn't required for what he wants. Dustin can take what he wants from me, and he knows I can't do anything about it. He wants to own me. That's all he wants. He spreads my thighs apart himself and holds them forcefully. I push against him to shut them again, but once Dustin Rathbone sets his mind on something, he goes all in.

I shudder and accept my fate. I'm going to have crazy ass Dustin's tongue between my legs and I don't know what he'll be like or what he'll do, or if the entire thing will be over in thirty seconds. I've heard horror stories about entitled male athletes. But Dustin just presses his nose between my legs, forcing another shudder out of me as he inhales my scent and makes a low, lusty growl in his throat.

I'm weak. Too weak and wet to close my legs as Dustin closes in on his prize, pressing his fingers between my lower lips and then sliding them up to my clit. As I gasp, he removes his fingers.

"You're all swollen," he whispers. "Fucking perfect."

Dustin's tongue slides between my legs, and he instantly sends a surge of pleasure straight through me. I moan loudly and my ass sinks into his palms deeper. He pulls my pussy closer to his face and allows his curly hair to cover his face as he buries himself between my legs.

My thighs and hips buck forward, but I can't move a muscle with Dustin pinning me in place. I have no choice but to submit to his desires and his control over me. I squeeze my eyes shut and let the sensations of the soft pink muscle against my clit push me close to the edge. How is he doing that so quickly?! Heat spreads through me and I feel tightening through my core like I'm about to burst.

His tongue is so big and so long. Holy shit. He can cover the entire length of my pussy with that thing. He moves his tongue slowly along my clit and then sucks on my outer lips as I scream before moving back to my clit and teasing me with the slow licking and sucking until my body squirms and wriggles relentlessly in his grasp from the pleasure. *Please, don't stop.*

It's like he can read my mind. Dustin grips my thighs and buries his face deeper between my legs. I have no control anymore — just a deep sense of euphoria spreading through me. My fingers sink into the sheet and my toes curl as Dustin's tongue hits the most sensitive part of my clit.

"I— I"

I sound foolish as I gasp desperately, attempting to warn Dustin that I'm about to cum all over his tongue. I feel the gushing wetness building within me and I attempt to warn Dustin that I'm going to cum again.

"Cum, kitten," he murmurs between passionate licks. "Cum all over me."

The very next touch of his tongue against my clit pushes me to the edge. I moan louder, and Dustin moves his tongue faster and sucks harder on my lips. The dam bursts and the most intense climax of my life spreads over me. Dustin grips my palms and runs his tongue over my pussy as I cum hard in his mouth.

He slurps up every drop and then sinks his nose between my lower lips, taking in one last breath of my soaking pussy before kissing my mound and pulling himself away from me reluctantly.

"Keep your legs open," he demands. "It's my turn to cum."

Dustin rises from his knees, his impressive 6'4" frame sending a shiver of fear and desire through me. He's a truly terrifying man, but there's something primal about his appearance that I can't help but find incredibly hot. Fear and attraction come from the same part of the brain, right? It's hard to tell the difference between the two and sometimes, our fear and attraction get all mixed up.

He unbuckles his belt as his hulking shadow blocks the light. His firm hands and broad shoulders get to work, releasing his cock from his dress pants. There's nothing formal about the way he does away with his clothes, however. They drop to the ground and my stomach lurches at the size of the bulge between his legs.

It really is that big. Worse... it's even bigger than I thought. My throat constricts like I swallowed a dinner roll whole. He can't expect me to fit that thing inside me, can he? Despite my terror, I can't take my eyes off Dustin Rathbone's enormous, pulsing bulge.

10

THIS ISN'T NORMAL

DUSTIN

I wet my lips as I await my property's reaction. Raven stares between my legs, but she still doesn't have a clue what to expect. It's a good sign that she hasn't looked away or high-tailed it for the door. The truth about half the women that make it to this bedroom is that they take one look between my legs and they run for their lives. Not every woman wants a giant cock. In my experience, most women don't. They see a dick the size of mine and they think I'll split them in half or break their bones.

One chick even cried when she couldn't get her mouth around the head. Now that was a bad fucking night. Raven isn't crying, but she isn't saying anything either. Normally, I'm not one to complain about a woman's silence, especially not a woman like Raven, whose constant quips keep me on my toes.

I let my boxer briefs drop to the floor and she whimpers. Fuck. She's definitely afraid. I worried about this. All this time I kept myself away from her wasn't for her own good, it was for mine. She takes one look at my cock and her body quakes. The pleasure my tongue provides for her no longer feels adequate now that she considers the pain of allowing a cock as big as mine between her legs.

"How do you fit that in your pants?" She blurts out. It's an annoyingly Raven question and I'm just glad she can't see my cheeks turning red. I don't want her to worry about how I fit my dick in my pants. I want her to spread her legs and stay wet so I can get my dick deep inside her. Get the whole dick in her. Remember when I said that? It's one of my best pieces of advice and it works every time. If I can get my entire dick inside Raven, she'll be mine and she'll be mine forever.

"Carefully," I say. "And by wearing sweatpants a lot."

She squirms to the edge of the bed, too motivated by terror to care about grazing her incredibly sore, bare ass on my sheets. My stomach flips when she winces. I thought I had her pegged, but maybe I was wrong... maybe I went too hard on Raven.

"Dustin, I'm a virgin. You know that."

"Yes."

"You know a lot about me."

"Yes."

She sighs. "That's it?"

"You signed a contract, kitten. I expect you to fulfill it."

My tongue darts over my lower lip again. I technically can't stop her from breaking the contract. It's not exactly like it would hold up in a court of law and as for that $50,000. I can't dip into my trust fund again to get my money back without having to explain how I lost 50k. My snitch ass accountant would run off to my dad to blab about how I'm spending my trust fund, and I'll be in deep shit.

"Your dick is going to break me in half," she protests.

"How can you be so sure, virgin?" I don't mean to sneer, but my voice emerges with a cruel sting. Raven flinches, but my darkness has yet to scare her off. I don't know what draws her to me like this. That dark part of me keeps trying to push her away, even after this contract, but she refuses to let me push. She refuses to let me dominate her, and she doesn't have a fucking clue what that does to a man.

Every word out of her mouth only gets me harder and more determined to pin her to my bed and take her.

"It's at least twelve inches long," she says. "Dustin... that isn't normal."

She neglects to mention the thickness — another problem most women have. I refuse to be ashamed of what I can't change. And as for Raven... she can't let this stand between us.

"I'll be gentle."

I've lost count of how many times I've made that promise. I've meant it each time, but that doesn't mean I haven't left a few women limping or begging me to never call them back because they can't take what I have to offer. Rejection barely hurts anymore, but rejection from Raven would devastate me. I can't handle it — not with hockey preseason about to start and our team on the line without our star player, Cole.

"Dustin… you can be as gentle as you want, but it's huge. I don't know if it can fit."

Before she can scramble away from the bed entirely, I close the distance between us, keeping my eyes on Raven like she could scuttle across the room and escape.

"Babe…"

"It's babe now?"

Fuck…

"Yes. It's babe. I want to try this. And… you don't want to lose your scholarship, do you?"

"Don't refer to your sick arrangement as a scholarship."

"I promise I will make you cum. Now get on the bed, kitten. Don't make me ask twice."

She narrows her eyes, but then she sighs and lays back. Her breasts jiggle beautifully on her chest and I let her lie there for a moment, just appreciating every inch of her physique. I've always found Raven Rose gorgeous. She's the forbidden fruit I've wanted for so long and nothing

I've done to keep away from her and stop myself from ruining her worked. I set this in motion and I need to follow through.

I wet my lips and get on my knees again.

"If you're worried about my dick, I can get you wet again. Relax, kitten. I'll take care of you."

Her thighs part slightly again. My heart quickens. This is working. Thank fuck it's working. I spread her lower lips and her slick juices are still keeping her soaked and sticky. My tongue works between her legs again. Raven moans when I brush against her clit and I easily make her cum twice before I scoot her over on my bed and press my body on top of hers. My cock stiffens against her leg and I face her as I press my weight into her. I'm clothed. She's safe. We just need to take this slowly.

I gaze into her gorgeous brown eyes and she stares back, unflinching. She doesn't mind my staring. She just looks right back and refuses to break the overly intense eye contact that I enjoy. Without fail, my gaze forces women to squirm and glance away with discomfort. Raven just stares back and then she touches my face.

"You aren't as fucked up as you want people to think," she whispers.

"I want you," I murmur back.

I don't want to talk about my feelings. I don't want to talk at all. Blood pumps fast throughout my body. I press my lips to hers and kiss her. Raven's perfect hand rushes to my cheek and she arches her hips up as she kisses back. When she pulls away, she rests her hand against my chest. She's touching me. By choice. My jaw clenches and moves nervously.

"If I didn't know any better," she whispers, running her hand through my smattering of chest hair. "I would say you were just as nervous as I am."

"I've waited a long time for this."

"How long?"

She runs her hand over my chest more. My cock jumps against her leg. I don't want to lie to her. I don't know why. Lying to women has never been a problem for me if it suited me. But I can't lie to her. Brett can't lie to her. I dry swallow.

"Since the day I met you."

"Bullshit."

"You felt what I felt last year," I whisper. "Didn't you?"

"Then why are we here like this?" She says. "Why did you trap me in a contract and trick me into your bed, Rathbone?"

Her hips hook around my thighs and if I didn't know any better, I would say that I fucked up somehow and gave Raven Rose the upper hand.

"Because," I murmur, hot shame coursing through me. "I'm a rich white guy and you're dirt poor. And you're black. The world isn't ready for that yet, is it? Even if it should be."

She runs her feet along my thighs. My cock wants to burst. I need to get inside her while she's nice and wet. I don't care if she's black. Fuck, I want her because she's black.

"That means we can't ever work then," she whispers seriously. "Because we're too different and I don't fit into your world."

I press my hips forward. I don't even want to entertain the thought of letting her go.

"I don't fit into yours either," I murmur, kissing her cheek and then her neck. "Come on… your friends think our fake relationship is a crisis."

"Let's not think about anyone else then," Raven says. "I want to lose it to you, Dustin. But… you can't break your promise. Be gentle. My ass is sore enough."

I nod, but I'm so hard she could have had my consent to just about anything.

"I won't break you, Raven. I promise."

I kiss her neck, sucking as much of her flesh as I can between my teeth. My heart pounds like crazy. I want her so fucking bad and I've waited so fucking long. This feels better than a hat trick, better than the sweet sweet rush of adrenaline from sailing across the ice. I run my hands over her hips and then allow my fingers to tease her large, flawless nipples. As I stroke the small bumps around her nipples, my cock stiffens more.

Her hands stroke the back of my neck, and I freeze. Going slow doesn't feel like it should be a real option with her. I don't want to take my time with Raven. I've waited so long to have her in my bed and my cock wants her. She's so sweet and soft, so gentle that I know it makes me a monster to keep her here. But I don't care. I want what I want.

I run my fingers along the length of her thighs and touch her mound again.

"You have a perfect pussy, Raven," I murmur, kissing her neck again. My fingers massage her clit a moment longer and then I slowly press one of those fingers against her entrance and as she gasps, I slide my finger inside her pussy. She's so fucking warm and tight...

Raven moans as I push my finger in deeper, right up to the knuckle. I can move my fingers inside her slightly, but she's still untouched and tight. I hook my finger inside her and slowly massage her walls from the inside. She moans and bucks her hips toward my palm.

"Dustin..." she moans.

"Shh," I whisper. "Feel good, huh?"

"Yes..." she whimpers. Fuck, her voice sounds so sexy when she's all weak with lust. I kiss her neck and keep massaging her inner walls as she gets wetter and closer to climaxing. One finger won't get her ready enough. I tease Raven as she moans until she's close to the edge and then I add another finger to her slowly. This time, she breathes slowly and as her moaning stops, I taste her earlobe and nibble a little.

"Does it hurt?"

"Yes…"

"You're tight," I whisper. "If I need to get you ready, I'll need to be gentle."

She whimpers again as I move my two fingers around inside her. Raven's hips swivel and she squirms beneath me. Holy fuck, she's tight. My heart quickens and worry surges through me. I've wanted her for so long that I never considered the possibility that she might be too tight, that my size and everything about me might ruin her too much for her to want me.

I push the thoughts out of my mind and push my fingers deeper instead. She moans with pleasure and my sense of pride surges. I can make her cum and once I can make her cum, I can keep her. Raven's body responds well to two fingers, but she's nowhere close to a climax and I'm nowhere close to getting my cock inside her. With two fingers, I massage her g-spot and use my remaining fingers to tease her clit to an engorged state. As I kiss her and fuck her with my hands, I push her over the edge to an intense orgasm and press my body against hers, pinning her to the bed with my weight as she cums.

Raven is so hot when she cums. Her hips move against my hand as she grinds her hips to take my fingers deeper. Her moans are fucking hot and every movement of her body has a dancer's grace. She's not just a chick you take to bed. She's a chick that a dude could fall in love with if he wasn't careful. If he watched her long enough. If he came to understand her little quirks and the way she moved, and her deepest desires.

If a guy wasn't careful, he could fall in love with her before getting the whole dick in her. That would be a problem.

I ease my fingers from Raven's cunt and press them to my nose. I don't see the point in resisting the urge. I want to smell her beautiful pussy, even if I've tasted her plenty already. I fucking want more.

"Dustin…" she whispers. "Don't smell me."

"Why not?" I murmur, tasting my index finger. "I like how you smell."

She rolls her eyes.

"You taste even better," I whisper.

As she opens her mouth to respond, I slide both my fingers between her lips and her instincts push her to suck on my fingers instead of violently biting down.

"Taste yourself," I whisper as she sucks on them. "Come on…"

Raven sucks her juices off her fingers and when I take them out of her mouth, I put those fingers right back in mine. She tastes so fucking good.

"Good?" I murmur.

"Weird," she replies. "I don't know."

"You get used to the taste," I whisper. "I like it. Obviously."

Raven wraps her perfect fucking thighs around mine, still tempting me to plunge into her without warning and just take what I want without caring about all the ways I could destroy her tight ass pussy. But there's something about her warm brown eyes that stops my monstrous urges from taking over.

"Your dick is much bigger than two fingers," she whispers. "How is it going to fit?"

"Do you trust me, kitten?"

"Um... do you really want me to answer that?"

But as she whispers her distrust, her body moves closer to mine. Our lips might lie, but our bodies don't and as Raven moves, I sense that she trusts me. She might not want to trust me and she might not know why any part of her bothers with trusting me at all, but she can't help it.

"No," I murmur, kissing her nose. "Don't answer, kitten. Let me prove myself."

She braces herself against me and wriggles, but I have her pinned to my bed and there's no way in hell I'm letting her go. I free my cock from its trapped position and maneuver the mushroom head against her entrance. The soft head pushes against her tightness and her resistant entrance pushes back. I can't ease my hips in, but I can't rush in and hurt her either.

Raven's body tenses and I kiss her until she softens again before attempting to press the head of my cock to her entrance again. I push my hips a little more forcefully and she gasps as the head of my cock stretches her open and I begin my entry. Just the head is enough to hurt her, and she hasn't even gotten to the widest part of my cock. She's mine — and I'm always careful with what's mine.

I'm the broken one. I don't need to break her, too. I stroke her cheek and kiss her slowly.

"I'll go easy, kitten."

I push my hips forward another inch. Her tightness registers around my stiff pole as her incredible pussy cinches me in its death grip. Blood rushes to my face and my hands grow incredibly cold as my blood fixates on two parts of my body. Raven's cool hand touches my face.

"You're all red," she whispers, mystified by the sudden change in my coloring. I grit my teeth as a vein bulges from my neck and I nod in response.

"You're tight," I manage through strained breathing. "Really fucking tight."

She runs her hands over my bare back next, forcing desire to shoot through me. Stay in control, Dustin.

When her hands grip my bare ass, I lose control. I grunt as my hips move forward again. This time Raven cries out and her pussy grips my dick so tight that I know it hurts her. I should stop. I can't do this to her.

Raven responds to more of my cock between her legs by running her fingernails over my ass. I'm frozen, torn between my fucked up desires to penetrate her and the fact that I can't bear the thought of hurting her this way. Spanking her is one thing. She'll be fine in a couple days. This could injure her.

"Why did you stop?" She murmurs. My heart thuds a million miles a minute. With my cock buried halfway between her legs and gripped so tightly by her cunt, I don't have control of any part of myself, especially not my words.

"I can't hurt you. I can't."

What the hell is wrong with me? How can I hesitate when I'm this far? What's this weird feeling like I actually give a shit? Hurt her. I just need to push through the pain and hurt her. But I can't.

"Put it in Dustin," she whimpers despite the slight contortions of pain registering on her face. "I want to feel you. I'm not scared."

She digs her nails into my ass and squeezes her thighs around me, drawing me deeper, willing me to bury my full length in her cunt. I bite down on my lower lip so hard that it bleeds. I wanted to be strong enough not to hurt her, but I can't help myself. I force my hips forward and

Raven screams as any woman would taking so many thick inches between her virgin thighs.

Her genuinely pained yelp forces anguish to surge through me, but the monster between my legs finally has what he wants and he doesn't want to stop. With our hips smashed together, our bodies have never been closer and the soft heat grabbing my cock isn't the only thing about Raven driving me wild.

She smells like rosehip oil and her skin tastes salty and delicious. She's so fucking soft it's crazy. I can't fuck her the way I wanted to. I can't.

"Baby, I can't," I growl, burying my face in her neck. She clutches my back with her thighs.

"Yes, you can," she whispers. "You feel... good."

She can't be serious. I heard her scream. If I move even slightly, pain returns to her face.

"Don't lie for me," I whisper. "Just don't."

"I think we both know we want this," she whispers back. "We're here. Now go easy... I'll be fine."

"No..."

"I'm tougher than I look, Dustin... now make love to me. Just the way you want to."

I meet her gaze and for a moment, I feel exposed. She knows. I don't know why the unfocused, panicked thought enters my head, but I suddenly wonder if I've seriously underestimated Raven Rose. I can't look away from her and I can't bring myself to move my hips and cause her any more undue pain.

"What did you say?"

"Make love to me," she whispers. "I'm not afraid of you. I'm just... not."

I bend my head to her neck again, inhaling that perfect scent and willing myself to try. My body wants to cum. I want to cum inside her. I know we're playing a dangerous game, but I want to take her permission and run with it. I withdraw my hips slightly. She gasps from the absence and then cries out again when I bury myself inside her. She's still so tight and it still hurts her so much for the next few strokes.

With each anguished cry, she refuses to push me away. Raven stubbornly kisses me and pulls me tighter until her pussy adjusts to my size and once it does... we set my bed on fire. I've never had anyone like her. I've never had anyone so perfectly soft and sweet, so patient with accepting my monstrous cock.

I've never felt this way about another woman. And fuck, the feeling scares the shit out of me. She pulls me in deeper and moans with pleasure this time. Her body squirms deliciously against mine, and she runs her fingers through my hair as I make love to her. Just the way I want to. How does she know what I want? How can she possibly know that more than fucking a woman in my bed, I want something slow and soft... and sweet?

I can't stop myself from kissing her. We kiss as my hips move slowly and with each slow movement, Raven gets closer and closer to cumming. I ease my hands between her legs to help her along and I don't take my lips off hers until I feel her body tremble with a climax. Once she cums, I keep fucking her slowly until she cums again and I keep her cumming on my cock with each stroke after that. I'm so big that once I awaken every nerve between her legs, she can't help but respond to each stroke with absolute euphoria.

I clutch her body close to mine and after I lose track of her orgasms, I push into her deeper and slower to make myself cum. She clutches my ass with her heels and runs her fingers through my hair as I get close.

"Cum inside me, Dustin," she whispers. "Cum inside me…"

Those words are kryptonite and I fucking lose it. I make a nearly humiliating animalistic grunt and empty my balls between her legs. I finish so hard that my cock aches. I don't want to remove myself. I want our bodies pressed like this forever. Raven surprises me by smiling once I finish and catch my breath.

"What are you looking at, kitten?" I whisper. But we're both grinning. Both caught up in the euphoria of having the best damn sex of both of our lives (although technically Raven doesn't have much to compare it to.)

"You. Duh," she whispers. "That was fun."

Fun? That was more than fun. My heart still hasn't caught up with my breath and I feel shit I haven't felt in… I'm feeling. For her. For someone else.

"Raven…"

"I know you had a good time," she says with that light-hearted smile on her face. She doesn't have a clue I'm about to wipe that smile away.

"I love you," I murmur. I want to pretend it's impulsive and stupid, but I actually fucking mean it. I'm that fucking sick in the head that I tell her right there exactly how I feel. She'll think I'm a creep and a stalker and a fucking sicko, but I don't care. I'm the type of guy who goes after what the fuck he wants and every part of me wants Raven.

I repeat the three words. "I love you."

I don't know why I tell her right then with my cock buried inside her, but I can't help myself. I know it's too soon. I know it makes me seem like I'm fucking crazy, but I can't help myself. I love her. I loved her the minute I laid eyes on her, but with all the shit I've been through, I guess I didn't see it. I didn't see her until I had her in my arms, until I knew she wasn't going to reject me for one of the many parts of myself I can't change.

"Dustin… um…"

I've broken the spell I put on her. No climax can stop her from coming to her senses. She presses her hands against my chest to push me away from her. No. I don't want that. I freeze, keeping her pinned to the bed with my hips.

"I mean it."

"Why?"

What kind of fucking question is that? I don't need an explanation and I don't have one. I can't exactly tell her what I did for a year, the ways I wormed my way into her heart and her secrets, and the way my fucked up plan to get with her turned into something more. There's a reason Brett kept coming back to her. There's a reason I kept coming back to her.

"Because Brett McClure loved you."

"Stop that, Dustin. Just stop it."

I push my hips forward, pinning her tighter and allowing my cock to come back to life. I can feel my cum moving around inside her as my cock stiffens to its full girth again. Raven squirms uncomfortably because she can't avoid feeling my dick as it engorges inside her tightness.

"I can't help what I feel."

"You don't have feelings," she says. "You've said so yourself."

My throat tightens, and then I lose it. My erection subsides between her legs. She's wrong about me and worse, I'm wrong about myself. See, I used to think exactly what Raven thinks. I used to think that I didn't have any feelings, but fuck, I was wrong.

"I was wrong," I whisper. "It's just... something really bad happened to me, Raven Rose. Something fucking awful. And it broke me into a thousand pieces."

Her thighs tighten around my torso. My cock grows again to half-arousal from her touch, but a confusing blend of emotions surge through me, threatening to take me over and pull me away from her again.

"What happened, Dustin?"

Her fingers are so fucking soft. I want to spill my guts to her, even if it's a bad fucking idea.

"I can't tell you," I murmur. "I can't tell anyone. Most days, I can't even admit it to myself."

"Then don't say anything tonight," she whispers. "I'm here. I'm yours. Let's just... enjoy it."

I would have set myself on fire if she asked me to. Thank God she's not that sadistic. She just moves her hips until my hardness grows to size and then she fucks herself on my dick until she cums. Her body moves beautifully against me and I cup her soft copper skin against mine as she orgasms. We rock our bodies together for the rest of the night, intertwined in bliss, until I climax again. This time, my cum gushes from between her legs and coats her thighs in stickiness. She's so full she can't accept any more of me. We keep making intense, sticky love until we can't breathe.

When I withdraw from Raven, we don't want our bodies to move apart, so we kiss until our lips are raw.

"You're sleeping right here tonight," I murmur. "I hope you know that."

She nods and nestles in my arms. After a long night of hot sex, Raven's perfectly scented body provides soft warmth to mine. She falls asleep quickly, but I still can't bring myself to fall asleep. I love her. I don't want to let her go.

11

THE LOVE STORIES WERE RIGHT

RAVEN

Last night was the least boring night of my life. *I lost my virginity to Dustin Rathbone.* I don't think I'll forget what he felt like between my legs, and not just because of all the orgasms. There's a tight ache between my legs from his immense size. I've done the research, and I know that whatever Dustin has between his legs is significantly larger than the average male organ. He wasn't just long, but thick, and fitting him inside me... let's just say I'll be limping today. A lot.

I think I'm awake before him and try to wriggle away from his grasp, but Dustin just pulls me back against him and snuggles me tightly. My chest tightens. Sex wasn't the only fascinating turn of events from the night before. I signed up for the sex. That's how I'm getting my money, right? But the everything else around the sex still drives me mad. I love you.

I don't know what possesses Dustin to say those words to me. I know his true darkness. He's cold and manipulative when he needs to be, and I know he will say anything to get what he wants, so I can't trust him. But that was before I felt his body against mine. That changes every-thing… My stories were right.

I sensed things in Dustin Rathbone that I'd never sensed before.

"Good morning, kitten," he whispers in my ear. That raspy voice does something to me that it's never done before. I squeeze my thighs together and unconsciously push my hips back against him. What the hell am I doing? I can feel him already as I rub my butt on his thigh and he's stiff.

He chuckles and wraps his arms around me tighter. I can't let go of anything that happened last night, especially not how close Dustin came to telling me his big secret – or what I assume is his big secret. I've never seen him show so much emotion before. But then he clammed right up. If any part of Dustin really loves me, he'll tell me the truth. You don't lie to the people you love. I let him stroke my hair and press my butt against his body. He's so damn muscular.

"What happened to you, Dustin?" I murmur. "I want to know."

"First thing in the morning, huh?"

I can feel his discomfort, but he doesn't stop pressing his nose into my neck.

"You don't have to tell me if you don't want to," I say.

But I know Brett would have told me. And even if I should hate Dustin for pretending to be Brett, there's a part of me that realizes... he's still Brett. He still shared those feelings and sent those messages. There's a part of Dustin Rathbone that I fell for last year and now that we're in bed like this, I'm weak to that part of him. He doesn't stop stroking me as he answers.

"If I tell you, you'll leave."

I've never heard emotions in Dustin's voice before. Not like this, at least. Even when he's angry or frustrated, he's always had utter discipline over his rage, controlling every note of his voice. This time, his voice rasps uncomfortably, and he shifts his body around me, clutching me tighter.

"You don't scare me."

"Liar," he murmurs.

"If you scared me, I would have tried to escape. I wouldn't have taken your money and I wouldn't be here right now. I'm not afraid of you."

I wriggle away from his grasp and turn to face him. I know that isn't what he wants. Dustin fears facing me, facing his heart, more than anything. I know that because he's Brett. He might think he knows everything about me, and that I'm the one who spilled all my secrets, but he hits his head all the time. I doubt he remembers every detail of our conversations. I'm a bookworm by nature. Words dance around my head all day, and I remember many words typed by "Brett", the crazy blue-eyed boy lying across from me.

Despite his reluctance to look at me, Dustin's eyes can't help but meet mine. They are so fucking terrifying, honestly. I remember the first time I saw someone with blue eyes when I was a toddler. I cried and offended my mixed auntie. Dustin's eyes have that same terrifying hue, giving his face an otherworldly intensity. There's a five o'clock shadow across his face, only accentuating his gorgeous jawline. I pull my body closer to his, never breaking his gaze.

His brow furrows again, expressing more emotion than I've seen from Dustin before.

"I... I can't," he whispers. "I want... fuck, Raven..."

"Tell me," I repeat. "I'm contractually obligated to keep your secrets, right?"

"I didn't write that in the contract."

"We can make a new contract – a verbal contract. Right now."

His throat tightens, and he nods. "Okay."

I'm surprised that he trusts me enough to tell the truth. Dustin Rathbone tells me his secret. Six years ago, one rainy night in Boston, the cruel hockey player's life changed forever.

"They're all dead now," Dustin whispers. "My dad made sure of that. But he's still the reason it happened. No one who has as much money as mine has clean hands, Raven. That's what you need to understand."

Hands. I want to touch his hands. Mine shuffle beneath the covers until I find his hands and I interlace our fingers. Dustin squeezes my hand tightly. His broad shoulders pull closer to his ears as his thighs push against mine and our bodies press so close, our lips nearly touch. Dustin's eyes flutter shut for a moment and he runs his tongue over his lips, biting down on his lower lip before he opens his mouth and allows the words to spill out.

"My dad pissed off some fucked up people. I played hockey for Milton Academy, huge team star, always in the Globe, rich fucking dad. I didn't know I was a walking target. Dad always kept his business private, you know?"

I wish I could relate. My heart races as I hear the slow beginnings of Dustin's confession. If any story or event can turn the eternally cool Dustin Rathbone into this tense and sensitive person, I can't imagine what it might be. Something dark enough to break him? Something dark enough to cover up the person he was when he hid behind a screen?

I want to be angry with him, but my curiosity gets the better of me. That's the problem with falling in love with stories, you can't break the habit of wanting to know more, even when you're pulling a deep dark secret out of a deep dark man and even when common sense tells you that it's so much smarter to run.

"I didn't know you went to a private school in Boston."

"Dad would have died before sending me to public school. He nearly died after that night. I remember we were playing Nobles & Greenough at home. They're tough kids, all coked out, but tough, and we kicked their asses. I scored my first hat trick that night. Wicked hat trick. Great night in that regard."

He continues about the hat trick for some time, and even if I want him to get to the point, I understand that's what athletes do… reminisce about their sports victories before getting to the point.

"Anyway…" Dustin whispers after telling me about the game. "My team went out that night to this place that didn't check IDs. Believe it or not, I was the quiet one. Didn't say much, I didn't drink much. That night I thought I could let loose."

He presses his forehead against mine.

"None of my friends know this," Dustin whispers. "So you have to promise to keep this secret, Raven… or I'll have to hurt you. I don't want to… but I'll have to."

"I won't tell anyone," I whisper back, squeezing his hand. "I promise."

"I drank too much," Dustin continues. "I went to throw up in the bathroom and that was the last thing I remembered for a while. When I woke up, I wasn't at the bar anymore. Six guys had me and they beat the shit out of me. They took away my dignity, and they left me for dead."

"Took away your–

"Rape, Raven," Dustin murmurs, refusing to change his tone of voice or show any genuine hurt from the horrific story he's telling me. "Lucky for me, I don't remember most of it."

He unlaces our fingers and takes my hand, pressing it against the hair on his chest and then sliding my hand down more on his abdomen. I flinch when I feel the raised skin. I didn't notice in the dark, but my hands notice the rough texture on Dustin's body. I assumed his scars were from hockey injuries and never thought twice about them.

"This was from a ten-inch serrated hunting knife and nearly pierced my kidney," he murmurs. "They left me for dead, but I woke up. Somehow. I don't think I should be alive, Raven… but I'm still here."

My chest shudders as Dustin runs my hands over different parts of his body, naming the weapons the men used, describing the ways they beat him and the horrors of the worst night of his life. He detaches as he continues describing the attack with clinical coldness until I can't take it anymore.

"Dustin, stop." My voice warbles and I'm surprised to find myself crying. I read novels that expose the most horrific parts of human nature. I don't have a sensitive stomach and I've never met a story I couldn't handle. This is the worst I've heard. Dustin drops my hands and murmurs an apology.

"Sorry, kitten. I'm so fucking sorry."

He bends his head, letting the brown curls flop casually around his face. I don't want him to break away from me. I pull his face close to mine and kiss him. He pulls away in surprise.

"Raven…"

"Stop talking," I whisper. "You told me. And now I know."

His brow furrows in an expression I might have mistaken for anger on another day. I don't think I'll misunderstand Dustin Rathbone the way I have before anymore.

"I don't understand."

"You aren't a monster, Dustin. I know you think you're a monster. I know you're scared to feel what happened to you, and I know you're scared to push people away. But you're not a kid anymore. You don't have to be afraid. And you don't have to care what people think."

"People would think I was a… you know…"

"You didn't cause that attack," I say. "You survived. Whether we're rich or poor, white or black, we all have dark shit to survive, Rathbone. I think you've done a damn good job making it out okay."

"I haven't been close to another person in six years." His cheeks darken. "I don't know why I let go with you, Raven. I made that fake profile to mess with you, but fuck, kitten… you got into my head."

"Brett got into mine."

Dustin nods. "Yeah. I guess he got into mine too. Because I forgot the part where it was all a game, and I started falling for the girl on the other side of the screen."

"You already know how I feel."

Dustin nods, then moves his hands between my thighs. "Shall you begin your duties for the day, kitten?"

I nod and push my head against his chest. I can feel his heart beating still and slow, calm throughout the storm. Maybe the love stories weren't all the way wrong about bad boys. Maybe even guys like Dustin have a heart of gold beneath it all. I rake my fingers over his chest and then pull him in for a kiss.

"I'm ready, Dustin."

"Then spread your legs, kitten. I want to feel you."

12

HOCKEY LIFE

DUSTIN

Our new forward is no match for the line we had with Cole Seabrook, but the new kid shows slow signs of improvement during our pre-season skates. Our first real game this year won't be until much later in the semester, but we still need to practice. Only problem with practice today is Logan Hargreaves won't stop sticking to my ass, pestering me about Raven Rose.

I don't want to answer questions about her.

"When did you start dating, eh?"

Jayce steals the puck from the distracted Canadian, ensuring I don't have to answer that stupid fucking question myself. Why the hell is Logan Hargreaves asking questions about Raven at all, huh? He needs to mind his fucking business and stick to poutine and beaver tails before I kick his fucking ass. It's bad enough that he kissed her and I've had to forgive him for that.

Well, I did put a Madagascar hissing cockroach in his skate every day last week. But aside from that, I forgave him. Roaches are old news anyway. I need to get a new snake to put in an enclosure next to Ovie.

Logan steals the puck back and shoots on Barkov, who catches the tough corner shot. He's much better this year than he was last year. Winning should be easy for us...

Three weeks of Raven in my bed, and I still can't make it through hockey practice without thinking of her. Weed doesn't help keep my mind off her. In fact, drugs only make me more obsessive towards her. It doesn't help that I've never told anyone my secret before her, and that every time she's alone, I panic that she'll betray my trust.

She's just a woman. I've never had a woman twist me up in knots like this before and the feeling absolutely fucking sucks ass. Raven's different too. If she broke my trust, that would legitimately hurt. I hate to admit it, but it's how I feel. Fucking feelings. Those are all her fault, really.

Jayce skates up to me after practice and asks to talk. He's all serious, like I've done something wrong, or somehow, he's done something wrong. Who am I kidding... he probably wants chick advice.

"I've got you, brah."

After a quick and dirty shower, I meet Jayce tapping his feet impatiently outside the locker room, his wet hair combed back like he's got somewhere important to be. I shake my curls out on him and ignore Jayce's irritated glare.

"What do you want, brah?"

"I need to talk to you about Makeba."

I grin because this is totally my specialty. I have so many great sex tips for Jayce. I can help him fix things with his girl if that's what he needs.

"Chick advice. I knew it."

"I want to marry her, dude."

Okay… I blink slowly to buy myself time. This is normal dude stuff. Normal human stuff. Raven keeps trying to tell me that it's okay to feel shit. Three weeks of living with her and it's worse than having a fucking therapist.

Therapists are easy to manipulate and get twisted around with the facts and their feelings and the fact that they're all women doesn't hurt. Raven has immunity to my looks. I can't get her twisted up, and she gets me to the truth.

It seriously fucks with my head.

"Marriage. Dude. That's permanent."

"I fucking know that," Jayce snaps. "But what do I do? How do I know she'll say yes?"

Feelings. I can have feelings about this. But the only thing I feel like is telling my best friend to run away from commitment. If he gets married to old Keeber (a pretty chill chick, no doubt) where the fuck does that leave us? What about hockey? What about boys' night? What about fishing trips and hunting trips?

Fuck. I'm frowning.

"Why bother, brah?" I mutter.

Jayce doesn't buy my bullshit. I don't even buy my bullshit anymore.

"Because I love her," Jayce says. "And there's not going to be another Makeba. We spent all summer together, and I never wanted to be away from her, dude. I just... I don't know. I want more."

I want more. Hearing those words from my best friend freaks me the fuck out. Jayce is the man I planned to live out my bachelor days with. I don't need him getting married. No fucking way.

"You're acting like a chick, Jayce."

This doesn't move him in the right direction. Nope. My best fucking friend just gets more pissed off.

"Jesus fucking Christ, man."

"What?"

Jayce scowls. "Can you cut the shit for a second?"

Why should I cut the shit?

"How can I possibly help you with this? I'm not the marrying type, brah."

My heart quickens. I don't want to talk about this because I can't handle it. Feelings. Women. Marriage. It's just too fucking much. It's all so… new. I don't know how Raven Rose wriggled her way into my head, but she has and I hear all those fucking words and ideas and I flip the hell out.

"Never mind."

"Right," I mutter. I should have given a better answer. For once, I'm not in fucking control and I hate that shit.

"You know, Dustin… I keep defending you, saying that you aren't really a dick, but I'm starting to think I'm wrong."

"Whatever, man. Propose to Makeba. Do whatever you want. You don't need my permission."

"I wasn't asking for your permission. I wanted your support. You're my best friend."

Jayce… Fuck man. I should appreciate having a best friend who cares about me, who cares about his girl, who would die for any of us. But I'm not comfortable with the new way people want me to live. I just can't fucking do it. I can't let go of myself.

"Right."

"Fuck off, Dustin."

Finally, I've pissed him off enough. But it doesn't feel good.

"Yeah. I'll do that."

Fuck. The second I turn away from him, I know I should turn back. Jayce is right. I'm acting like a fucking dick and it's ugly to watch first hand. I know what Raven would tell me to do. I can't think of her right now. I burst out of the rink and storm off to my truck. Marriage. Why the fuck does Jayce want to get married? Why does anyone? What's the point of all that shit, anyway?

I start the truck and put on something soothing – a little Slipknot – to drive back to Pesthouse. Raven had better be waiting for me in my bedroom. I need to talk to her about this Jayce shit. I need her.

I fucking hate that I feel that way. She still hasn't responded to the fact that I love her, or the fact that I'm still keeping her in my room as a strictly financial arrangement despite that. Maybe I have a messed up way of showing how I feel, but fuck, I try to show it. I kiss her like I love her. I treat her like I love her. I just needed that contract so she wouldn't run – so she could hear my shit and give me a fucking chance.

I don't think it's working. She doesn't love me and whatever she feels for me... I don't know what the fuck she feels. That's the problem. For a hopeless romantic, she keeps her cards close. I don't have a fucking clue what's going on in her head. All I know is that I want her, I want to be with her, and I want her advice on all the bullshit I have to deal with. She's the only one who knows my secret... she's the closest I've ever been to trusting someone.

When I get back to Pesthouse, there are too many cars in the driveway. Fucking Hargreaves probably has a bunch of damn Canadians in there playing Beirut. I don't want to deal with this shit right now... but I walk through the door and plaster a party-Dustin smile on my face.

"Yo gentlemen, what's popping?"

"Hey man," Logan calls out from the other side of our pong table, stinking like PBR and soaked in sweat. "You've been gone for a while. We started already."

Fuckers.

"Toss me two beers."

"One for Raven?"

If this motherfucker doesn't stop asking me questions about Raven Rose, I'm going to put his ass through a wall.

"Yeah. One for Raven." I can barely contain the rage in my voice and Logan's beer-flushed cheeks lose their color. The damn Canadian's finally getting the fucking hint.

"She's not here, bro," Logan replies. What?

He'd better have a suitable answer for me about where the hell Raven went and whether he had anything to do with it.

"What do you mean, she's not here? I left her upstairs."

I don't know why the fuck I'm explaining myself to this idiot. He probably means that Raven stepped out for a walk or she trotted off to the library to trade in her new romance novels for something fresh to read tonight. (She reads while she monitors my homework.)

"Her friends came and snuck her out the window," Logan says.

"That was hilarious, eh?" some dark-haired Canadian kid adds. Hilarious? What the fuck about this sounds hilarious?

"Raven was fighting and screaming the entire way down," Logan continues calmly. "We thought it best not to stop them, eh? Women. They do what they want."

Maybe Raven's right that the guys on my team are all fucking idiots. I might be an idiot too, but I at least went to prep school long enough to learn how to cover it up. Fuck. Why the hell did Raven's friends kidnap her out of my room?

I tell myself there's an innocent explanation that these motherfuckers are too drunk to explain to me, so I pull out my phone to call Raven. Kitten, pick up the fucking phone. Her call sends me straight to voicemail. I call again. Then I call Jayce, but he doesn't answer and texts back, "Fuck off."

I deserve that for being a dick, I guess. I still need to fix this shit. First with Raven, then with my best fucking friend. Raven would tell me I need to stop being an asshole. Probably. Maybe I've finally found my way to some type of moral compass on my own.

I wouldn't bet on it considering what I want to do to Kya and Makeba for kidnapping my girl. Cole's long gone and he won't be any help. Shit. I take one of the cups off the pong table and hurry upstairs, finishing the PBR before I get to my door. When I thrust the door to my bedroom open, I have an even bigger problem than Raven Rose's disappearance.

The timing of this crap couldn't get any worse. Holy shit. Kitten was right about Big Sexy.

I've got babies. Baby tarantulas. And some of them are free. Fuck. Shit. Fuck. Baby spiders… Jayce told me not to get tarantulas, but what's a guy to do when he's three blunts deep and armed with a no limits credit card?

This has to be the worst possible time, but three of them have already escaped their enclosure and there are four more who are probably minutes from figuring it out. Fuck. I was sure Big Sexy was male. 100% sure. This is a fucking nightmare.

I hunt down two of the babies and then find the third on my pillow, next to a handwritten note. My throat tightens. I know it's from Raven, but I don't want to read it. I can't bear the thought of her running away from me. I just can't.

But the message isn't from Raven at all. *Fuck.*

13

SEE YOU SOON, KITTEN

RAVEN

"Did you guys really have to tie me up!?"

"Don't answer her," Kya whispers. "We need to get her to the second location."

My best friends kidnapped me and now they're treating me like I'm a real life prisoner. *Oh, hell no. I need to get out of here. I need my damn money...* or at least a chance to explain so we can all go back together... and get my damn money.

Kya keeps "whispering", but I can hear every word of their little plan in the front seat, even with Makeba crunching merrily away on her stick shaped pretzels.

"I can hear you, Kya!" I grunt as I wriggle in the backseat to free myself from the tight knot my friends used to tie me up. I know they used teamwork, but it was way too easy for them to overpower me. Shit!

I thrash again, to no avail.

Makeba turns around with a bag of pretzels. "Want some?"

"No!" I don't want any damn pretzels. I want to know why the hell my friends broke into Dustin Rathbone's room and kidnapped me.

Makeba gives Kya a funny look and stuffs three pretzels into her mouth. I regret turning down her offer for the pretzels because my tummy is rumbling. Dustin likes ordering dinner instead of struggling against the dining hall's questionable 'meals' for his macros and tonight he was going to do Pad Thai with some crazy sounding veggie side dish.

Dustin... What the hell is he going to do when he finds out I'm gone? *I need to get back.*

"Guys! This isn't funny. We need to go back to Pesthouse immediately."

He's going to get back to his place and realize I'm gone, then it'll be game over for me and my money. My friends don't know what the hell they're doing. They need to get me back to Pesthouse before I lose my tuition money

"We found evidence of a disturbing plot," Kya explains calmly. "We need to get you to safety. Now."

A disturbing plot? I don't know what they're talking about.

"Are you sure you don't want some pretzels?" Makeba offers.

"I can't eat pretzels with my hands tied. And where the hell are we going?"

I grunt and fight against my binds again, still doing nothing to loosen my binds. I could theoretically kick the back of Kya's seat, but her driving is questionable enough as it is because she drives like she's still in L.A. when we're in the middle of nowhere…

Looking out the window, we're even more in the middle of nowhere than Laguna Grove College.

"We're transporting the subject to an undisclosed location," Kya says, but she glances sympathetically at me in the rearview mirror. "But we can stop and untie you."

"Thank you…"

Well, that was easy. Once they untie me, I can stop freaking out long enough to think of a plan to convince them to take me back. I don't know what 'disturbing plot' Kya thinks she uncovered, though. Maybe it's serious, but I doubt it's serious enough to require tying me up.

Kya nearly swerves off the highway into a sketchy looking rest stop with three eighteen-wheelers parked there and nobody else. It's dark out and not exactly where I want to stop for the night to stretch my legs.

There's thick fog in the trees around the rest stop and running away from my friends seems like a horrible decision anyway, considering it's dark out and I don't even know where I am. I wait in the backseat for Makeba to untie me. She apologizes profusely through a mouthful of pretzels as she works through her shockingly effective knots.

They didn't even play a romance audiobook for me in the car. Kya knows I hate riding in cars without a book. I am not happy. Kya stretches as she gets out of the car and seems to do some sort of balanced yoga pose, curling her right leg up and balancing on her left leg with her eyes closed. Is now really the damn time?

I scramble out of her sedan and fold my arms.

"Can you quit with the yoga and explain what you two are doing?"

"We signed us all out for a week of medical leave," Makeba explains. "Don't worry, it won't affect our grades."

"That's not an explanation!"

Kya stops her yoga and frowns. "Raven. You had fifty-thousand dollars under your bed. Cash. We investigated."

Shit. Dustin told me not to put the money in the bank yet because of some stupid rich guy tax thing. I thought under my bed would be a safe space, but my best friend apparently thought the right thing to do was to sneak into my stuff and violate my privacy. My voice stiffens defensively.

"Why were you under my bed?"

"Fair point…" Makeba says, forgetting that we are not on the same side right now.

Kya doesn't budge against my defensiveness.

"You told me to look in the blue suitcase for the green sweater, remember? You even gave me a key and told me to 'knock myself out'."

Shit. I totally did that. To be fair, the green sweater was in my blue suitcase until my sudden influx of cash from Dustin. I forgot I moved it. My dumb mistake…

Between telling Kya about the green sweater and stashing my moolah, I had a lot of other crap going on. I didn't expect my best friends to find the money and go haywire. As for the money… I'm not trying to be that girl, but it was $50,000.

"Did y'all do anything with the money?"

"That would be my first question too," Makeba said. "It's fine. It's in the trunk."

"It's in the trunk?!" I squeal. "Kya, are you crazy? What if we get pulled over?!"

"By who? It's night."

"Kya, cops come out at night," Makeba murmurs.

"Not in my neighborhood."

Makeba and I exchange glances and hold our tongues. Kya would never let me change the subject, anyway. She has the investigative skills of a woman who helps her mother track down her dad's several mistresses. Imagine Nancy Drew with a cellphone and several subscriptions to websites that conduct thorough background checks... and then give her an afro. That's Kya.

Kya continues proudly. "We investigated your stash of funds to make sure you weren't in trouble with some kind of drug dealer, and do you know what we found?"

"If I did, I probably would have tried to avoid this kidnapping."

"A contract," Makeba blurts out before Kya can get to it. "We found a very disturbing contract."

Where did they even find the contract?

"Then we made a plan to rescue you and here we are. One week of medical leave, a secret road trip, and an undisclosed location that Dustin will never find."

I wouldn't count on Dustin not finding our location. Haven't my friends encountered Dustin's crazy side before? I've been with him long enough to figure out that he's more than a little possessive. And his feelings for me... they're strong. Too strong, maybe.

He's different from the guys in the novels. He might be mysterious, like a romance novel hero, but he's too unpredictable to belong in a proper story.

Heroes in books are easy to fall in love with, but they all eventually blend into one indistinguishable perfect guy. They can be almost too perfect. Dustin doesn't have to worry about that. He's spanked me, tied me up, kissed me in public, convinced me to lie to my friends... He's far from perfect.

But fuck, he makes me question everything. I have feelings for him too. They don't know how that scares the crap out of me more than anything Dustin Rathbone could cook up in his twisted guy-brain.

At least when I fall in love with unrealistic fictional men and over-the-top romance, I can't break my heart. Fiction is safer than real life because I can always close the book or move on to another one.

Dustin could break my heart, and honestly, it would be easy for him. He likes games and chasing me down, but I don't think he could handle the real thing. If I said 'I love you' back, he would change and then he would break me. All it would take is one blond woman in his bed and all those feelings he thinks he has would melt away. I have to remind myself who he really is. I won't let him worm his way in deep enough to break me.

Despite all that, I need to get back to him. I don't want my friends to end up in Dustin's line of fire. I can handle his crazy ass, but only if I get to him first.

"Can I have some of those pretzels?" I ask Makeba as I rub my wrists. Sigh. I get where Kya and Makeba were coming from, but they totally have the wrong idea. And now that they freaking kidnapped me from Dustin's bedroom, he's going to assume I orchestrated this and there goes my damn student loan money — scaling down the fire escape with me and my best friends.

I take the bag of pretzels and empty the remaining half of the party-sized bag of pretzel sticks into my mouth. Makeba shrieks as I devour her precious pretzels like a starving orc.

"RAVEN!"

"What are you doing?!" Kya yells.

"REVENGE!" I scream, but I absolutely filled my mouth with pretzels and pretzel-dust, so it comes out as a desperate choking sound.

"Oh my God, she's CHOKING!" Kya screeches. I chew the pretzels and as a large ball of chewed up pretzel forms, getting larger and larger with each chewing motion, I wonder if maybe… oh crap… I for-real gag as the pretzels get stuck and I freak out.

My dumb ass is really choking out here.

"Do the Heimlich!" Kya yells.

"Why do I have to do it!?" Makeba screeches. "What if I kill her?!"

"She's going to choke to death if we don't do it now," Kya says. "We'll both do it."

My friends wrap their arms around me and after several dramatic minutes where I really was choking, I finally hawk up the bolus of pretzel dust and pretty much every soggy half-chewed pretzel in my digestive tract. Kya and Makeba pull away from me out of breath and gape at me like I'm crazy.

"You nearly died," Kya says.

Tears stream down my face from the choking and I'm gasping for breath. Okay, fine. Not my best revenge plan yet, literally choking on my best friend's pretzels, but I needed to do something dramatic.

"I'm fine."

"You are not fine," Kya says. "Your revenge plan nearly killed you."

"I said I'm fine. I just don't want to be here. I don't need you guys kidnapping me because you don't trust that I can handle myself."

"I don't want to be here either," Makeba says. "She has a point."

I give another unwillingly dramatic cough and Kya wraps her arms around me.

"Don't die on us. Oh my God, Raven… Come back to life!"

I cough again and roll my eyes. Kya is so dramatic sometimes, but damn, we love each other. She wraps her arms around me and shakes her head. "We killed you!"

"Kya, I'm fine! This place is just giving me the creeps. It's a weird rest stop in God knows what state. We should go."

Makeba wraps her arms around her shoulders and nods. "I have more snacks in the car, anyway."

"I don't want you making another suicide attempt," Kya says. "So we can leave. But promise you're fine?"

I cough again and promise her I'm fine, but honestly, there's still a little pretzel dust coating my esophagus. I need to get better at escape plans.

Makeba glances around furtively, but everyone knows she stays strapped since last year. Jayce gives off gun nut vibes the way he's always scanning catalogs for baby Glocks to gift his girlfriend. They think Dustin's crazy? What about Jayce or Cole? They can be just as crazy, and who knows what Dustin might say to them to recruit them into hunting us down?

"Hold on. I'm not leaving to go just anywhere," I say, putting my foot down. "I want you to take me back to Dustin so I can explain that I'm not breaking the contract, and this was all a simple misunderstanding."

This vanquishes any notion I may have had that my friends could come around to seeing my side of things. Without warning, they lunge at me and holy shit, they're both strong this time. Kya and Makeba wrestle my ass hard into the back of the car again, even with me putting up a complete fight, and they shut the door, which is so obviously dumb. I grab the handles to free myself and fuck... I speak too soon. Kya has the damn child locks on so I can't escape.

No problem, I'll just crawl to the front... I try to squeeze my body between the seats, but I get stuck. I wriggle my ass, trying to fit it through before Kya and Makeba settle into their seats in the front, but I can't fit and my butt just flails in the air like I'm a street cat trying to attract a mate. I make a frustrated sound that sounds like a yowl, making the situation worse.

"Are you trying to climb through?" Kya accuses me as she slams her butt into the driver's seat. There goes my freaking chance at escape.

"No! And I'm not stuck either…"

I push myself back through to the back seat and plant my ass with a frustrated sigh. They're seriously going through with this.

"You two don't understand. Dustin and I have an agreement. We have an understanding."

"You don't have to recite from his little script. Raven… Dustin lied to you. He catfished you. He stalked you. He drugged you. He kidnapped you. And then… I don't even know. You had sex?!"

Kya sounds like she's some kind of nun. She was the first one out of all three of us to sleep with a guy. And how does she even know the part about where Dustin kidnapped me and drugged me? And they call Dustin the stalker…

Friends are supposed to let you live your life, not throw you in the back of their fancy cars and drive you to undisclosed locations. Now that's some stalker shit.

"How do you know all this stuff?"

Kya pulls onto the highway, nearly slamming the side of her car into a little turquoise Prius that angrily beeps its horn at her as she zooms around.

"Oops."

"Remember you told us about your secret fan fiction blog last year?" Makeba says. "You pretty much write about whatever's happening in your life with code names. We figured it out."

"It's fiction. It's not real."

"Really?" Kya says. "So 'Justin' couldn't be based on anyone at all. Interesting…"

What's the point in trusting your friends if they're going to use all the little details against you?

"You have it all wrong. That's all I'm saying."

"How?! Dustin stalked you, Raven. He lied," Makeba says. "Kya and I have a plan, so you don't have to worry about the money. If that's an issue or whatever."

This is so awkward. I don't want to talk to my friends about money. I mean, Makeba gets money issues, but Kya's rich. She probably grew up wiping her butt with disposable cashmere wipes. She got her first pair of diamonds before she could walk.

The only stones I've ever owned are rhinestones, and even those were hand-me-downs.

They're the last people I want to talk to about money and

I don't want to explain how or why I'm getting my money either.

"You two have no right to invade my privacy like this."

"Dustin is dangerous," Kya insists. "You know that. He tortured Makeba and threatened to rape her last year. He got information from B.J. to mess with you. He's sick in the head."

My stomach tightens. Dustin might have some character flaws, but Kya and Makeba don't know what he's been through.

They don't know his sweet side, just the grim, tough face he shows to everyone at Laguna Grove. He isn't perfect and sure. Our contract might look a little fucked up from the outside. But everything has been different since the night we first made love.

First, my butt has finally stopped hurting from the spanking. And the next spanking didn't hurt half as badly. Plus, I can't lie... the post-spanking sex always pushes me to another universe. Now isn't the time to get into all that, but they need to know one thing: I'm not afraid of Dustin. I might be his 'property' on paper, but I understand Dustin. I have a plan...

And now it looks like I'll need another one to get out of here. Running into the woods off the interstate isn't my best option, either. I'll need to let my friends take me to that second location and try as I might until then to talk them out of this little escape strategy. That's assuming Dustin doesn't get to us first. If they think he's such a creep, they should know he has ways of tracking people down.

I don't have any idea how Dustin will react to what my friends have done. They aren't completely wrong about him, but they aren't completely right either.

"He's not sick in the head," I say. "I mean… he's a little sick in the head. But he never hurt me. He's never messed with me. Our contract is working."

"Did you actually sleep with him by choice?" Kya says. "Where are your consent forms?"

"Girl, we didn't even use those consent forms," Makeba says, throwing me a sympathetic glance over her shoulder. "She seems like she's for real."

Kya sighs. "I know that. I get that. But I'm scared! Look what B.J. did last year. I let my guard down for one second and Makeba nearly got shot to death. I don't want the same thing to happen again. I got a bad vibe from B.J. and I get a worse vibe from Dustin."

"You don't know him the way I do."

"And what way is that?" Kya asks with all the haughtiness of a private investigator.

"We might have had sex like… I don't know. Every night for a while."

"Oh my God," Kya says, her voice suddenly changing in tone. "You lost your virginity to him!? I assumed you did that over the summer or something. You stopped bringing it up!"

I did kinda give the impression I was keeping my business private, but only because I didn't want to just be 'the virgin friend' anymore. I guess I took care of that with Dustin.

"Damn, girl," Makeba says. "I kinda saw it coming… but I'm low-key surprised."

"Well, it happened."

"Is it bad if I ask how it was?" Makeba probes.

"Yes," I snap. "Considering you're both kidnapping me and treating me like I'm too dumb to make my own decisions."

"Maybe we're trying to keep you from getting dickmatized so you don't end up having to sleep next to hockey pads every night," Makeba says, a smile slinking across her face. I knew she would be easier to crack than Kya. I mean that literally, since Kya's resistance has only increased.

"I'm checking for signs of consent," Kya says.

"Well, I literally signed a contract," I point out.

Kya shrugs and shows signs she's close to cracking. Finally, I get through to her stubborn ass.

"Damn. You right," she concedes. "So… was it good?"

Kya can't keep her kidnapper persona straight for long. I should have known that salacious gossip would get both my friends to lower their guard long enough for me to come up with an escape plan. I roll my eyes in the back seat, grateful that they can't see how easily they fell for my accidental but totally working new strategy.

"Yes... understatement of the century. I had a sexual awakening."

Saying it out loud makes me realize it's the truth. Fuck.

"With Dustin? The guy who stalked you?" Kya says.

"Yes, girl! With Dustin. It wasn't just this rough, gross, weird sex between strangers. It was deep, slow... and sensual."

"Wait, we are talking about Dustin Rathbone, right?" Makeba says. "Because he's the only white boy I've ever seen eat bone marrow in the dining hall."

"I've seen him put a turkey heart in his protein shake," Kya says seriously, following up with a gagging sound.

"Yes," I answer impatiently. "It's the same Dustin."

Everyone in the car falls into an oddly contemplative silence until Makeba breaks the silence by crunching on something extremely loudly.

"Sorry," Makeba mutters through her chewing sounds.

"Please, y'all. Can you at least give me a chance to explain the Dustin situation? I see how it can look all scary, but I've got it under control. I'm securing the bag. Isn't that every black woman's dream?"

Kya and Makeba exchange glances and shrug. They know I'm right. There's a reason that black women are the fastest growing group of college graduates in America. There's a reason our interracial relationships are the longest lasting out of any other race. We're visionaries. I have a 'vision' that works well with Dustin's. I complete all his stupid tasks and pretend to be afraid of him once in a while… all while securing my bag. My college tuition. My trip to Italy. Everything.

It's not the only reason I don't want to run away with him — but it's the only reason I'm ready to admit to my friends.

"He's making you sleep with him for the bag," Makeba says. "He wants to call you his property. That's messed up."

"Jayce called you his pet. How is that any better?"

"Pets have rights," Makeba says.

"That's not what you said when you called us up, afraid they were going to get your ass," I hit back. "But I accepted when you got with Jayce. I didn't judge you."

"We aren't judging you," Kya says, which thankfully snaps Makeba into reality.

There's rarely a moment when Kya isn't judging someone. We love her anyway, and she's become way better about her judgmental ways since Cole, but her old habits still die hard.

"Maybe we are," Makeba admits. "Okay, be honest… are you seriously chill with the fact Dustin stalked you?"

"Did he really stalk me if I participated in the conversations?"

"Uh… we aren't talking about the conversations," Kya says. She isn't?

"Then what are you talking about?"

"We got further evidence from hacking into Dustin's email. His password is just 'hockeybutt'. One word. No caps. Very insecure, just like Roxanna's… too easy to hack," Kya says calmly, like hacking into a hockey player's school email is the most normal pastime in the world.

I'm also guessing Roxanna is one of her dad's mistresses, but honestly with Kya, you never know.

"What evidence?"

"He has like… hundreds of pictures of you, Raven," Makeba says. "All from freshman year and a couple from the summer. It's like he's been following you or something. It's weird."

"What?"

"We thought he confessed that to you before the contract," Kya says. They both seem genuinely surprised. My friends can also tell that I'm genuinely surprised too. I don't want to believe what I'm hearing.

"Pictures of me?"

I keep repeating what they've said to me, hoping that once I hear it from some fresh angle, the accusation will sound different.

"Yes, girl. It's that deep. Dustin's like an IRL stalker," Makeba says. "Not just an internet stalker. We thought maybe you figured it out, and that's why you agreed to be his property. He has naked pictures. A lot of naked pictures."

I feel sick to my stomach. Here I was feeling all smug, like I really understood Dustin, when he had a secret even bigger than the one he told me while we cuddled up in bed.

"Pull over," I murmur.

"What?" Kya asks. I didn't speak loudly enough.

"Please, Kya. Just pull over."

She doesn't miss a beat. Kya pulls over onto the shoulder as soon as she can. I need air. I burst out of the car and race toward the guard rails. I grip the icy metal and lean over, throwing up more pretzels and then the remaining contents of my stomach. I feel sick and my hands feel like they've immediately frozen around the metal guard rails.

I can't think. Dustin has secret pictures of me on his computer. Hundreds. He lied to me. I thought he was opening up and telling the truth. I thought I could at least trust him enough to make it through the year, but it's all falling apart. I don't want to go back to campus anymore. I just want to curl up into a ball and die.

He had more leverage on me than he let on, and he's Dustin Rathbone. They're right. He was probably using those pictures and this entire situation to get something so much worse from me than sex… but what? More blackmail?

"What should I do?" I ask my friends. "I need to talk to him. I need to get the truth. I need to stop him from potentially coming up here and killing you both."

"He do be crazy like that," Makeba agrees.

"Honey, we don't think you should talk to him," Kya says. "But we understand if you need to. In a few days, once we're sure you're thinking straight, we'll take you back. So… get him off the trail if you talk to him and we won't stop you from calling him to preserve your contract… But you can change your mind anytime and we'll drive you to our backup second location to ensure he can't trace you."

How many backup plans does Kya have for this?

"I'll explain when I'll be back and get him off the trail — if he doesn't already know where we are. Who has my phone?"

"Trust me," Kya says. "He won't find us."

She doesn't know Dustin as well as I do if she thinks that.

Makeba hands me my cell phone. I call Dustin, but he doesn't pick up. I call again and this time, Dustin answers after the first ring.

"Hello, kitten."

He sounds eerily calm, and I hear his fingers tapping lightly against his desk. I expected him to be totally losing his cool or something.

"Hey. You good?"

My voice sounds shakier than I want it to.

"I'm coming to get you, don't worry," he says.

"Wait, Dustin… There's no need to–"

"See you soon, kitten."

He hangs up before I can get in another word. What does he mean "see you soon"? My stomach sinks once I hang up.

"What happened? What did he say?" Makeba asks.

"He says he's on his way," I tell them. "And that he'll see me soon."

"Shit," Kya says. "Coming from Dustin, you know what that means, right?"

"Get in the car," Makeba says. "He won't find us tonight, okay? And tomorrow you can talk his beefy ass down from turning us into kebabs."

"Yeah," I mutter, but I feel uncertain. And I feel like Dustin's playing a game. The thing is, Dustin Rathbone doesn't play any games that he can't win.

14

BOYFRIEND SLAVES

DUSTIN

I crumple the note from my bed as if I can squeeze blood from it. Kya and Makeba have gone too far this time. I've allowed them to cause trouble in my life before. They steal my best friends and turn them into little boyfriend slaves and I say nothing. I do nothing. This time, they steal my property and think they can get away with it? I don't think so.

Unfortunately, I don't want to piss off Jayce or Cole, which means I have to plan this out carefully and make sure they don't find out. I scoop up my baby tarantulas, getting all the little bastards in a smaller enclosure with a soft mesh lid so they can breathe. They'll come in handy later.

As for Big Sexy... She doesn't look so good. Childbirth takes a lot out of a woman, I guess... even a spider woman. With a smaller abdomen, she scuttles around the cage with enthusiasm that's as close to joy as you can expect for a big hairy spider. Good girl… and thanks for all the free babies. I hope she makes it. Female spiders don't live long after they breed. The spiders rear up the side of the large plastic container, urging for freedom.

Then again, by all rights, Big Sexy ought to have devoured her male counterpart right now. She's different… I gift her another mealworm and watch her thrashing pedipalps devour her fresh meal.

Wicked.

I don't need to work too hard to find Raven. I prepared for all contingencies, including the one where she makes a hair-brained plan to run away. Thing is, I don't think Raven had anything to do with this plan. No… This has Kya Ambrose written all over it.

Before I retrieve my property from her 'secure' mental health trip, I need to get hockey out of the way. I can't miss practice tomorrow, even if I need to track down Raven. At least I know she's safe and she can survive the night without me.

I'm the one who doesn't want to sleep without her. It's chilly in my bed without her and I miss that thigh swinging over me as she wraps her body around mine and rests her head on my chest. I miss what's mine…

I head to bed alone, replaying my nights with Raven in my head and then succumbing to my desires, staring at all the pictures of her I have on my phone. This is what I turn into when I resist her… a creep. I couldn't stop myself from following her, especially after those stupid freshman parties where creeps hunt for chicks like her. I know I'm a creep too, but... I just wanted to protect her. I just wanted... I don't fucking know.

How the fuck did I let this chick get into my head? And how the hell did it happen? She signed my contract. I'm the one who should have control here.

You know you aren't in control with her. That's what fucking sucks. I never wanted to give up control again. I can't handle it.

I can't sleep, so I get out of bed, crank out a few hundred push ups and open my stash of Hindu Kush, allowing the pungent smell to overwhelm the smell of reptile substrate and skink goo. Bergie needs a good clean—Raven's job. Fuck, I miss her. I roll a fat joint and seal it with resin for an extra kick. I smoke until she's all I can think about. I can conjure the scent of her hair or the soft oil she wears on her feet... I don't remember falling asleep.

Thank fuck I wake up in time for practice. I stumble out of bed and search for my workout shit in my room and my hockey bag. Jayce Clutterbuck pounds his fist on the door to my bedroom.

"Hey asshole, wake up."

"I'm up."

He pushes the door open without waiting for a response. I can tell that he's still pretty pissed at me about the Makeba thing. If I'm smart, I'll make it right so I can smooth shit out with my best friend and get information from him.

"Smells like shit in here."

"Jealous?"

"How much pot did you smoke last night?"

"Not enough."

Jayce wrinkles his nose, his eyes darting around the room. There are still painful signs of Raven's presence. I just fucking wish she were still here.

"Where's the girlfriend?" Jayce probes. "Feed her to Ovie?"

My jaw clicks as I drag it back and forth to repress a far more unsavory answer to Jayce.

"Nah, brah. She's gone rogue."

"Sure she isn't on that weekend trip or whatever with Makeba and Kya?"

Does he know where she is? I examine Jayce's face to see if there's any chance he knows exactly where Raven is. I'll be tracking her on my phone when I'm ready, but Jayce compels me to test his loyalty.

"Don't think so."

"She wouldn't even tell me where she was going. She called me racist when I asked. How is it racist to ask where your girlfriend is going for her hippie spa weekend?"

"Brah, it's assuming black people don't go to the spa. Fucked up."

Jayce tilts his head curiously and then nods. I fucking love my dumb ass best friend.

"What about that proposal, huh?" I ask him, hoping to make up for being a dick. We're dudes. We don't need to talk about feelings to move on from them.

Jayce glares. "You were right. I should talk to Cole about that."

"No way, brah. I've got you. As soon as she gets back, you ask her. Make it all romantic."

"How? She loves pretzels, but… if I bake it into a pretzel, she might eat it."

"Bake what?"

"The ring, dumbass."

I nod agreeably. "We'll get this shit sorted after practice. Let's hit the ice."

"Dude, what happened to Big Sexy?"

I tuck my tub of spiders out of Jayce's line of sight.

"Long story, Clutterbuck…"

We hit the ice earlier than the rest of the team, putting in the extra work it takes to be the top of the team. Skating clears my head, allowing me to think clearly about my plan for retrieving Raven and getting revenge on her best friends for daring to steal her from me. Jayce senses I've got a problem, but he's too smart to ask and thankfully suspects nothing.

It's a gritty practice and the first one that makes me feel like I have a shot at getting anywhere near pro. I love the game, but I don't know if I have what it takes to dedicate myself to it. I just want a simple life. Me, my kitten, our menagerie of exotic pets. Is that too much to ask for?

Once I'm back in my bedroom, I pack a large black duffel bag with everything I need to retrieve Raven Rose. Duct tape, a pump-action shotgun (just in case), a hunting knife with a serrated 8-inch blade, soft ropes that won't cut skin, a few plastic bags, my trusty blue tarp, and my new pets. Baby spiders grow quickly, but these are still too small to terrify anyone on their own. If they don't work out, I'll just set them free.

I skip my morning class after sending my prof an email complaining about a migraine. Professors view it as a blessing when athletes skip class, anyway. When I finally get in the truck, I use my phone to track her down. I slipped that little tracker into the back of her phone case. Wherever Raven Rose rested her little head last night will be up on my screen in seconds.

Fuck. The location that pops up has Kya Ambrose written all over it and apparently, Raven's crew told Jayce enough that he essentially spilled their 'secret location' with little effort required on my part. Perfect.

It's not a long drive to the New Hampshire hotel and spa. Their secret hideout lies well tucked away from any prying eyes, about ten minutes out from Mt. Monadnock — a popular day hike when I was in high school.

I roll another Hindu Kush joint in the truck and soak myself in calm before I get out. Fall in Massachusetts smells like apple blossoms and crunchy dead leaves. I love that smell. I can almost smell Raven along with it, but I know it's my imagination. I hold every detail about her so perfectly captured in my head.

The only problem I have now that I'm in the hotel parking lot is finding out what room they're in without raising suspicions. The best way to discover the information you want is patient observation. Asking questions helps sometimes, but I don't need anyone here seeing my face.

I wait about three hours in the car playing some old school Snoop Dogg tracks and bouncing my head to the beat, thinking about Raven… Raven. Raven. Raven. Fuck, it's like an obsession.

I notice Kya Ambrose's hair first. Anyone who needs to track down a member of their crew only needs the single skill of identifying a large afro in a crowd. Kya's hair bounces with each step. Makeba and Raven follow closely. I know they'll spot me, but it doesn't matter. My plan doesn't depend entirely on secrecy. I just need to know where they are and I need to know that Raven isn't hurt or held against her will.

Makeba's the first to spot my truck, which doesn't surprise me, considering the last time she saw my truck was the night I helped Jayce torture and scare the crap out of her with a few of the animals. It wasn't a big deal or anything, but Makeba still kinda hates me. She's going to hate me a bit more after tonight.

Makeba points and grabs Kya's arm, but it's too late. I start the truck and set my plan in motion...

Subduing three women takes less time than I thought it would, even in broad daylight, and even without help. I start with Makeba. She's the best fighter of the three. Raven and Kya scream while trying to pull me off her, but I get her in the back of the truck and then work on Kya next.

They're too loyal to run away from their friends in danger, a risk I was willing to take. Thanks to Raven, I understand their bond well. Loyalty keeps them together and fighting hard as I secure their captivity.

Raven keeps hitting my back with her fists and screaming at me to "chill the fuck out". No fucking way. I already made the mistake of letting my guard down around her friends. No more Mr. Nice Guy.

"Get in the car," I snarl at her, once Raven is the only one of her friends standing outside.

"No!" She pushes hard against my chest in protest. Not like that really does anything.

The problem with choosing an isolated mountain resort during the off-season for their little hideaway is that there really isn't anyone around to hear their screams. The girl at the front desk has her headphones in and she's watching some type of video. She never looks up once as I subdue all three women with relative ease.

Not my problem. Unfortunately, Raven's little tantrum is definitely my problem.

"I said, get in the car, kitten."

She flinches when I call her kitten. Maybe she wasn't so against this kidnapping as she wants me to think. Maybe she wanted to get away from me. I can't let that happen. No fucking way.

"Dustin, what are you even doing here?" she snaps. "I don't need you to rescue me."

"Damn it, Raven…"

"Dustin, stop!"

She keeps screaming until I hoist her over my shoulder and throw her into the front seat of the car. Kya and Makeba sit in the back with their restraints, glaring at me as hard as they can. Raven turns around to them, restraint free.

"I'm untying my friends!"

"Do whatever you want," I tell her. "But if you three try to carjack me, I'm going to take us off the highway and down a mountain."

"You have a problem, Dustin," Kya says. "A serious problem. A misogynist problem—

Here we go again. Now kidnapping three women for defying your direct orders makes you a 'misogynist'? I don't know what kind of fucking classes Kya takes at our school, but I don't want to get anywhere near them.

Once Kya finishes lecturing me, I'm ten miles down the highway. Raven waits for a break in her monologue.

"Where are you taking us? And can you slow down so I can untie my friends? How did you even find me?!"

"I put a tracker in your phone."

"Stalker alert," Makeba mumbles.

Stalker? I don't like that word. I'm more of a research-based Raven enthusiast.

"Listen, ladies. I promise if you comply, no harm will come to you at all."

"Do you think we're idiots, Dustin? Everyone in this truck knows exactly what you're capable of. Raven, punch his lights out."

"He's behind the wheel and going 85 miles an hour. I don't think that's a good idea."

"We need to do something!" Kya says.

"Keep planning out loud and I'll blast some music to cover it up."

Kya doesn't stop talking — that isn't really her forte — so the ladies get a solid thirty minutes of Party Up by DMX on repeat before I pull over to my special super secret location. I park the truck behind the cabin, a few miles outside of Boston, but the perfect Rathbone getaway – my family's second home…

Raven jumps out of the truck before me, desperate to run around and free her friends from their binds. Not so fucking fast, kitten. I race around and grab her by the hips to stop her.

"Dustin! Let go of me!"

"We still have a contract, kitten," I whisper as she thrashes violently, and I need more force to subdue her.

"Let go! I won't let you torture my friends!"

"Torture? Who said anything about torture?" I grunt as she elbows me several times in the stomach and then kicks me hard in the shins. Fuck. She can throw a good elbow when she needs to.

"LET GO!"

"If I let go, will you promise not to do anything stupid?"

"You mean promise to choose you over my friends?"

"No, don't open the truck doors. Don't set them free, because it's just the four of us out here and my pump-action shotgun. Things could get ugly."

Raven pushes me away from her, and I let her go. She's bewildered and furious. Fuck. What the hell did I do now?

"How dare you!" she screams at me.

I have a few critical seconds to judge how angry with me she really is. Punch to the face angry or slap to the face angry? It's unfortunate that Raven is drop-dead gorgeous when she's angry. I find it truly distracting…

"What's the problem?"

"You stalked me, Dustin! Makeba's right. You're a stalker, and that violates our contract. And after what we've been through, how dare you threaten us with a gun?"

"How the hell am I a stalker?"

"I wouldn't have signed that contract if I knew you had hundreds of pictures of me on your computer. Naked pictures. Clothed pictures. How long have you been following me?"

My fists clench against my will as I swallow dry to quench the rage and humiliation coursing through me. I'm sorry about threatening her with the gun, but only because I think another threat might have worked better. Fuck. She's really pissed.

Under normal circumstances, I would lie my ass off, but unfortunately, I really love Raven Rose. I haven't been able to let go of her since I first laid eyes on her at that Pesthouse party last year. I can't lie to a woman I love, even if she doesn't love me back.

"A year."

"Dustin!"

"Sorry. I would have told you eventually if you didn't run off."

"I didn't run off."

"You were no longer under my possession. I did what I had to get you back."

"You need to let my friends go. They were only trying to help."

Has she lost her mind? Trying to help?

"I don't want to let them go."

"Too damn bad."

Raven opens the back door to my truck. Makeba and Kya leap out, free from their bonds, which I admit to hastily tying together. Kya hits some karate stance and Makeba has an empty and half-crushed plastic water bottle from the floor of my car as the world's weakest makeshift weapon.

I change my tune when the bottle flies at my head, smacking me right in the temple.

"Raven, get him! Kick him in the nuts!" Kya yells.

"Guys! Calm down, we can talk this out. We don't need to kick him in the—

Kya has other plans for my nuts and before I can subdue the wild-haired sophomore, she kicks me right in the groin and fuck, it's the most painful kick in the nuts of my life. Blood rushes to my cheeks as my knees wobble together and I keel over, lying on the ground like a damn puppy, groaning for my life.

"Kya!" Raven shrieks. "You killed him!"

"He'll be fine…"

Raven rushes over to me and I close my eyes and wish that I was doing anything else except suffering this humiliation. I groan again and roll over, bright sparkles flashing in front of my eyes. Kya Ambrose kicks like a fucking donkey.

"Dustin, it's okay. Take deep breaths…"

Raven's attempts to comfort me only make me feel worse. Fuck, I must look like such a pussy. I have to get my shit together.

"Raven, stand back," Makeba says. "I'm ready for another beat down…"

I groan. Fuck. If I'm going to get jumped by three black women, I need to have my wits about me. There's no way in hell I can let that happen. My reputation would lie in tatters and I can't imagine the number of hockey fights it would take to put me back on top.

Thankfully, Raven intervenes before Makeba can throw her retrieved plastic bottle at my head again. She stands between me and her friends with her arms stretched out.

"Stop! No fighting. Dustin, you stay right there."

I'm on the ground groaning in pain, so I don't exactly know where she thinks I'm going.

"Kya, Makeba. Stand still. We have a lot to work out and it's very complicated, but we won't be fighting each other. We will talk this out like civilized adults."

"How can we talk things out with the guy who followed you in secret for a year, snapping pictures like the damn paparazzi?"

"Dustin and I had an understanding. Sure, he was a little passionate back then, but… you don't get him."

My ears perk up. Is Raven Rose actually defending me?

"Honey, he's pure evil," Kya says.

"He's not!" Raven insists. "Seriously, guys. I was so supportive of you and Cole and then you and Jayce… I just want you guys to give Dustin a chance."

"A chance at what?" Makeba asks. "He made you sign a contract saying you were his property. That's not a proper relationship. That's a transaction."

"And it would have been a profitable transaction," Raven continues. "But I think Dustin and I have sort of changed our minds about… that."

She glances over at me nervously and then back at her friends, who keep staring on as if Raven has suddenly sprouted a second and significantly uglier head. Once I get on my feet again, I approach her slowly. She's defending me. After all of this, there's a part of Raven Rose that genuinely cares. My heart thuds in my chest.

I have a chance to get her, and I'll take it.

"I want to date Raven for real," I groan, surprising not just her friends, but Raven herself. "The contract was a dumb bid to get her attention and maybe I went a little far kidnapping all of you in broad daylight like that. But I care about Raven, and this only proves that I'll do anything to keep her safe."

I'm still groaning and my crotch hurts like hell, but if I actually have a chance at talking them into giving me Raven back... I'm game.

"Really? Because you tortured me with spiders and I don't see any spiders in that truck," Makeba says. "So it sounds like you haven't even pulled out all the stops."

What is she talking about?

"Uh... there were spiders in the back of the truck. That little plastic container between the seats..."

Kya emits a blood-curdling shriek. We all turn to look at her. Oh fuck. Big Sexy's brood. One of them crawls across Kya's collarbone and there's another one on her cheek. When she realizes there's a third spider on her forearm — and once she sees what a tarantula baby looks like up close, Kya goes fucking wild.

"I'M DYING!" she yells. "They're biting me! Oh God! Get them off! Get them off!"

"Tarantula babies don't really eat yet at that age, so I doubt they're—

"FUCK YOU DUSTIN!" she screams, brushing the babies off her arm and sending them scattering in the surrounding gravel — most of them surviving the fall. She shrieks even louder as a baby tarantula scuttles back to her foot, mistaking her for a friend. Most of the fallen baby tarantulas sprint away from Kya, who keeps screaming and even steps on one.

"Did you just step on my spider?!"

"It's disgusting!" Kya shrieks. "I'd do it again too!"

"I've given you a wide berth, Ambrose," I snarl. "Kill another one of my–

SQUISH. She steps on another one.

"That's it…"

I lunge for Kya, but Raven gets between us.

"Dustin, stop!"

"Raven…"

"Stop attacking my friends and Kya, Makeba, don't antagonize him. Can't you see he's crazy?"

"I am not crazy."

"You are a bit, honestly," Makeba blurts out.

"Crazy? If you understood what I felt about you–

"You love me," she blurts out. "You keep saying that. But I don't know what that means when you stalk me, creep on me, kidnap my friends and make me sign a crazy contract."

"Fine. Fuck the contract, Raven. I'll give you the money, anyway. I'm doing all of this because… I want you. I want you to be my girlfriend. For real."

Kya lets out an untimely shriek as the last baby tarantula scuttles across her forehead. It doesn't exactly set the mood, but nothing can take my gaze away from Raven or my attention off of her. I'm for real this time. I'll let go of all my bullshit just for a chance with her. That's what all of this was about anyway and I can't win big unless I put all my chips down and lay my cards out on the table.

She can take it or leave it and I'll just have to accept that…

"Sorry," Kya mumbles. Raven ignores her, and she pays no mind to Makeba, who opens a fresh packet of pretzels a few feet away. Jayce was right about her. She needs snacks and man, she loves pretzels.

"I can't have a boyfriend who lies to me, Dustin."

I knew it. I already blew it with her. I'm such a fuckup. I'm ready to head back into my truck and accept defeat. I fucking care about this chick, but if I blew it… maybe it's time for me to accept that and… give up. I don't know if I can, but for Raven… I could at least try.

"I understand."

"So you have to promise no more lying, no more stalking, and no more kidnapping and acting up. And you need to admit publicly that I was right about Big Sexy being female. Which was obvious to anyone with eyes."

Holy fuck. She's not giving up on me. She's not… leaving.

"I used my eyes to look away from that nasty thing," Kya mutters, meticulously parting her afro to search for more baby spiders.

"Fine. Big Sexy might have been female."

"Dustin!"

"Fine. You were right. And I promise to stop being a dick to you, to your friends and to everyone else. I'm officially reformed."

"That didn't convince me," Makeba says through a mouthful of pretzels.

"It's not up to you," Raven says. "It's up to me. And for now, I agree to give you a chance."

Seriously? This fucking worked? Dustin Rathbone wins again... Since I'm here, since I'm getting what I want... I have one more question for Raven Rose.

"If you say yes, I want to take you on a proper date, kitten."

"Kitten?" Makeba pipes up anxiously. "You ain't keeping her as no damn kitten."

"It's a pet name," Raven says defensively. "A stupid one. That might be growing on me."

"Ugh!" Kya lunges for me and smacks me on the shoulder. "What is wrong with you? You seriously did all of this instead of just asking her out?!"

I shrug.

"You're an idiot, Dustin… and I'm sorry, but Raven deserves the best damned first date with you of all time, so when you're done… you'll have to face the tribunal."

"Do we have to do another tribunal?" Raven grumbles.

"Yes," Makeba said. "But we'll be fair. We just need Dustin to prove he's not a creepy criminal."

"Can I start by driving you back to campus?" I offer.

"Take me back to my car first," Kya says. "I can drive myself and Makeba back. Raven? Who do you want to ride with?"

15

DATE NIGHT WITH A CRAZY GUY

RAVEN

"I have two dresses for a date in Makeba's hands. One of them is a velvet, forest green Betsey Johnson dress with a gorgeous low-cut and ¾ sleeves. The second dress in Makeba's hands is a gorgeous red Balmain bandage dress."

"I don't even know where we're going."

Makeba grins. "That's the best part, isn't it?"

Kya sighs. "I have mixed feelings. Are you sure that you want to go?"

"Yes. We've been talking. It's been weird not having the contract and not sleeping in his room, but I want to see him. I want to give him a chance."

"Why?" Kya asks. "Please, just remind me."

"Because I believe he has a good heart. Despite every-thing. I wish you both trusted me."

"He's the one we don't trust," Makeba says. "Now pick a dress because my hands hurt, and he's going to be here in like fifteen minutes."

"I don't want to do too much. I pick the Betsey Johnson."

"Yay!"

"I knew you would pick that one. Let's get you ready, girl..." Makeba says.

My friends squeeze me into Kya's dress. I must have put on a few pounds this semester. They warn you about the Freshman 15, but they don't warn you about the Sopho-more 20.

"Your boobs look great!" Kya says once they get the zipper all the way up my back.

"Are you sure it's not too tight?"

"You look like a video vixen," Makeba teases, shaking her hips dramatically.

I look in the mirror and holy shit. I look better than I thought I would, considering how much effort it took to squeeze myself into the dress.

"I hope he's not taking me mountain climbing or anything."

"He's Dustin Rathbone," Kya says. "Don't you know what his family does?"

"Um, his dad is a lawyer or judge or politician or something," I add.

Kya shakes her head. "I seriously thought this was common knowledge."

"You always think that rich people tea is common knowledge," Makeba says. "Where'd his daddy get his money?"

"They only come from the biggest land-owning dynasty on the East Coast. They own like half of Nantucket, several homes in Boston, and a few hundred acres out in Idaho. Haven't you ever heard of the epic Rathbone Ranch parties in Idaho?"

"Girl, nobody in this room has even been to Idaho," Makeba says.

"Whatever. He's classy. He'll take you somewhere classy. You look good."

"But do I look good enough for Dustin Rathbone?"

Makeba and Kya fold their arms. "Don't you dare," Makeba says. "You look beyond good enough. If Dustin can't appreciate you, he can fuck right off."

"If he says the slightest thing about you that you don't like, I'll fuck him up myself," Kya says.

My friends have a strange way of boosting my mood before my date, but it works. When I see Dustin's truck through the window, my stomach does a little flip. Having secret sex with Dustin or a fake relationship is one thing, but going on a real date freaks me out.

"Please tell me I'm not making a mistake," I whisper as I watch him get out of his truck from the window. He leans against it and pulls out his phone. Damn, he looks good.

"You aren't making a mistake," Kya whispers. "You're taking a chance. We're right here for you if you need us. Don't let him kidnap you again."

"I can handle him."

"He looks good," Makeba says. "Don't let those crazy eyes suck you in. Keep your head on straight and let him impress you."

"Thanks for the advice, queens. But I can take it from here."

My friends give me a big fat hug and I hurry downstairs to meet Dustin Rathbone in front of his truck. When I appear in the doorway, he looks up from his phone and smiles. There's something magical about standing beneath a rare smile from Dustin Rathbone. His gorgeous blue eyes crinkle slightly at the corners and his perfect white teeth beam at me from across the parking lot. He sticks his phone into his pockets and does that little white boy half-run to see me.

"Wow. You look good."

"Thank you. I could say the same."

"Can I kiss you, kitten?"

I nod nervously.

This is our first kiss outside of our contract. I don't know what kissing Dustin will be like now, but I agree to kiss him, anyway. He touches my cheek and pulls me in, kissing me with a soft, slow kiss. I can't believe I thought this would be different. He's still an amazing kisser. His lips are still soft and full. Dustin kisses me with so much romance that my heart flutters and my knees feel weak.

I didn't think knees could actually get weak when you kissed a guy, but Dustin has to catch my hips in his grasp and pull me against his chest.

"Don't fall apart from one kiss, kitten."

"Shut up. I wasn't falling apart."

Dustin grins and he doesn't seem so serious and out of my league when he grins.

"Ready for our date? I have a great night planned."

"You don't have a great history with plans."

"No. Maybe not. But come."

I take Dustin's extended hand and follow him to the truck. He swings the back door open and I half-expect a giant tarantula to jump on my face. Instead… roses.

"Six dozen roses," Dustin says as the scent flows out of the truck and surrounds me. He takes one of the vases and hands it to me.

"Smell those."

"Dustin!" I squeal as I take the roses. My last name is 'Rose', so I've always loved roses. I used to get teased for my last name in Georgia, but how can anyone care when they have such a pretty last name, named after such a pretty flower? I press my nose into the bouquet and they smell so fresh.

"What am I supposed to do with these?"

"I know your friends are upstairs. Let's get them into your room and then I'll take you out. You look great, kitten. I can't fucking wait."

Kya and Makeba eagerly coo over the flowers as they help me and Dustin unload them from the truck. When we return downstairs together, the truck still smells delicious. I can't help but want to roll around in the backseat with the flower scent. Dustin helps me up into his truck and I just want to revel in it. Once he climbs up into the driver's seat, he's grinning.

"I hope you came prepared to eat."

"Um… always."

"Good. Let's go, kitten. I went all out for you."

Dustin still insists on keeping our final destination a surprise, but I can tell that we're going towards Boston. I spent the summer with my friends in the city, so I recognize the roads leading into the city. Dustin keeps me talking all the way, asking me questions about romance novels and acting sweeter than I've ever heard him. If I didn't know any better, I would guess Dustin Rathbone was... nervous?

But he can't be nervous. He's been with dozens of women before and I'm just another in a long line. We don't get all the way into the city before Dustin pulls off on an exit and drives into Cambridge. That's where Jayce and Makeba lived, but I don't know all the neighborhoods around here well.

"My uncle owns a restaurant around here," Dustin said. "I want to treat you tonight, Raven. Dating me won't just be spiders, ropes, and spankings. I want to give you the Rath-bone experience."

He reaches over the seat of the car and puts his firm hand on my thigh. Dustin. I don't know what the hell I'm doing with him, but I don't want to stop either.

"I'm fucking nervous," he says. "I've slept with women before, Raven... but I've never brought a woman this far into my life. Do you think you can handle this?"

"It's dinner, Dustin. Unless you're making me eat raw squid..."

"Not this time."

"Hilarious."

"Come on, kitten. We're here..."

When Dustin told me his uncle owned a restaurant, I don't know why I imagined something somewhere between a chicken shack and a diner. Instead, we park in front of a luxurious restaurant with huge fire pits outside, some outdoor seating and a well-dressed host standing out front. Dustin helps me down from the truck and glances at the sign.

"Dramatic, huh?" he mutters, suddenly sounding shy, not a character trait I usually associate with Dustin. His shyness makes me feel better.

"Moonlight Harvest. It sounds romantic."

"Good," Dustin says. "I booked us a private suite for dinner. Come on."

Dustin slips his hand into mine and squeezes. I like his possessive touch and I interlace my hands with his. He towers over me, smelling like expensive cologne. I want to press my nose into his wool blazer, but if Dustin's nervous, I'm on pins. I forgot how horrible I am at walking in heels when I allowed Kya to convince me to wear them.

The host leads us into the dark, cool restaurant. There's live music and a few couples, all dressed in fancy clothes and leaning into their romantic conversations. They all look so expensive. And none of them are black. Once the host learns the reservation is for Rathbone, all the staff snap to attention. I don't have to pull out my chair or wait a second for water and Dustin immediately orders sparkling water and red wine for the table – two bottles so I can have my pick.

"I'm not 21," I tell him. "They're going to card me."

"They won't," he says confidently. "Relax, Raven. Enjoy this."

He still does that creepy staring thing. When he catches me looking, he smiles.

"I can't believe your friends helped you get ready. I thought I'd have to fly out to St. Louis to get you."

"St. Louis?"

"After what happened, I started keeping tabs on Kya. Don't worry about it."

The server arrives with warm fresh bread, a garlic herb butter and the bottles of wine. Dustin and I order appetizers, and Dustin pours me a glass from the colder bottle of wine. He pours a glass twice its size for himself and takes a huge gulp.

"Keeping tabs? Is that what you call your internet stalking?" I tease him.

He sets his wineglass down and twirls the stem, his blue eyes never leaving me. What the hell is it with me and those eyes? They're so impossible to look away from. Instead of responding with humor, he's serious…

"I don't want to lose you, Raven."

"You don't have me anymore, Dustin. This is just a date. A regular date. Our contract ended."

I'm making it clear for myself as much as I am for Dustin. He fluffs his curls and reaches into his coat pocket for a stack of paper.

"Right," he says, sliding the stack across the table. "But we still have unfinished business."

"Is this another contract?"

"No."

He won't talk unless I unfold the stack of papers and look at it. Financial statements. Okay, I'm an English major, one of the people who never clicked with numbers, so the numbers jumble together in my head. I squint to see the numbers a little better and try to piece everything together.

"This is what I owe you. I… might be in a little trouble with my dad, but it's not your fault the deal fell through. I want you to have the best of the best, Raven. It's the least I can do. I'm sorry for lying. I'm sorry for stalking you."

I flip a few pages and glance at the final number.

"Dustin. This is more than we agreed to."

"Yes."

"Dustin, you can't just give me $400,000."

"I didn't. I gave you $427,560.50."

"Dustin, I'm serious."

"Can we save arguing until we have appetizers, at least?"

"We can't, actually."

The server emerges with the appetizers, oblivious to the tension. He lists out the entrees. Dustin and I order the same thing, which only serves to make the tension greater as I scowl at him for copying my order. We can't wait for the server to disappear, which takes several minutes.

I'm suddenly not in the mood for spinach artichoke dip, and I'm always in the mood for spinach artichoke dip. Dustin enjoys a guilt-free bite of his seafood appetizer.

"Well?" I snap. "Say you're not giving me the money."

"I'm giving you the money, kitten. I don't want to argue. I want you to enjoy this beautiful… green soup."

"It's spinach artichoke dip."

"Right."

"You can't buy me, Dustin. If that's what you're trying to do, I don't want the money. I want to be with someone because I love them. I'm not a mistress. I'm not a prostitute. I'm not your… property."

"I understand that, kitten."

"Do you?"

"Take the money. Please. I was a dick to you and your friends. I want you to be comfortable. I don't care if you want to walk away. I just want to look after you."

"You understand how this is confusing, right?"

"This isn't easy for me, Raven."

His voice tightens with tension. I know this Dustin. He wants to hold back. He wants to keep his walls up and lock himself away, but if any part of this is going to work,

I can't keep scaling his walls to get inside his head. He'll have to tell the truth.

"Explain, Dustin," I tell him. "If we're not honest with each other, we don't have a chance."

Dustin's cheeks turn red.

"I didn't think I could feel again until I met you, Raven. You saved me. Even if you walk away from our lovely dinner and the other surprise–

"Wait, what other surprise?"

"It's a surprise. That's the point of surprises."

"Dustin…"

"You saved me, kitten. I've even been thinking… if it's not too late, I'm going to do what Cole and Jayce want from me. I'm going to take hockey more seriously. I might not be good enough to play in America, but… there are other places that might take me."

"Like Canada?"

I smirk. "No. Like Italy. If they'll have me."

I've made it halfway through my spinach artichoke dip, somehow. Once I saw those numbers, I told myself I'd turn Dustin down. I don't know why I'm drawn to his crazy.

"You wouldn't leave being with your friends and life to go to Italy."

"I would if it meant being with you. I want to give us a shot, Raven. I don't want this to be our first and last date. I want it to be our first of hundreds."

"I should turn you down. But…"

"But what?"

It's finally time for me to tell him. These weird feelings crept up on me the way those tarantulas crawled across my best friend's forehead. Those creepy, crawly feelings turned into something big and overwhelming. My feelings scare me more than Dustin.

"I love you. The way you love me. I should have been so angry when I found out you were posing as Brett McClure. But I was crazy in love with that guy behind the screen. If any part of that guy is right here in front of me… I want him."

Dustin's stern face cracks a smile.

"I'm not as smooth as Brett."

"Standing outside my window watching me change definitely isn't smooth." He reaches for my hand, earnestly rubbing his thumb over my palm. His touch spreads fire through me.

"Will you let me make it up to you, kitten?"

I can't say no to him anymore. If there's one thing my friends helped me realize with their kidnapping plot… I enjoy Dustin's company. I want more nights in his bed with his firm chest propping up my head and his fingers lightly stroking my back as I fall asleep.

Why couldn't we both see this coming? From the moment we met each other, we wanted this. But our friends, our school, the worlds we came from kept us apart. I don't want to keep dodging Dustin Rathbone. I want to fall… I want to fall hard with no parachute, just my belief in that happily ever after waiting for us at the end.

"Yes."

"And you'll take the money?"

"Yes." I feel an exhalation of relief as I agree and Dustin pulls out his phone, tapping for a few seconds before exclaiming, "Done."

"What do I do now?"

"Paperwork in the mail. Don't worry. It's handled."

When our dinner arrives, talk about relationships, money and contracts subsides and it's just us in the private room with no one else to judge us or screw with us, or make us second guess these weird feelings blossoming between us. Sometimes you love the guy with the pet spiders and snakes, with the scars on his thighs and his heart. Dustin reaches for my hand on top of the table and strokes my forearm throughout dinner.

I want to jump him by the time we finish the chocolate mousse cake we split for dessert. Slow, gentle touching puts me in a romantic mood. I forget that I have an unfinished romance novel in my purse for the first time in forever. There's a genuine romance unfolding in front of me and it's with Dustin… the last guy I expected to look twice at me if he didn't have some twisted ulterior motive.

We walk back to his truck slowly, but instead of helping me in, Dustin presses me against the clean chassis and kisses me. I'm tall enough in my heels to reach his lips without getting on my tiptoes. He runs his hands over my velvet dress, settling on my hips.

"I want to get that dress off," he whispers. "But we have a long night ahead, kitten."

"Don't we have to get back to campus?"

"We aren't going back to campus."

Dustin insists on upholding this air of mystery until we get to his 'second location'. He drives so fast, I think my braids will fall off. But he's so confident and calm behind the wheel. I run my hands over his thighs and he shifts in his seat, the slightest hint of a grin teasing across his face.

"Careful, kitten."

I move my hand closer to his crotch and he shifts again. *Fuck.* He's already hard. I hope wherever we're going has a bed.

❦ 16 ❦

I CAN'T WAIT FOR HER

DUSTIN

"**D**ustin!" Raven shrieks.

I violently swerve my truck off the road and park... wherever the fuck this is.

"Sorry."

It's a half-hearted apology, but Raven has to know I'm not really sorry. I just need her. Immediately. I don't care where we are or what the fuck was happening before. The second her fingers graze my cock, I lose control.

"This is an... abandoned parking lot!?"

"Seems like it."

"There are three tents halfway across the damn parking lot. There are probably people sleeping in there."

"Yes."

"This isn't your second date location, right?" Raven squeaks, slamming on the locks on the truck ferociously several times in succession and hiding her purse underneath her seat.

I'm normally patient with her quirky expressions of nerves, but right now, I need her naked, not nervous.

"Damn it, kitten. Get your dress off."

Isn't it obvious why I pulled over? Sure, it's not the most romantic spot, but that'll change once I'm inside her.

"Are you serious?" Raven squeaks as I unknot my tie. I want those fucking clothes off her now. No more waiting. No more excuses. I need to touch her body…

"I can't wait for you. Climb into the backseat and get that dress off."

"You pull off the highway, driving like a maniac, I might add, dragging my ass into an abandoned parking lot so we can–

"Fuck? Bang? Screw like rabbits? Yes. Now hurry."

I have my hand down my trousers already, adjusting my cock so I don't actually burst through my pants. I need her badly and I don't care who sees us. Raven's hand near my cock is enough to set me off.

"Dustin, we're going to get caught!"

"We aren't."

I reach over and unbuckle her seatbelt, attempting to hoist her into the back seat. Raven squeals.

"Dustin, let go of me!"

"If you won't go back there, I'll bring you there myself."

"You can't drag me off like a caveman every time you want sex!"

"I definitely don't do this every time I want sex," I grunt, as I maintain my efforts to carry Raven over my shoulders into the back seat with me. She doesn't know how often I want to rip her clothes off, but I control myself. She doesn't know how many times I've seen her half-naked in some sexy fucking outfit and resisted her.

I'm done resisting Raven Rose.

We're in a contorted and tangled mess by the time we push and crawl over each other into the backseat of my truck. I pin Raven beneath my weight on the leather seats and she squirms beneath me, aggressively pawing my chest.

"Dustin, you've lost your mind," she gasps as I kiss her neck, then her shoulders.

"I want you."

"I can tell!" Her hands reach into my pants and she cups my boner. Jesus fucking Christ, I'm going to burst.

"Relax, kitten," I murmur.

"Please tell me you brought a condom."

Since when? Maybe she wants one now that our arrangement ended. I thought we handled things pretty well before... no need to mess with condoms now, right? I want to feel her tightness wrapped around me.

"I did not."

"Dustin!"

I move my hips forward and press them into hers. Raven wriggles her hips to get away from me, but only pins her body tighter beneath mine. She lets out a desperate gasp for air and then strikes my shoulder.

"Ouch. What was that for?"

"You're crushing me."

"Right," I whisper. "I should eat you out instead. Scoot up..."

"Dustin, is this really the time and the–eek!"

I scoop her butt cheeks up with my palms and slide her up the seat so I can contort my body well enough to fit my face between her thighs. I've been dreaming about those juicy brown thighs throughout all of dinner.

"Dustin!"

"Quiet."

I raise her dress over those smooth thighs to expose them to my palms. Raven squirms again, but I'm too close to her pussy for her to stop me. I slip her underwear off and my tongue finds Raven's soft, slippery entrance. I know I hit the right spots when she moans out loud and I push my tongue in deeper to respond. Raven arches her back, squeezing her thighs around my face.

I run my tongue over the length of her slit, nibbling on her outer lips and then focusing on her clit until she gasps and edges toward a climax. Her fingers tease my curls apart as she gets closer.

"Cum for me."

"Dustin..." she whimpers my name, forcing me to tease her faster and use my fingers on her to push her over the edge. I fucking love when she moans my name. I get her screaming again and Raven's thighs clamp around my face when she cums. I fucking love making her cum and use my tongue to lick up every last drop. She is fucking delicious.

I run my tongue over her juicy thighs and lick her clean before I drive my tongue between her legs to make her cum again. Her girl juices taste delicious and I easily make her cum again. Raven kicks her heels off and uses her toes to press against my oblique muscles.

"Enough..." she gasps. "We're fogging up the windows."

"Enough? I'm nowhere near done."

"We can't fuck in a parking lot on our first date, Dustin."

"Why not?"

"It's not... romantic..."

I distract her by easing a finger inside her cunt.

"Are you sure?"

Raven gasps and squirms, attempting to pull her pussy away from my hand but failing miserably. I press another finger inside her.

"Fingering you feels romantic to me. I like being close to you, Raven."

"Dustin…" she gasps. "That's not the…"

I kiss her before she finishes her sentence and use my hands to make her cum again. I love watching her melt into putty in the back of my truck. After she cums, I reach around to unzip the back of her dress.

"Kiss me," I murmur. "Kiss me while I strip you."

She kisses my shoulders. My neck. My cheek. She touches me ravenously as I work the zipper down the length of her back and slip the sleeves of her velvet dress over her soft shoulders. Her breasts heave beneath me and I press my chest against her, pushing her deeper into the seats.

She's totally right that screwing here is a risky, terrible idea. If the Boston police department catches us, both our names will show up printed in the paper, and that will definitely piss my dad off. I don't want him to find out I have a black girlfriend in the Boston Globe. I still don't know how he'll react. Probably not well, but right now… I don't give a shit.

Once I have Raven naked, she helps get my shirt off and uses her feet to slide my boxers over my ass. I want to put her cute ass toes in my mouth. But I'll save that for later.

Now, I just need her pussy. Raven shudders as she feels the head of my cock against her entrance. It's been too long since I've had her, and I'm done waiting for Raven. As the head of my cock parts her thighs, Raven freezes. I bend my lips to meet hers.

I don't want her scared. I want her to be open, willing, and mine. Her soft body eases against mine and I push the head of my cock between her perfect legs. She moans from just my round cock head, teasing her open and cries out louder as the first inch slides inside her. I already have her pinned to the backseat from my girth. I need to go slower.

I kiss her cheek and then lick and suck her nipples until she cries out and gets even wetter, so her pussy can adjust to my cock entering her slowly. I move my hips again to ease another inch inside her. Raven responds perfectly, by wrapping her ankles around my hips and pulling me closer.

"More," she whispers. "I can take it."

She grunts as I slide more inside her and her slippery cunt resists taking more than half of me. Color rushes to Raven's face and I know it hurts her.

"I should stop," I whisper. "It's too big."

"No," she gasps. "It will feel good once you're inside me. Don't stop. Don't stop, Dustin… Please…"

Fuck, she's hot when she gets all throaty and desperate for my dick. I grunt and forcefully push the rest of my dick inside her. We both groan together as our hips join and I bury my enormous length inside Raven's tightness. I soak in her perfection as I steady my body against hers.

"Easy, kitten," I whisper. "I don't want to cum too early."

She eases her hips and gasps for breath. "You're so big."

I slightly withdraw my hips and kiss her as I slide into her again. Raven cries out louder and her cunt offers milder resistance. She's so fucking tight I could explode. No. I'm not ready yet. I hold her close and fuck her slowly in the back of the truck. I don't want to wait to make love to her again. I want Raven when I want her. I don't care about the consequences, just smelling the perfume on her skin or the shampoo in her hair. If I'm crazy for how I feel, then I fucking embrace it. I just want to be with her over anyone else. She's the only person I want. Mine.

I clutch Raven's body against mine and lose myself making love to her. Her fingers tangle in my curls and her legs wrap tightly around me. I don't want to let go of her until I finish. Our lips join and kissing her sends a jolt of desire through me, changing my slow love-making to forceful thrusting. Raven shudders and climaxes again, her juices spilling between her slick thighs, drawing me to the edge of a climax.

"I'm going to cum inside you," I whisper.

Her hips thrust upwards to meet mine, and she moans as my big cock slides into her deep. I can't hold myself back anymore, and I hold Raven's body against mine as I finish.

Dripping in sweat and glued together by desire, we don't pull away from each other for several minutes.

"You are crazy," she whispers, but there's a pretty smile on her face and she smells even better than she did before we made love.

"I know," I murmur. "And see? We didn't get caught. Hotel, kitten. Now."

I ease my hips apart from her and we both gasp as we pull apart from each other. We share one last deep look and then break away to search for our clothes in the back seat mess. Neither of us wants this to end.

Raven pulls her bra over her breasts and flips over so I can slide the zip of her dress back up her back. Fuck. Looking at her from behind only makes me want to do incredibly wicked things to her ass. My throat tightens. No way she would let me spank her again without the contract. She wants me to be a boyfriend now, right? Not some creep. But fuck, her ass is so perfect and jiggly. I want to squeeze it.

I kiss her shoulder as she gets her dress on and work my cock back into my pants. Raven turns to face me again.

"Why the hell do I like your crazy?"

I grin. I don't mind when she calls me crazy.

"You make me feel sane, kitten."

"But you're not," she says, grinning. "You're crazy as hell. And I don't know why I like it."

"It's all those books. I've read some of them, by the way. All those knives and ropes… I think you have a dark side, kitten."

"A virgin with a dark side?"

"You are not a virgin anymore."

Raven bites her lower lip and nods nervously. I take several minutes to realize what she means with that half nod. She isn't a virgin. We took care of that, didn't we?

By the time I 'get it', we're halfway to the hotel. Was she talking about… anal? I don't want to believe my innocent Raven could want my cock in her ass. When we make love, she struggled to accept me between her legs, squirming and reddening in pain as I ease my dick between her thighs. I bite my lips until they turn red, but Raven doesn't notice.

She just had an orgasm and she dances in the seat along to *50 Cent* as we approach *The Rathbone*–a boutique hotel a couple miles away from my uncle's restaurant.

"Is everything in Boston named after you?" Raven teases when we drive into the parking lot.

"Not quite," I murmur. "Come here, babe. Give me another kiss."

I kiss her and reach around for her butt, giving it a good squeeze. Raven squirms as I palm her ass. Maybe she wants me back there. Fuck.

I take her into the lobby, check us in, and Raven sticks close to me. She looks nervous.

"Everything okay, kitten?"

"How much did you spend on this date, Dustin? This place is really nice."

"Doesn't matter. You're worth it."

We ride the elevator to the top and once the doors open, Raven gasps, clasping her hands to her mouth.

"Dustin!"

"Did I do something wrong somehow?"

"This place is enormous!"

"Shame we only have one night. But we can spend Christmas break here… if you want."

She rushes into the room and kicks her heels off. Score.

"I'm running into the bed!"

Good move, kitten. She scurries ahead and jumps onto the California king, bouncing off the mattress and squealing. I can't help but grin, watching her all wild and joyful. She's so emotional. She's so open with those feelings, and that scares the crap out of me.

Raven bounces off the bed and runs over to me, grabbing my hand. "We should jump on the bed," Raven says, grinning. "Right now."

"You serious?"

"Yes!"

"I take you to the nicest hotel in Boston and you want to jump on the bed?"

"If you're crazy, Dustin, I'm ten times worse."

"I doubt that."

"Come here, stupid."

Raven grabs my hand and steps on my feet until I take my shoes off. She certainly has her methods of getting me out of my shell.

"You really want me to jump on the bed?"

"You need to relax, Dustin. I think half the reason you're so crazy is you never let go. You never give up control."

"Correct."

And why should I give up control? I want what I want and whenever I want something, I get it.

"That won't work tonight. Get on the bed."

I'll do anything she wants.

Raven drags me over to the bed and I jump on with her. She doesn't hesitate before she jumps high.

"Wee!" As she lands on the mattress, she nearly slams into my chest.

"You aren't jumping, Dustin!"

I bounce on my heels a little. "I'm good."

"You'd better jump, Rathbone."

She presses against my chest and I jump a little as Raven springs into the air excitedly.

"Higher!" she squeals.

"Raven... I'm not a child."

"I know," she says with wild eyes. "I just don't care."

She grabs my hands and leaps into the air, squealing with delight. Fuck. I want to stay in control, but her joy spreads like a contagion. I love her 'I don't give a fuck' grin and the way she jumps like she's trying to touch the insanely high ceilings. Game on, kitten.

I jump really high and Raven screams with delight. "Yes! Higher!" I jump really high again, this time bouncing Raven off the bed. She loses control and falls directly into my chest, screaming in delight.

I grunt as her body thuds against me, and I catch her, setting her on the bed.

"You are wild," I whisper. "Very wild."

"Let me keep jumping, Rathbone."

"No way, kitten. I'm not letting go of you."

My hands squeeze her hips and Raven gazes up at me with those pretty, innocent eyes.

"What are you going to do to me, spank me for jumping on the bed?"

My heart pounds. Is she joking or does she really want that? Raven's hand touches my chest.

"I knew it," she whispers. "You want to, don't you?"

My throat tightens. "We're dating. I want to treat you right, Raven."

"I'm the same girl you spanked before. I'm not breakable just because we went on a date."

"You only did that for money," I whisper, running my thumb over her lips, promising myself that I won't hurt her anymore. I won't do any of the sick, kinky things I wanted her to do. I can't hurt her.

"Really?" she says. "You don't know how stupidly hot you are."

I chuckle. "Oh, I do."

"It's enough to scramble a woman's brain."

"Enough to want a spanking?"

"Why do you think I defied your orders and jumped on the bed?"

"Hm," I murmur, kissing her forehead. "That's a good point."

My hands tease over her lower back and I grab her round, juicy ass as gently as I can. Damn, she has a perfect ass. My cock jumps to attention.

"If you're crazy, I'm crazy," she whispers. I squeeze her ass and she bites down on her lower lip hard enough to turn those perfect full lips deep red.

"You're going to have to get off the bed for me to spank you."

"No way, Dustin. You like a chase? You're going to have to catch me."

She doesn't give me a moment to react. Raven springs off the bed and sprints away like she's serious. The hotel room is big enough for this to be a real chase, and there are obstacles. She's fucking serious. Raven runs quick for a chick in a tight dress, but once she activates my competitive side, I sprint. Raven squeals and dodges me around the mini-bar, leaping over it like a trick pony and escaping my clutches again.

Raven knows how to get my juices flowing. She runs around the small dining table and then back to the bed. Once she gets close to the bed, I go wild. I sprint for her and wrap my hand around her forearm. She screams as I catch her with a mixture of fear and delight.

"Gotcha, kitten."

"Oh no," she whispers, struggling to hide the smile on her face. "You caught me."

"I'm going to bruise your ass so hard…"

She pretends to struggle. I'm not gripping her. She could get away if she wanted to.

"I've been terrible," she teases. "I understand, Mr. Rathbone."

"Mr. Rathbone?" I grin. "Very fancy."

"Would you prefer 'sir'?"

"Hm. I thought we weren't doing that anymore."

"We don't need a contract to mess around, sir. We can just… play."

"Get on my lap, kitten. You've been a very bad girl."

If I didn't know better, I'd say Raven Rose looks relieved at my threat. I don't know why the fuck we work, but somehow, we do.

THE PACT

RAVEN

My ass is so sore. I wake up with Dustin's large leg swung over me and his nose pressed into my neck. We got into the champagne after his big spanking and that helped ease the pain, but it wasn't enough. If my butt so much as jiggles, it hurts.

But the sex after was… beyond amazing. Sex so good I don't even want to read my latest romance novel. The real thing is so much better. So much better. I don't know if that would be true with every guy, or if it's just Dustin.

I wriggle a little so my butt hurts less, but the slightest movement wakes Dustin. He pushes his curls out of his face and kisses my cheek with a sloppy kiss. "Good morning, kitten."

"My butt hurts."

"Uh huh." Dustin kisses my neck. If I don't stop him now, I'm going to be in the same position I was yesterday – powerless against Dustin's lusty desires.

"No…" I whimper. "Too tired."

"Hm. Breakfast then. And I have to get back to campus. Hockey game tonight. You coming?"

It's just a preseason game, but I don't want to miss it. I think my friends all plan to go too. I don't know how we all ended up dating guys on the same team, but it makes planning convenient.

"Yeah. Duh."

"Good."

I move my butt again and wince. Dustin grins and kisses my neck again when my phone rings. Ugh.

"Ignore it," Dustin murmurs. I glance at my phone. It's Makeba. I can't ignore the call. I wriggle away from Dustin and pick up my phone.

"AIEEEEEEEEE! OH MY GOD!! Raven!!!"

I fly out of bed and sprint to the door.

"What's wrong?! I'm on my way!"

"Nothing's wrong!! Jayce proposed! He proposed, and I said yes!"

Now I'm shrieking as loudly as Makeba.

"Oh my God! You're engaged!!"

I jump around and squeal for a while, taking notice of Dustin ordering room service over the phone. He looks so sexy while he orders, his fierce eyes fixating on the menu and his tattooed back hulking over the menu. He's so hot. But is what we have like Jayce and Makeba? Dustin's a sex God, no doubt… but I want marriage. I want the happily ever after.

Once Makeba and I share excitement for a while, she has to call her parents and tell them. They've never met Jayce, but she won't be able to avoid telling her Jamaican daddy she's dating a white boy if they get married.

I hang up and Dustin gets out of bed. I always stare at his body. I can't help it. Dustin towers over me and he's just big. Everywhere. He doesn't even mind when he catches me staring. This morning, he flexes instead.

"Need fuel to keep these muscles for ya. What's old Keeber saying?"

"She's getting married to your best friend. And we've told you not to call her Keeber."

"Jayce finally did it. Nice."

Dustin leans forward and kisses me. Marriage. It's a really awkward subject this early in our relationship… or whatever this is. Technically, we just went on a date. I try not to be 'that girl' and rest my head on Dustin's chest. It's too soon to ask "what are we".

"You're my girlfriend, you know that, right?" Dustin murmurs.

"Huh?"

"I know you, Raven. I'm Brett, remember? You never want to be that girl who asks 'what are we'. You told me that. I don't want confusion between us. I love you. I meant it when I said that. You're mine... in every sense of the word."

"Dustin..."

"I know... You're not ready for–

"I love you too."

"Good," he answers, a tiny smirk crossing his handsome face.

"Yes. Even if it's crazy and possibly the worst decision ever since my butt is totally sore."

"Need a massage?"

"If you even think about touching my ass today, I'll spank yours next."

"That's an enormous threat, kitten."

"Uh huh. Believe it..."

After breakfast, Dustin and I dress in our clothes from last night and I don't even care about doing the walk of shame – mostly because Dustin insists on cajoling me into Pest-house first.

We sneak upstairs to his bedroom and Dustin becomes visibly more relaxed in his dark red, oddly humid bedroom. He rushes straight to Ovie's cage, checking the latch twice and finding his snake chilling peacefully.

"He's about two weeks away from hacking this one," Dustin mutters. "He's an escape artist."

"You really love these creatures, huh?"

"Most people don't see the beauty in reptiles, spiders or scorpions. I like monsters."

"For monsters, they're pretty quiet," I admit. "And if I look away, it's not so bad feeding them the creepy crawlies."

"Are you saying you finally accept my menagerie?"

I shrug, glancing nervously at the various enclosures in Dustin's bedroom. I don't know if I'll ever completely accept them, but once Dustin keeps Ovie safely latched away, they can't be that bad, can they?

Dustin and I have to shower separately if there's any hope of him making it to practice. We both know there's no chance of seeing each other naked and keeping our hands off each other. I shower first and change into one of Dustin's old t-shirts and a pair of leggings he claims I left over at his place. I'm 98% sure he stole them from me last year, but at least I don't have to fit into Dustin's gigantic sweats.

"Will you read here and wait for me to get back?" Dustin asks after his shower. He smells delicious and his workout clothes highlight the rippling muscles on his back and arms. Yum.

"I'm heading out with the girls tonight to celebrate Makeba's engagement," I tell him. "So we can hang out for a bit after practice."

"Cool. See you then, kitten."

Dustin kisses me, then slings his hockey bag over his shoulders before leaving his bedroom. Normally, I would freak out left alone with the creepy crawlies. This time, I decide to inspect the enclosures and see what Dustin likes about these 'pets'. It's not like they can jump out of their cages or anything – unlike those baby spiders.

Poor Kya will probably have nightmares for weeks. Ovie sleeps most of the time and he keeps sleeping as I approach his cage. Dustin has some elaborate latch set up that I don't even think a human could get through.

His skink basks under a warm orange lamp, also fast asleep. I'll never find love in my heart for his scorpion, so I just ignore it. As for the spiders... I peer close to the cage and notice Pastrnak feasting on some gross fly in the corner and then... there's Big Sexy. Oh shit.

Dustin won't like this at all.

Kya flips the plantains she's frying in the dorm common room. No one ever uses this space, so we spread out all our ingredients to cook together and celebrate Makeba's engagement. Makeba prefers home cooking to restaurant food because she 'likes to know who touched her plate'.

She insists it's a Jamaican thing, but I've never met another Jamaican who made these claims.

"Let me get this straight... he wants us to all attend a funeral for his tarantula?" Kya grumbles. "Dustin doesn't have nearly as many brownie points as he thinks he does."

Makeba swipes some of the buttercream frosting that we're supposed to use for the cupcakes and eats the entire spoonful in one bite.

"I'm only going to go if there's a eulogy."

"We aren't going to a spider funeral," Kya says. "Raven... I get that you and Dustin are weirdly into each other, but I have to draw the line."

"It's not a regular funeral. He's buying kegs. He's throwing it at Pesthouse like every other hockey party. It should be cool."

Plus, there's no way Jayce and Cole are getting out of Big Sexy's funeral.

Makeba lifts her ring to the light and watches the giant 2 carat stone in the middle sparkle. I don't blame her for spending the past two days staring at the giant rock Jayce Clutterbuck got her. He made the perfect choice and we're all mesmerized by the gorgeous (and enormous) rocks Makeba now sports on her elegant hands.

"Jayce is going," Makeba adds dreamily. "So I guess I'm going. But don't expect me to sing Amazing Grace."

"Cole wants to send flowers," Kya huffs. "Can you believe it? Big Sexy will have more flowers this year than me."

"Are you and Cole arguing?" I ask her, scooping the last bit of cupcake batter into the tray.

Kya shrugs. "He got all weird when I told him about Jayce's proposal. I thought we were going to get married, but now… I don't know. Maybe he's not as committed to me as I thought. He's always treated hockey like his wife…"

"Don't be so down!" Makeba says cheerily. "Love wins, Kya. Love wins. He just wants to wait for the right time."

"Easy for the girl with the ring to say," Kya says. "Maybe I gave it up to him too easily."

"Kya, you're a strong, independent woman who don't need a ring!" Makeba says. "You and Cole are happy. Maybe he's waiting for you to graduate. Jayce is way more impulsive. You know that."

Kya steps away from the plantains and sighs. "Guys, it's not about me rushing things. The last time Cole visited… things got a little… oh fuck it. I'm pregnant."

"The Pregnant Feminist…" Makeba muses. "Sounds like one of Raven's romance novels."

"Makeba!" Kya says. "I'm serious. I'm pregnant in college and my dad will kill me when he finds out. Kill me."

Considering what her dad did to Cole Seabrook's face when he found out about their relationship, it's partially believable that he'll at the very least get 'very disappointed' in Kya over the news. In a rare move for Kya Ambrose, she tears up and then tries to get a hold of herself, wiping her cheek and pulling herself together.

"I'm sorry. This is about celebrating Makeba. I didn't mean to steal your thunder…"

"You're not stealing my thunder. This is a big deal," Makeba says. "And once I have fried plantain in my belly, I will be ready to discuss the situation…"

"Makeba! I'm not done frying that one!"

"I'm testing it."

"You're going to burn your tongue…" Kya warns. Sure enough, Makeba burns her tongue.

I confiscate the fork from her and stick her bitten plantain back into the hot oil. Makeba makes a sad whining noise, but then gives up and puts an ice cube on her tongue — a much better choice than going in for another hot oil burn.

"Just as long as we're all going to the funeral. I called Sydney and invited her up too. She's been wanting to visit Laguna Grove for a while and she has time off from school."

"We're going to meet the legendary Sydney?" Makeba asks as she dabs her tongue with an ice cube. "I'm in."

"She thinks Laguna Grove is a lame white people school. I don't know how we're going to prove her otherwise."

"It is a lame white people school," Makeba says. "But we're getting an excellent education here. Who cares about parties? We're leveling up."

Sydney cares. She also cares about boys, hooking up and having a wild ass time. I don't know how she's going to get along with Kya and Makeba.

"Sydney cares. She'll want to party. I think she's even bringing someone from her school, but I don't know who. She won't tell me."

"Fine," Kya says. "We can show her and whoever she brings a good time. Can't have her thinking that all we do up here is go to hockey games and do homework."

"That is all we do," I remind Kya. "Sydney goes to a cool ass state school. I'm hoping this spider funeral rager is enough to entertain her."

"Sure. A spider funeral. That's going to convince her our nerdy ass liberal arts college is normal."

"Kya has a point," Makeba attempts to say, but she froze her tongue a bit with the ice, so it comes out all muffled.

"She's my friend," I explain. "Can we just make an effort to show her a good time?"

My friends agree, even if we all know we aren't exactly the school's biggest party animals. Hopefully, Sydney doesn't cause a scene or anything.

Luckily, by the time we finish cooking, Makeba regains use of her tastebuds and piles her plate high with treats.

Kya and Makeba grill me about Dustin a bit more and then we talk about other things: our plans for Thanksgiving break, our classes and upcoming midterms, the crazy shit that happened last semester with B.J. and how close we grew over the summer.

Kya tears up a little. "I hope having a baby doesn't change everything."

"Relax," Makeba says. "It's a baby with Cole. He won't let anything happen to your kid."

"But what about us? I don't want to lose my best friends."

"We could make a pregnancy pact," I say.

Makeba grins. "Ha-ha."

"I'm serious."

"I think you've been hanging out with Dustin a little too long," Kya agrees with a smirk.

I shrug and roll my eyes. "Whatever, y'all. All I'm saying is... we can make a pact to stick by you through your pregnancy, through any future pregnancies that may occur and to never let guys or babies get between us. Not saying we should all get knocked up."

Makeba shrugs. "Jayce wants a baby. I could let it happen."

"Jayce wants a baby?" Kya says. "Isn't he responsible for like... half of Ovie's escapes over the years?"

"I know," Makeba says. "I don't know if I'm ready to be a mom, either. I'm ready to eat for two, though."

"If I told Dustin I wanted a baby–

Makeba and Kya threw me a sharp glare and warned, "Don't!"

"Damn, y'all! I thought you were supporting me now."

"Dustin will say yes to a baby," Kya says. "He's like… beyond obsessed with you."

"Go to Italy first," Makeba agreed. "Dustin can be your sugar daddy and then he can get his baby."

"He is not my sugar daddy!"

Kya smirks. "Girl, ain't that the dream, though? Securing the bag with a crazy ass white boy who spoils you?"

"And stalks me," I remind them. "That part was a bit of a problem. And y'all had a problem with it like two weeks ago."

"We've got a plan for that," Makeba says. "Don't worry. We'll make two pacts at once, a pregnancy pact and a beat down pact."

"Agreed," Kya says. "We all stick through it with each other, and if we need to beat a bitch's ass, we'll do it."

We make a deal and finish up our food, singing and dancing along to Makeba's reggae playlist as we clean up the common room. It's the most fun we've had in a long time and I can't wait for all of us to have a great night together, even if the occasion happens to be a spider funeral. I also can't wait to see Sydney... I haven't told her about Dustin, and I don't know how she'll react to my new boyfriend. It's a party, right?

How hard can it be to get along?

❧ 18 ❧

THE FUNERAL CHAPTER

DUSTIN

"Do you have the urn?" I knew this day would come, but I didn't know losing Big Sexy would hurt this much... She deserves a proper sendoff. Finally. I'm getting choked up just thinking about her sitting there with those crunched up legs in her urn.

Bergie scuttles across his enclosure, settling beneath the heat lamps for a long day of basking. Our party starts in forty minutes. I haven't planned a eulogy or anything, but I smoked a blunt and texted Raven a poem I wrote about her smile. It's dumb, and it sounds like a nursery rhyme, but she's all romantic as fuck, so I try to write something to her every day, even if I feel stupid.

Jayce slams the urn on my desk, and I flinch. No one gets how this loss eats me up inside. If I knew Big Sexy would

286

die after giving birth… I would have given her one last dubia roach. Those were her favorite.

"I told you cremating him in the oven would only fry him," Jayce snaps. "This is too weird, Dustin. Half the school is too afraid of you to decline the invitation, but do you really think a kegger is the best way to celebrate your spider's death?"

I really wish Jayce would shut up sometimes. This isn't just about Big Sexy. I have a plan. And it's too big to tell anyone else – especially not Raven and especially not my dough-brained best friend.

"Big Sexy was female, you idiot. Show some respect."

Jayce sighs and opens the box on my desk, pulling out one of my thick ass pre-rolls. Since I started seeing Raven, hiding my emotions isn't as easy. I don't know how I let her get under my skin so easily.

"You good?"

Jayce taps the glass on my emperor scorpion's enclosure, flinching backwards when the scorpion aggressively lunges towards the glass.

"No," I murmur, flopping down on my bed and sticking the joint in my mouth.

I don't want to fucking do this right now.

"Is this about the tarantula?"

"It's not about the fucking tarantula. It's about Raven…"

Jayce puts his arm around my shoulders. "What's going on, big guy?"

I light the joint and pass it to Jayce, who enjoys a deep inhalation and then coughs like a newbie. You would think I smoked him out enough that he won't spray his cough juices all over me, but you know what you get when you're dealing with Clutterbuck – a big lovable dumbass with a heart of gold beneath his aggressive exterior.

"They won't let me play in Italy next year," I say calmly. "I'm graduating, Raven's going away, and I'm only going to drag her down."

I don't want to think about this and I definitely don't want to talk about it, but I guess Big Sexy's funeral might make me sentimental. That spider helped me through so many dark times.

"Relax, brah. You can go long distance for a while. Visit the country. Hang out."

"You don't understand. I'm banned from the Schengen zone. I forgot about… that."

I did so much stupid shit when I was a kid. It's hard to keep track of.

"What the fuck did you do?"

"Some shit went down in Amsterdam after my sophomore year at Milton. Dad sent me to rehab for a couple months. I barely remember what the fuck happened, but I fucked up. Again."

"Raven will understand."

My best friend doesn't get it. Raven puts love first – always. If she hears I can't come to Italy with her next year, she'll want to fix things. She'll want to cancel her plans, change her flight, fuck her life up… all because of me.

I care about Raven enough to know that I'm not worth the fucking trouble.

"She'll want to screw her life up for me, man. I've got to dump her. Tonight."

Jayce wouldn't understand. If there's one thing the past few weeks taught me, it's that Raven Rose is too good for me. I need to let her go before I screw up her life. She could end up like Big Sexy… and that would be my fault. It's not just the grief. I love her too much to ruin her. That's why I stayed away for so long.

"Are you serious, bro?" Jayce says, his hand tightening on my shoulder. "Aren't you like… fucking in love with her?"

"Who told you that?"

"Uh, my fucking fiancée, who spent hours organizing the roses you had her carrying up fucking flights of stairs?"

"Stop bragging about having a fiancée. Can't you tell this is difficult for me?"

"Relax, brah. Don't do anything hasty. Raven's probably going to be pissed off if you dump her at Big Sexy's funeral."

"Why? I'll make it memorable."

"She'll be sad. This will hurt her. Fuck, Dustin... I swear you don't understand people sometimes."

"I don't." I understand weed. Snakes. Spiders. Scorpions. But people? That's an entirely different fucking story. Raven was the closest I came to understanding someone, and she's the only person who gave enough of a shit to try to understand me. But I can't ruin her life and stand in the way of her dreams. I need to let her go to Italy without me and I'll just stay here... with Ovie.

"Listen, don't do anything stupid. Enjoy tonight. Bring her upstairs. A few minutes with her and you'll change your mind, 100%."

"Yeah. Whatever you say..."

Jayce won't change my mind. Once I decide, I'm all in. Unfortunately, I have to break Raven's heart. She won't see this coming, but I don't want her to know the reason we have to fall apart is that I'm a fuckup. I'll still do what I promised, but I can't take her away from her dream.

I head downstairs to drink and play Beirut for a while with the assholes on our team. Logan and Barkov play against me and Jayce. Damn, I wish Cole were here. He's not as sloppy as Jayce is after a few drinks and I don't want to stand here losing this fucking game to Logan.

"Where's the spider, eh?" Logan asks. "Are we going to send him floating away on a river of beer?"

"No, asshole. I'm not letting Big Sexy get passed around this party. We're just going to chill, make a couple speeches, and get fucking wasted. Then... I'll bury her under the big tree outside."

"Chill out," Logan says. "I didn't mean anything by it."

Barkov sinks the ball three times in our red solo cups. Fuck. I elbow Jayce, who keeps furiously texting every five fucking seconds instead of focusing on the game.

"What?" he grunts.

"We're losing asshole. Get your shit together."

Jayce is too busy on his phone to pay attention. Girlfriend shit, most likely.

"Makeba's almost here." He sounds so fucking happy. I never thought old Keeber could bring that out of Clutterbuck's cranky and frankly unstable ass, but she's done it. Now my best friend's getting married. Big Sexy would have definitely wanted us to celebrate.

I throw back more beer. I should text Raven, but I know she has her friends from home here for tonight and I want to give her some space before I break the bad news... I don't want to hurt her, but if I stay with her, I'll hurt her in exactly the way I don't want to by holding her back from all the shit she wants to accomplish.

I just want her to be happy, with or without me.

"Great," I tell him, sinking a ball. "What about Cole? He's supposed to keep these motherfuckers in line tonight."

"Cole is five minutes out. They should get here together."

"Perfect. I need someone who can actually play this fucking game."

Jayce elbows me hard and then struggles to prove his prowess. He's no good when drunk, but at least the big bastard sinks one ball, but the other one veers off the mark. Fucking A, Jayce... It's up to me to save this game.

By the time I save the game from Jayce's shitty play, I'm fucking drunk and I can hardly keep my shit together. When Raven and her friends get there, I push through the crowd to the door and give her a warm hug. She looks fucking gorgeous and delivers a box of chocolates to help get me through my grief.

I know she doesn't exactly enjoy my pets, but she's so... supportive. Sweet. It's too bad I don't deserve her.

I wave and greet her friends — a tall black dude and a caramel-skinned black chick. Hakeem and Sydney. They don't seem too interested in talking to me, but before I can say more than a quick hello, Raven promises to see me later and drags them toward the drinks.

I hope I didn't somehow fuck that up...

I want to get to know her friends from home, even if I'm sure she'd call me 'racist' or whatever for saying something out of line. Hm.

She texts me a few minutes after zooming off.

Raven: I'll find you in 40 minutes. Big plans tonight.

Me: For what?

Raven: Proving I'm cool, haha

I smile. People at this school care too much about being cool. Maybe it's easy for me to say as a big white guy and an athlete, as Raven loves to point out, but what makes someone cool isn't a huge social group or getting approval from all the fuckups. It's just being a good fucking person. With a big heart. Like Raven.

Too bad in forty minutes… I'm going to break up with her. And probably spend the rest of the night dodging assaults from her friends. I can handle that, honestly. What I can't handle is costing Raven her chance at travel, excitement, or all the dreams she's told me about. She deserves those dreams and I don't know what the fuck I deserve.

Killing time, I check the crowd, pump some fists, rage a little, and drink even more. If I have to break up with Raven, I'll need enough liquor in my system to get me there. I don't want to leave her…

There's a line out the fucking door and Foote keeps turning people away so we don't pack the house over the legal limit. Big Sexy would have loved this. Well, probably not since she was a tarantula, and they get spooked pretty easy. But I think she would have at least appreciated the sentiment.

After forty minutes, I head to our meeting spot, but Raven isn't there, and she doesn't answer my texts either. I can't see Kya or Makeba either. Jayce and Cole play Beirut together with a couple sophomores on the team, but I can't

Where the fuck is Raven?

I feel a tug on my arm after I struggle through the crowd of grinding freshmen on the dance floor. Ever since the college shut down all Greek life, our parties have only become wilder and wilder. I turn around, expecting to see Raven, but it's only her friend. Sydney, I think her name was?

I'm so drunk that I barely recognize her, but she recognizes me. She has to know where Raven has run off to, but I'm slow to speak and Sydney speaks first as she touches my arm.

"Hey Dustin. We need to talk."

"We do?"

"It's about Raven. It's serious."

Shit. Maybe she's dumping me first, and that's why she's sending her friend here. My stomach tightens, but that might be from the liquor. There's something fucking weird about this chick's face. Again, that might be the alcohol, but I get the nagging sense that... she's smiling.

It's the slightest glimmer of a smile on the corner of her face, something that most people wouldn't detect. But I notice.

"Where's Raven?"

"Cheating on you," Sydney says flatly. Cheating on me? No way.

"Is she now?"

"I'm sorry but... I told her friends they should come tell you the truth right away, but they refused. I know you don't know me, but... a guy like you doesn't deserve to get cheated on. Especially not in your own bedroom."

I don't know what the fuck this chick is talking about, but something is seriously fucking wrong here. Raven isn't cheating on me. She can't be. But I don't trust that she's safe.

"Is that where she is right now?" I'm stern. Serious. And she has that smile on her face again, like she knows something I don't.

"Yes. Listen, Dustin," she says, grabbing my arm. "I'm sure she didn't mean to cheat on you, but... that's just what Raven does. Trust me, I've known her my whole life."

I pull my arm away from Sydney and thank her. Calmly. This chick might claim to know Raven, but she definitely fucking doesn't, and she seriously underestimates me. I don't have to have known Raven her entire life to know that the hopeless romantic who always has her nose stuck in a book would never cheat on me. Never. It's just not Raven.

"Thanks for your help. I'll... confront her."

"I'll come with you."

Another trick... I'm torn. It's a bad idea to let this one out of my sight, but some shit is definitely going down upstairs and I don't want this chick to get the upper hand, either.

"Don't worry. I can handle it. Just... enjoy the party. And thanks for being a true friend, Sydney."

"You deserve to know the truth."

I nod and disappear into the crowd, heart racing. I move towards the stairs and get past Logan, flirting with some lacrosse chick in the stairwell.

I lose track of Sydney quickly as my mind focuses on Raven Rose, possibly in danger, and likely in my bedroom.

I don't buy this bullshit story and I don't know where the fuck Makeba or Kya are, but they're nowhere downstairs and I find it highly unlikely they're helping my girlfriend cheat on me. They call themselves the 'boring' black girls, but maybe they should call themselves the 'loyal' black chicks because I know these women and they live and breathe their love for each other.

They have real love. Real friendship. They call each other out and they're not bad fucking people.

I should have never let Raven out of my ·sight. Maybe Jayce was right about tying the woman you want to the bed...

I push through the crowd at the top of the stairs more forcefully and break up four separate couples making out on the stairs as I rush to my bedroom, sloshing beer from my red solo cup all over my shirt. Fuck the beer. I toss it over the railing as I open the door to my hall and stop in front of my bedroom door.

I hear a piercing scream as my hand touches the handle, but the handle won't budge. She's locked in there. And there's that piercing scream again. Fuck. I shove my body into the door. The wood refuses to budge. I'm going to have to hit this door a lot fucking harder to get in there. Blood rushes past my ears as adrenaline surges. I hear a deep, low voice and then the sound of breaking glass.

"RAVEN! RAVEN, OPEN THE DOOR!"

"DUSTIN!" I hear her shriek. Then she screams again and I imagine some motherfucker putting his hands around her neck or doing some fucking thing to hurt her. I lose my shit and I don't know how I do it, but I break the fucking door down.

I don't even get a good look at the fucking guy. I just grab him by the back of the neck and shove him against the wall. I feel broken glass crunching beneath my feet. I hear him say something, and then my fist cracks his jaw. It's Sydney's friend Hakeem, not like it matters. I'm breaking his nose, anyway.

"DUSTIN!" Raven screeches. I can't look at her. I throw another fist at the guy's face and feel the familiar squelch and crack of bones breaking. There goes that motherfucker's nose...

He cries out and lunges at me with a fist. Fists don't scare me, even from guys nearly my height and almost double my weight. I slam my leg into his side and push him over, wrapping my hands around his throat. All it would take is three minutes to kill him, but there are more efficient ways to get this fucking job done.

I can hear Raven on the phone. He tore her dress. Her makeup covers her face and she's shaking as she speaks into the receiver. He raped her. Or at least he tried to. It doesn't matter which one it is — I'm kicking this motherfucker's ass or putting him in the ground, depending on how quickly the cops get here.

I throw another punch and throw the guy against the wall. I need a weapon.

"Raven, get my knife."

She knows exactly where it is, and we can end this bullshit in a goddamned second.

"Dustin, stop! I don't want you to go to jail. I called for backup... just stop."

"No," I snarl, rage coursing through me as the desire to watch this man bleed surges. Raven leaps on me, wrapping her arms around me and doing her best to pin my arms at my side. Let go of me, kitten. Fuck... just let me kill him.

"Dustin! Please!"

"I ain't gonna hit you back," Hakeem chokes. I loosen my grip on his neck, satisfied that I've caused enough damage. For now. He stumbles back against the wall and then lunges for the door.

"Not so fucking fast," I snarl. "You leave this room, you're dead, motherfucker."

I drag my desk chair out and slam the back against the wall. "Sit. Now."

Hakeem sits and buries his head in his hands. He can't breathe. If he had any blood flowing through his brain, he would have run, regardless of my threats. He grabs his throat and gasps. He won't be a threat for another minute or two and by then, hopefully, Raven's backup materializes.

I can't avoid looking at her for another second. I turn around and my heart cracks. My brows pinch together and my jaw tightens. I know I should have more of a reaction. He tore her clothes in several places, exposing her matching bras and panties, not to mention her bare flesh with bruising on her legs and arms from where he held her.

There's blood on her shoulder and a bite mark on her neck.

I feel sick.

"What did he do to you?" I ask.

"No," she says. "Don't kill him, Dustin."

"Answer the question, Raven."

"Dustin..." she says, her voice warbling and tears welling in her eyes. I forget about containing the big motherfucker sitting in the chair and I rush over to her, wrapping my arms around her and letting Raven's head fall against my chest. She sobs softly as I cradle her head in my chest. I know she can hear my heart race.

"What did he do to you?" I growl. I want answers. I want to know just how badly to fuck this guy up.

"I'm sorry..." she sobs. "I'm sorry. This was all my fault."

"I don't know what happened," I whisper. "But this wasn't your fault. Stay here..."

"Dustin..."

I push her away from me, even if it kills me, and I open my top drawer for my hunting knife.

"Dustin!" Raven says, rushing in front of me and grabbing my forearm. She's too fucking pure for this world. I don't know what that bastard did to her, but even if he hurt her, she doesn't want to watch him die. She doesn't want him to suffer. Too fucking bad.

"Why did you hurt her?" I ask the motherfucker as I grip the handle of my knife, planning which parts of his body I'll stab first. He's still out of it with his head buried in his hands. Raven shakes her head.

"He came with Sydney... Dustin... I think... I think Sydney set this up."

Hakeem doesn't answer, but Raven might be right. That fucking smirk. Raven rubs her arms with her hands and shivers, glancing away from me the moment she makes the accusation.

"You think she's responsible for this?"

Raven shrugs and mutters. "Partially."

Well, yes. We have the perpetrator here. That's good.

"Don't worry, kitten. I'll find out. Grab some of my clothes."

"Our friends are on the way," she mutters, stepping aside and allowing me to face the motherfucker who hurt her with a hunting knife. All she says when she steps aside is, "Don't hurt him."

I don't know how she can ask me to do that. I'm obviously going to hurt the fucking guy. If he's lucky, I'll paralyze him or cut off a finger. If he's unlucky, I'll put his ass in the morgue.

"Listen, buddy. What the fuck did you think you were doing here?"

He sits up and looks at me, confused. His eyes are bloodshot and his skin several shades darker than Raven's. His skinny dreadlocks hang down to his neck, and he inhales slowly several times before trying to speak. He winces as he talks and his voice comes out raspy.

"She... she wanted it."

"Don't fucking lie to me."

He glances nervously at the knife in my hand. "You can't assault me, man. It's not my fault your girlfriend's a slut."

Blood rushes past my ears. Every bone in my body wants to drive the knife into this motherfucker. The only thing stopping me is Raven gripping my arm — and having bigger fish to fry.

"I need you to tell me what the fuck you're doing here."

Raven's grip loosens, and she draws her body against my back. I might have to kill to protect her and it doesn't scare me. Losing her scares me more. I reach back with a free hand and snake it through hers.

"Call my girlfriend a slut one more time and I promise I'll gut you. Now tell me why you got her up here and what the fuck you think you were doing."

"Sydney told me she was good to go. She's the whole reason I came up here. Easy pussy."

Raven squeezes my hand, sensing the torrent of rage pulsing through me. Slut? Easy pussy? Does this guy want to survive until tomorrow?

"Some other chick tells you Raven wants you and that's enough for you to attack her?"

He shrugs. "Listen, man. I know how bitches like that get. They have to act all innocent, so you won't think they're fast."

"I'm not fast," Raven quips. I squeeze her hand. "I told you I had a boyfriend."

"I thought we were role-playing."

This guy is fucked up. I don't know if he's just an idiot or both an idiot and a creep. I'm gonna go with both.

"You're a liar," Raven says. "And you need to call Sydney and bring her up here."

Before Raven's attacker can respond, the door to my bedroom swings open, the handle nearly hitting him in the back of the head as Kya Ambrose thrusts the door into the back of his chair.

"LET ME IN!" Kya yells.

I drag the dude's chair out of the way and Kya struts in, wielding an empty fifth of vodka made of plastic. She brought an empty $6 bottle of vodka as a weapon? Kya whacks the guy in the head the second she sees him and he yelps like a hurt dog.

"Kya!" Raven says.

"Oh, I'm not done." Kya whacks the guy again, and then she turns her fearsome gaze on me. Thankfully, she's small enough that even her angriest expression doesn't scare me. But maybe it should. Kya swings the bottle at my head and when I duck, she twists her hand and whacks me hard in the stomach.

"Ow! What the fuck was that for?"

Makeba pushes the door in after Kya, panting and out of breath, followed by Jayce and Cole.

My bedroom can hardly take so many people in it. The guy on the chair looks scared as shit when he sees Jayce and Cole lumbering into my room. Makeba looks around at the unfolding scene, confused. I'm still doubled over and glaring at Kya. Meanwhile, Raven jumps between us with her hands out. I wouldn't hit Kya, but I get why Raven worries. I'm also wielding a knife, so there's that.

Raven's attacker thumps in the chair. "Let me out of here, bro! Let me out! I didn't do nothing wrong."

"Like hell you did," Kya snarls. "You and Raven's bitch ass so-called friend set this shit up and we're going to sort this out... after Big Sexy's eulogy. Cole. Jayce. Tie his ass up."

Jayce and Cole immediately bend to Kya's wishes. Hell, even I move out of the way, but only to put my arms around Raven. My throat tightens. I was going to leave her. I can't fucking do that.

I have to be up front about Italy, but right here, right now... I can't leave Raven Rose.

"Raven," I murmur. "I want to get you out of here, away from this guy."

"Sydney's downstairs," Raven says. "I don't want you to hurt her. Please Dustin. Promise you won't."

My jaw clenches. How can she ask me this? Her friend set her up to get assaulted by some guy. I don't want to make a promise I can't keep. Kya, Makeba and the guys get Raven's attacker all tied up – and they bind his mouth. Kya puts her hands on her hips once they're done.

"Weirdly enough, I can see why Dustin likes doing this," Kya says.

I tighten my grasp on Raven but give Kya a measured response. "I don't like kidnapping. I'm skilled at it, that's all."

Kya rolls her eyes. "You're going to tell that to a judge one day."

Jayce scoffs. "He's probably going to be a judge one day."

The sobering thought quiets the room.

"Drinks downstairs?" Cole offers. "Then we can decide what to do with this dick head."

The dick head in question glares, but he can't do much. There are too many of us against one guy. That might not be an advantage for finding Sydney.

"We should stick together downstairs," Makeba suggests. "No offense, Raven, but your homegirl is a dark ass hoe."

"Babe, that's racist," Jayce says, gently resting his palm on Makeba's shoulder.

"Jayce, I didn't mean her skin color. Obviously. But thanks for trying."

"Oh. Carry on, then."

"Downstairs," Raven commands, her voice finding some of its steadiness. I wrap my arm around her tighter. "We'll come up with a plan after a few drinks. I'm fine, y'all. Just a little shaken up."

"Let's go then," I murmur, kissing the top of her head. "Anything for you, kitten."

19

BETRAYAL

RAVEN

Sydney could be anywhere in the party crowd. Hell, she could be halfway back to our hometown or to her state school. I sense she's still here, lurking in the crowd, eager to gloat at my downfall.

Betrayal comes from where you least expect it, doesn't it? I'm too angry to be shaky now. I need to find her.

Somehow, Big Sexy has the biggest funeral turnout I've ever seen in my life and I'm talking compared to black funerals. Although, this party ain't anything like a black funeral since it's a white boy's house party and creeping up on sunrise. The party has degenerated.

There's a hipster giving out free spider tattoos on the couch while a teensy platinum blond girl does cocaine off a hand mirror on the same couch, whooping with each fresh hit up her nostrils. She's really just sitting out there doing cocaine in public. White people are different. I ignore the fact that those spider tattoos are totally off too. Big Sexy wasn't a black widow, she was a tarantula.

I know Dustin wants to dart out of here and find Sydney, but I'm still numb from what happened. Everything felt normal at first. I immediately noticed that Hakeem fit Sydney's prophecy almost exactly. He was tall, dark-skinned, churchgoing, and while he wasn't bald-headed, I figure prophesies have some wiggle room. He was a gentleman, she said. He went to school down in Virginia and she met him through church.

She already knew about Dustin, so I stupidly thought she had brought Hakeem as her date. By the time we were up in Dustin's room and things went so horribly wrong, I froze. I didn't even try to fight back. I wanted to, but my body responded differently than I expected, my limbs turning rigid and useless as this man attempted to have his way with me. I attempted to kick him in the nuts, but he was so big... it was just so easy for him to overpower me.

Remembering that feeling makes me sick to my stomach. Giving up control only feels good when you trust the person you're doing it with — not when a man forces himself on you. Tears prickle my eyes and I push them back. Finding Sydney is more important than crying. I can cry later.

Dustin picks up on my shifting mood.

"Hey," Dustin whispers. "You okay?"

"No."

"Why would your friend do this?"

"Does it matter?" I murmur. Dustin kisses the top of my head.

"No. It doesn't. I'm going to kick both their asses, anyway. Here, have some gin."

I wrinkle my nose. "Gin is nasty, Dustin. I prefer Henny, Crown Royal... something like that."

Dustin chuckles. "Fine. Whatever you need to take your mind off shit. We've never done this together before, but... there's always weed."

"How have we never smoked weed together before?"

"I was trying to be proper," Dustin says. "You know... I want you in your right mind for everything."

I wrap my arms around his waist and hug my big, tall boyfriend. Holding him close, I sense there's something off. He's hiding something. I don't think it's malicious, but I can definitely tell when Dustin Rathbone is holding back.

"We should probably find Sydney first... and when we get through it, we'll smoke. Okay?"

Kya and Makeba stumble back in our direction holding drinks.

"I'm saving you from the white boy drinks," Makeba announces, passing me a red solo cup with two shots of some mysterious brown liquor mixed with coke. I welcome the sip anyway. I just need to calm down and until I can smoke a fattie with Dustin, liquor will have to do the trick.

Sydney… I guess there might have been signs of her betrayal all along. She always made fun of me for going to a school with so many white people. She loved when I was sad and single — when I was just her lonely brown-skinned friend. Guys always liked Sydney better in church, honestly. She had golden skin, bright greenish eyes and her hair was always done. Her mother never let even a centimeter of nappy coils emerge before dragging Sydney back to the salon.

She loves her image. She loves being the cool friend. But I didn't expect her to go this far. That's not the Sydney I grew up with. Maybe college changed her, maybe I changed. I don't know which one it is. Dustin rubs my shoulder, sensing I'm lost in thought again.

I lean against him, never wanting to let him go but fearing that after this, he'll leave me. I know how possessive he is and I'm ashamed that another man's teeth marks are on my neck.

Kya tips a non-alcoholic kombucha can back into her throat. "Sydney probably high-tailed it out of here. Let's be real. She wouldn't stay. She knows what her friend planned to do."

"Unless she planned to gloat," Dustin says, his grasp on my shoulder tightening. I know he could have killed

Hakeem. I saw it in his eyes. I don't want him to hurt anyone. The problem with inflicting pain and violence on others is that it always comes back to you. I could have fought Dustin like a wildcat, but that wouldn't have helped, would it?

"I agree with Dustin," Makeba says after she and Jayce throw back a shot of tequila together. Tequila has special meaning to them. I don't get it.

"Keeber agreeing with me? Am I hallucinating?" Dustin mutters, waving his own hand in front of his face like that would even help.

"No, you're actually agreeing," I reply with genuine surprise. "I'm shook."

"Girl, Sydney's shady," Makeba says. "I swear I heard her cough 'no edges' walking past me when we first met."

"She helped Hakeem violate a woman, and he's totally unrepentant. We need to do another beat down," Kya says while throwing her fist into her palm for extra flair.

"Hopefully, this one doesn't shoot up a school," Cole blurts out. We all turn to look at him.

"Insensitive, Cole," Kya says. "But I don't have time for a lecture. Think like a little rat... where would you go to hide and then gloat?"

"Back to the bedroom?" I suggest, although I can't explain why the thought pops into my head. "She could be nearby in another room waiting or something."

"We locked Dustin's room, right?" Kya asks, taking the lead as usual. Even Cole knows better than to step into the leading role when Kya gets her girl boss groove going.

"Yes. I have the key," Jayce says, pulling out Dustin's keys from his pocket.

"We have to start the eulogy," Dustin says. "That's going to get the house quiet for a while and calm everyone down."

"There are people doing coke off the kitchen counter," Kya says. "A speech won't calm them down."

"What's going to calm them down, then?" Dustin grumbles.

"You might not like this very slightly dangerous idea," Kya says to everyone. "But... a gunshot."

"Absolutely the fuck not," Cole steps up. "Kya, have you lost your fucking mind?"

"I'm serious! There will be livestreams, people fleeing the party... There are only a few people who would stay no matter what, and Sydney could be one of them if Dustin's theory is correct. Jayce can message the hockey guy group chat so they know it's a hoax. Makeba can get one of Jayce's guns and fire it a couple times into the ceiling beneath Logan's room. Sorry, but I hate the Canadian kid."

"This is a risky plan, Ambrose," Dustin says, but I can tell he's considering it. I can tell they're all considering it.

"The cops will come if we fire a gun," I point out. "It's a decent plan, but… we're going to get in huge trouble."

"No, we're not," Makeba says. "Because we're going to come up with a good story and we're going to make sure Sydney and Hakeem go down for what they tried to do to our best friend."

"Ride or die," Jayce says. "That's what Makeba's always trying to explain to me."

"It's not even that complicated to understand," Makeba mutters. "But whatever, we're working on it."

"We'd better work on it quickly," Dustin says, towering over most of us and pointing to something he notices in the corner of the party. "I think those freshmen are doing it doggy-style on the pong table."

Me and my friends screech in horror while the guys laugh. Unfortunately, Dustin has a good idea. Seriously, ew. I suppose Big Sexy would appreciate it, but I certainly don't. Dustin clears his throat.

"On that note… it's time for my pet tarantula's eulogy. Anyone got liquor leftover?"

Dustin easily pushes his way through the crowd. I can tell he doesn't want to let go of me and that he also must have whispered strict instructions to Cole and Jayce, because they form a wall of muscle around me as Dustin emerges on the other side of the room at the DJ booth, bringing the music and then the party to a stop. He grabs the mic at the front of the room and clears his throat.

"You motherfuckers better stop what you're doing and listen up," he says. "This is a fucking funeral, so can I get an AMEN?"

I shake my head. I don't think Dustin's ever been inside a church. He probably would have turned into a pillar of salt before crossing the threshold anyway, so maybe I should count my lucky stars that he seems utterly unfamiliar with funeral proceedings.

Dustin talks about the first time he got Big Sexy, punctuating his speech with funny anecdotes and opportunities for the crowd of wasted college students to cheer and raise their red solo cups. By the time he finishes, with the iconic line of "that fat sexy tarantula would want us to fucking party", some girls in the front cry real tears... Doing the most, if you ask me.

Kya grabs my hand once he finishes. "Makeba got a gun during the lull. With or without the boys, we're doing this. She's scurrying off to warn Logan, but Sydney's nowhere on this floor. I had Barkov and the others check. Dustin might still be right... she's close."

"Just make sure Makeba doesn't hurt anyone. Please."

"Girl, don't worry. It's not even going to be loaded. We just need it to make the sound, you know."

Okay, this plan sounds a lot better now that I know there won't be real bullets flying around. My throat tightens, but I nod.

"What are you whispering about?" Cole says. "We're waiting for Dustin before we do anything… right?"

Kya wraps her arm around Cole and nuzzles him, nearly suffocating him with a cloud of her hair. "We would never do anything wrong, ever…"

She sounds incredibly suspicious and I don't think Cole buys her story for a second, especially since when Kya tiptoes to kiss him, we all hear a gunshot — and all hell breaks loose. I'm not the only person in the room low-key re-traumatized by the sound.

Makeba's weapon sounds more like a pistol than what B.J. used to attack our dorm, but the initial deafening crack still scares the shit out of me. I would freeze, but Dustin emerges next to me within seconds, his arm around me soothing me instantly.

"You three are so much trouble…" Cole hisses. Kya shrugs. Nothing gets between that woman and a plan. My heart quickens as I imagine Sydney's reaction. If I were Sydney, what would I do? Probably not set up my best friend to get raped… so there's that…

I can't predict her next move, and that's what I hate the most.

"Let's go upstairs and search. They cleared downstairs, and the team knows what's up."

Jayce and Cole eye me, Dustin and Kya.

"New plan, deal with the fallout from your plan," Cole

says, giving Kya a glare, which she replies to with a mischievous grin and a half-hearted apology.

Cole sighs. He definitely loves her crazy ass. Good. Because I love my best friends too.

The freshman hockey guys guard the exits as the crowd mobs them trying to escape. They make sure they make eye contact with every single person, even when angry dudes try to punch them in the face or chest, they take hits like hockey players and search for the girl with the green eyes.

Kya and Cole take the top floor. Jayce runs into the crowd to find Makeba, and I head to Dustin's floor with him. I half expect to hear screaming coming from Dustin's room, but I remember we left Hakeem bound and gagged. I don't relish the idea of my white boyfriend having a black man tied up in his room, but considering the circumstances, I can't exactly think of it that way.

Dustin presses his ear to the door, anyway.

"I can't hear anything," I tell him. "He's fine."

"I don't think so," Dustin says. "He would at least be shuffling his feet... something like that. We should open the door and check."

"I'll text Jayce."

"No need, kitten. I've got a key."

He kisses the top of my head, sending a rush of warmth through me, and then he unlocks his bedroom door, swinging it open. The first thing I notice is the temperature. Dustin always keeps his room warm, with several thermostats and heat checkers for his reptiles. He notices the cold too because he flips on his daytime lights instead of the red nightlights he keeps on for the menagerie.

Someone flung open his bedroom window. That's not the worst part. It looks like Hakeem might have been making an escape attempt. Except that's not what happened because Hakeem's still in the chair, he's still tied up, but he's slumped over and he looks...

"Dustin..." I whisper. "I think he's dead. I think Hakeem's dead."

Dustin rushes to the window and scans the grass outside.

"Fuck."

"It's cold."

Dustin glances at his enclosures, his shoulders tensing and his eyes narrowing with rage.

"I'll shut the window and get the heat back on..."

"Wait... Dustin... It's the other spider. I think..."

Dustin glances over and then glances away. "Dead. Most of them are probably dead."

I glance around Dustin's bedroom and I won't lie. It's grim. Bergie seems fine, at least. The scorpion seems shriveled up. I keep looking around for the biggest of Dustin's pets...

"Except Ovie," I tell him. "Where's Ovie?"

That snake always gets out at the worst times, I swear.

"Fuck," Dustin says, raking his fingers through his curls. "Raven, you get the hell out of here. I'm calling the cops."

"What? You can't do that!"

"There's a dead guy in my bedroom. My dad's a judge. That's 100% what I have to do. Kitten… leave."

"I'm not leaving. Sydney could be out there. Your snake could freeze to death or worse, get stepped on… I'm not going anywhere."

"The cops find a dead guy in my room, they're putting me under arrest. There's no way around it. I don't want you here."

"I'm not going to leave you to deal with my shit. I trusted Sydney. I invited her to visit me and I got myself into this situation. I'm not letting you handle it for me. We can handle it together or… actually… there are no other options."

Dustin's fierce blue eyes narrow. You don't scare me, Dustin Rathbone.

"Don't you dare blame yourself."

"It's not about blame, Dustin. There's a dead guy in my boyfriend's bedroom. It's a test. If we can get through this, we can get through everything."

Dustin's jaw clenches.

"You have a strange way of looking at the world, kitten."

"Call the cops. I'm not leaving."

He pulls out his phone and my breath catches. Dustin's right. When the cops get here, we'll probably all go to jail. That will be the end of my college dreams, a year abroad in Italy and it will definitely be the end of our relationship. I can't let Dustin take the fall for this. I approach Hakeem for any signs of what may have happened to him.

I don't want to get near him. I can still smell the liquor on him from before, and the scent turns my stomach. He wasn't too drunk not to know what he was doing. And he knew that I didn't want him. I couldn't stop talking about Dustin.

I press my finger to his skin and search for a pulse, but his body is so cold that I know I won't find one. Before I can throw up, there's a knock on Dustin's door and I hear Jayce and Makeba on the other side. Makeba sounds shrill, but I can't quite make out what she's saying. I drag her by the arm into Dustin's bedroom. Jayce follows, holding Ovie around his shoulders.

"It's fucking cold in here," Jayce says. Ovie wraps his head around Jayce's forearm. Dustin nods and gestures towards the chair.

"Holy shit. You killed him?!" Makeba hisses.

"He didn't kill him!" I blurt out. "I walked in here with him and we found Dustin's window open and Hakeem dead."

"Guys, Ovie's squeezing," Jayce interjects.

Dustin's still on the phone, speaking calmly, leaving me to explain everything to Jayce and Makeba in a hushed voice. Dustin leans against the window and covers the receiver.

"They want me to stay on the line until they get here," he says. Jayce nods and puts his hands on my shoulder and Makeba's. We both grimace as both ends of Ovie graze our arms. What is it with these boys and this snake? Jayce ushers us just outside of Dustin's bedroom and turns to both of us with a stern look in his eye.

"This isn't appropriate for you all to be here. Go down-stairs, wait for my step-dad to get here. We'll need lawyers and we'll need to find that girl."

"You think Sydney did this?" Makeba asks, dodging Ovie's head as he curiously reaches out to her. Jayce restrains the snake slightly better than before.

"Yes," Jayce replies. "We all know Dustin has a few screws loose, sorry Raven, but if he killed a guy, he wouldn't leave the guy's body in his bedroom to get cold."

"Do you think Ovie did it?" I whisper.

Jayce shakes his head. "Turns out, Ovie really doesn't eat people. He might try, but… he wouldn't get very far."

"I don't believe that," Makeba says. "He tried to eat you once."

"If he tried to eat Hakeem, we wouldn't have found Ovie

in Cole's old bedroom," Jayce says. "This was that chick who hurt Raven."

I want to argue with Jayce's excellent point. Sydney's my friend, and I want to defend her, but there's nothing left to defend. She did this.

I read so many romance novels, I feel like I should have seen this plot twist coming. I would have expected Dustin to break up with me or something tonight, especially since he was acting so weird, but I never expected this.

"Did Kya come up here yet?" Makeba asks.

"Not yet," I reply, wrapping my arms around myself. "I hope she gets here soon."

Loud footsteps on the stairs freeze us all in place. Jayce's body tightens, ready to fight even with a snake on his shoulder. It's Cole and Logan – and they have Sydney between them, fighting for her freedom but unable to escape from the two strong hockey boys holding her arms.

Sydney thrashes and makes a sound like a wild animal.

"She's a fighter, eh?" Logan says, as they drag Sydney toward us. Cole grunts and dodges an attempted kick from Sydney, who retaliates further by dropping her weight to the ground in an attempt to escape. Between Cole and Logan, she's powerless.

"The cops are on their way," Jayce says. "Hakeem's dead."

Sydney yowls and thrashes again. Cole squeezes tighter and grunts as Logan helps restrain her.

"Good. Where's Kya?"

"We don't know," Makeba says. "I thought she would be with you."

"Shit…"

"What about Dustin?" Logan asks.

"Calling the cops."

"And hopefully a fucking lawyer," Cole grunts as Sydney lands another kick in his thighs. I notice when Sydney lands, she winces. Something's wrong with her feet, which is why she can't get away. She's thrashing and kicking, but each one hurts her.

"Sydney, stop it," I snap, and my acknowledgement actually works to get her to stop kicking Cole Seabrook.

"Now you got something to say to me?" Sydney says. "After you get these white boys to drag me up here? HELP! SOMEBODY HELP!"

"Are you serious? How the hell are you the victim here? You killed somebody, Sydney."

"First of all, that was an accident."

"And second?" Makeba asks.

Sydney wriggles again. "Y'all let go of me! I didn't do shit, okay? He was in your boyfriend's bedroom. Maybe your gay ass boyfriend did something to him."

Jayce yanks Makeba back before she can fight. While I want to beat Sydney's ass, I want to keep my boyfriend out of prison even more. If we hurt her, we're all going down for at least assault. We need to keep calm. I glance at Cole and Logan. They understand.

"We're going to let you go," Cole says. "And you're going to talk to Raven until the cops get here. Make any wrong moves and we're going to break your fucking legs."

"Cole!" Kya balks, emerging at the top of the stairs. "Please tell me that was warranted."

"Trust me, it was," Makeba says. "We got her. Where the hell have you been?"

"Cops outside," Kya huffs. "I didn't know what the hell was going on, but I called my dad and he has three lawyers on the way here. I think I saw Judge Clutterbuck's car out front."

Jayce still gets uncomfortable when his step-dad's name comes up, but according to Makeba, they've been healing. If he's here already, he might have been in a nearby county for work. Maybe everything will be okay.

Cole and Logan let go of Sydney's arms. She glances down the hall like she's thinking about running for it, but Kya folds her arms and snaps, "Don't even think about it."

"Why did you do this, Sydney?" I ask. "Seriously? We've been friends for years. I don't know how long you've known Hakeem, but… you killed him."

"First of all, I didn't kill him and if I killed him, it was an accident."

"Sydney… he hurt me. You hurt me. I just want an answer."

"You think you're all that, Raven. That's the problem with you. You think you're better than everybody because you like books and got a scholarship. You're not better than any of us."

"I never said I was better than anybody."

"But you sure acted like it. We joke about dating white men. We don't actually do it."

"Well, I do it," Makeba blurts out, failing to read the room, but somehow lightening the tension, anyway.

"So do I," Kya says, folding her arms and sensing the opportunity to give a lecture about equality that she can't give up on. "Are you calling us race traitors because of who we choose to date? Didn't our forefathers and our foremothers fight for this little thing called equality?"

"Maybe I should bring Ovie back in…" Jayce mutters.

"You keep your ass right here for this," Kya says. "Listen, Sydney. We might not know Raven as long as you have, but we clearly know her better. She doesn't hate her race, and she doesn't hate her people because of Dustin. She sees the best in everybody – which is probably how your trifling ass even got to her."

I don't think anyone has ever told Sydney off like that in her life. But that's Kya for you, always ready to tell somebody off like an angry first-grade teacher.

"You don't get it," Sydney says. "None of you get it."

"I don't want to get it," I tell her. "You betrayed me. I'm sorry, but there's no reason to treat a friend that way."

Sydney glowers at me with a seething rage that stuns me. She was my best friend…

Dustin pushes the door to his bedroom open. "The cops are on their way up."

I move closer to him and wrap my arm around Dustin's waist. I don't want to let go.

20

OUR FUTURE

DUSTIN

We have a long night before the cops let us go. My dad waits in the police station waiting room for me and Raven to emerge from questioning with the lawyers. Jayce and Makeba are already with the judge. Kya and Cole are staying at a nearby hotel at her dad's expense before Cole heads back to Boston tomorrow. I'm not ready for my dad to meet Raven.

I don't know how he'll react to her. I can venture a guess, but I hope he doesn't embarrass me the way he says I always embarrass him. I'm just his fuck up kid. He can't pay enough money to keep out of trouble.

"Ready to meet my dad?"

"I know nothing about him. So... no. If he's anything like you, he's probably terrifying."

I shrug. There's some truth to that.

"Maybe you'll understand me better after you meet him. He says anything that pisses you off. Just let me know."

"I can handle myself."

Yeah. She can. She can handle herself, she can handle me… I don't think there's a beast on this earth that Raven Rose couldn't tame. She's a walking romantic and even if I prefer darkness, shuttering myself up alone, getting lost in my own thoughts, Raven makes me want to look for light. Even now, after a night of shenanigans that nearly ended in some really awful shit, she has a fucking glow around her.

I can't believe I wanted to let her go. Breaking up with Raven seems incredibly stupid now. But what seems like an even dumber idea is introducing her to my dad. She knows its him the second we walk into the waiting room. Dad's older, taller than me by a couple inches, and people mistake us for brothers regularly. If it weren't for his greying hair, we could pass for brothers. We have the same eyes. The same piercing stare.

"You came down to the police station without a collared shirt?" he lectures, ignoring Raven's existence and scrutinizing me instead. If he wanted boarding school to fix me up, he shouldn't have sent me to Milton. Everyone knows Middlesex or St. Mark's boys are more polished.

I ignore him.

"Dad, this is my girlfriend, Raven."

"Girlfriend? What woman would waste her time with you?"

Dad turns his gaze on her and Raven sticks her hand out with a broad smile on her face as if my dad's insults are nothing.

"Nice to meet you, Mr. Rathbone. I'm Raven."

"Raven. Call me George. It's nice to meet you. I assume you attend college with my son and you aren't... a stripper."

"Dad!"

Raven doesn't seem to mind. My father smirks at her. "Sorry. His last so-called girlfriend was a stripper."

"Do you mind not telling that to my current girlfriend?"

"Dustin has questionable taste in women. I can see why you might be concerned."

Dad grins. "I like this one. Why didn't you introduce me to her earlier?"

"Probably because of how we got together," Raven says.

"I see. I'm sure that's a good story. Dustin? I'll get you out of this. Why don't you take your girlfriend somewhere more... clean?"

"Yes, dad. Thanks for coming down here."

"Just keep your nose clean. Raven? Nice to meet you."

He shakes both of our hands before walking off. It's not like I expected more emotions from George Rathbone, but I hope he doesn't disappoint Raven. She doesn't seem to take my dad's attitude personally. She still has a pretty smile on her face and slips her hand into mine.

"We should get out of here. Your dad's right."

"That went…"

"Dustin. I get it. You and your dad aren't close, and he's probably a bit of a dick. I can handle him just like I can handle you."

"You don't handle me…" I protest.

"Yes, I do."

"Fine," I grumble. There's no point in arguing with her. "I'll take you back to campus. I have a lot of shit to take care of over there, anyway."

Raven's hand wraps around mine. There's going to be a colossal mess when I get back to the room. We got Ovie back in the enclosure before I left, but several of my animals are… dead. I could get all choked up, but I'm just happy to have Raven back and happy we don't have to worry about Sydney or anyone hurting her anymore.

"I let this shit happen to you," I murmur. "It won't happen again, babe. I promise."

And I fucking mean that promise, even if it changes my entire plan for the night and forever.

"Come on," Raven says. "Let's get in the truck. I'm exhausted and I have to call my mom back. She already heard about Sydney through the church grapevine and they're blaming Satan."

"Satan? Is that what you called me to your family?"

"Hilarious."

"I distinctly heard you referring to me as the white devil."

"I don't remember that, white devil," Raven says, yawning and resting her cute little head on my shoulders. "Let's get out of here."

I drive her back to Pesthouse. She's half-asleep the entire way, but I don't mind. Tonight was too crazy. I came too close to losing her, and a guy died in my fucking bedroom, not to mention half the pets in my collection. I guess I'll have to start over… and maybe when I graduate, I can get Raven a pet she'll actually like. A cat. I'll have to get her a cat.

Logan whipped the other guys into shape, cleaning the house while we were gone. The cops questioned him outside, but didn't bring him down to the station. Maybe I had the dumbass Canadian wrong, and he's a good guy at heart. The house is fucking spotless when we get back. It's time to face the carnage of my bedroom. Raven doesn't hesitate to burst up the stairs, and she opens the door to my bedroom first.

It's a little warmer, but still not warm enough for all my animals. My tarantulas and scorpion are dead. Bergie huddles under his heat lamp for as much warmth as he can absorb. Ovie sits still in his enclosure too, not likely to get out again for at least another week.

"We'll have to have more funerals," Raven says. "But judging by the last one… maybe we should tone it down."

"A private memorial service seems more appropriate."

"I'll help you clean up."

Raven dutifully helps me clean up, but I want her to rest and sit back. When I instruct her to obey me in logical terms, she snaps that she isn't my property and that she'll do what she wants. Sigh. This is the woman I love. She's the woman that I want to spend the rest of my time with. Once my room looks significantly better, I call Raven over to me and wrap her in a big, warm hug.

"I don't want you to leave tonight."

"I'm not going anywhere."

"Good. But kitten… I have a confession to make."

Her body relaxes. "Finally. I knew something was weird."

"Yeah."

I don't want to let go of her, but I need to tell her. I pull away from Raven and keep her hand in mine.

"I wanted to end things tonight."

"I knew it."

"Not for the reasons you think. I can't play in Italy next year, Raven. I can't be with you. And I don't want to hold you back... but maybe there's another way out. I didn't want to leave you and last night, I definitely don't want to leave you. I want to marry you."

My voice doesn't tremble or hesitate because I fucking mean it.

"I didn't think you were the marrying type of guy."

She's genuinely fucking shocked. I hate that there's any part of her that might be unclear in my intentions. I can't let that happen.

"Come here, you," I whisper, grabbing her hips and pulling her body against mine. "I want to marry you. I want you to go to Italy. I want... We're going to make this work. If you want it to work, I'm all in."

She leans against me, her gorgeous copper skin contrasting against mine. She's so fucking beautiful.

"How can I go to Italy and leave you here? It's not fair. You're already paying for everything."

I knew she would say this. There's no arguing with Raven, but I can't let her give up on her dream of going to Italy.

"I'm not letting you give up because of me."

"I wouldn't. I'm not. It's just..."

"Raven. I know you. You love romance. You love being in love. But your dreams matter too."

"Don't tell me what matters to me, Dustin. You're not my owner anymore."

"I'm not trying to be your owner." I try to give a level-headed response, but Raven's getting under my skin. I won't let her give up on this dream just because of me.

"I'm not going to Italy."

"You're not staying. I won't allow it," I command her, but Raven folds her arms and seems to have no intention of listening to me.

"I'm not giving up on a dream, Dustin."

"I can't make you stay because of me. I won't allow it."

"I'm not staying for you," she blurts out. "I just... I wanted to go to Italy, but honestly, my cousin Lisa's staying over there right now and it's not all it's cracked up to be on social media."

"That's it?"

"It sounds dumb but... I'd rather go somewhere I can sit inside and just read my books."

"Somewhere grey and rainy?"

"Yeah. Sure."

"What about London?"

Raven raises an eyebrow. "What about it?"

"Laguna Grove has study abroad programs in London.

Duh. You apply, I can still travel to the UK. My dad has a place there. It could be perfect."

"That's a shockingly good idea."

"What's so shocking about it?"

Raven quickly moves on from her potentially insulting comment.

"What about your menagerie?"

"Jayce wouldn't mind looking after them for a year. I think."

"You trust Jayce not to let Ovie out for an entire year?"

"He's getting more responsible. I think he can handle it."

"If we do this," Raven says. "Promise we don't miss Makeba's wedding or Kya's baby. I still want to be there for my friends. My real friends."

"You will have whatever you want, kitten. You've been my greatest obsession for... a long time. I'll do anything to keep you."

Raven moves closer to me and I kiss the top of her forehead. Don't let her go, you idiot. Whatever you do, don't let her go.

"Good," she whispers. "Because sometimes I think you'll get tired of it and run away, and stand outside some other girl's window."

I chuckle. That could never happen. There isn't another woman like Raven.

"Never. You're one of a kind, Raven. You're the only person I've ever met who didn't see my darkness and run away. I want that... forever."

"Dustin..."

"I mean it. After England, whenever you're ready... I'm going to ask and I'm going to make you my wife."

"What about hockey? What about... I don't know. Everything else."

"Nothing is more important to me than you, Raven."

"Not even weed? Or Ovie?"

"Not even weed or Ovie. Now come, kitten. I need you in my bed tonight. I need you close."

21

THE DREAM LIFE

A YEAR AND A HALF LATER

RAVEN

Dustin wraps his arm around me.

"Mind the bump!"

"Sorry," he murmurs, pressing his nose into my shoulders. "It's been hell to keep this secret, Mrs. Rathbone."

"I know... I know... but after the Jamaica vs. Boston family drama at Makeba's wedding and Kya with the surprise twin boys... I just wanted us to get away. Just you and me."

Dustin's palm rests against my baby bump. When we finally get back to America, we have a lot of news for our friends. A baby, an elopement in Italy, a book deal in London and then Dustin's biggest surprise...

"What I really can't wait for is getting your ass into bed

when we land," Dustin says. "I want the entire apartment turned into a giant sex dungeon."

"Dustin. I'm pregnant. We have to keep the sex dungeon in the sex dungeon."

"Fine…" Dustin murmurs, nuzzling me closer. "I can't help my deepest obsession."

The announcer calls for First Class to board and Dustin leaps out of his seat. He has no patience for airports, but at least he carries all my bags for me. Everyone I see congratulates me on the baby bump. It's been nearly impossible to keep this secret from my best friends for four months. Dustin's better at keeping secrets – much better.

When we nestle in our seats, Dustin immediately pulls me close and throws a large blanket over me. "Rest, kitten. I'll see you on the other side of the Atlantic."

When we arrive in Boston, Dustin gets all our bags into the limo and I can't stop squirming excitedly in my seat. We're moving into our first apartment together for the summer. After I have the babies, we're moving to a house closer to campus so I can finish my degree and Dustin's going to be… a stay at home dad. After that, he wants to open a rink in Boston and start running hockey camps.

The car takes us to our building. 100 Bank Street. Dustin bought us the penthouse at the top and we don't even need a key to get in. It's a 'biometrics only' building and I've never even conceived of living somewhere so fancy. The staff helps us with our bags and we get into the elevator together, exhausted from our flight and the massive time difference. Going backwards is hard…

Dustin presses his palm to the small of my back as we ride to the P floor. The ride takes almost a minute and when the doors swing open, my head rushes. I spent my teen years reading billionaire romance novels, stories about rich men and regular women, and I never expected those novels to exist as anything more than a fantasy.

"Kitten, we're home," Dustin announces.

"This is really ours. All of this."

"Yes," he says. "I can't wait to see the baby room."

"You spent ages planning it. Come on, let's go."

"No," Dustin says. "I want to fuck you in every room before we get to the bedroom. So we need to start here."

"Dustin! Is your mind seriously on sex after hours on a plane, then an hour in a car?"

"Yes…"

He wraps his arms around me and then presses that thing into my back. My pussy throbs. Pregnancy hormones have weakened me against Dustin's advances. His big dick pressing into me isn't doing me any favors. I turn around and lock eyes with him. I'm never going to get tired of those gorgeous eyes and the way they stare so intensely.

He has stalker eyes. But those obsessive blue eyes are also lover's eyes. Father's eyes. I know Dustin will throw himself into what he loves 100%, the way he did with me. Sometimes, 150%.

"You want to have sex before we see Ovie? I got Jayce's text that he was 'successfully transferred'."

"Yes," Dustin murmurs. "So take your panties off, kitten. Just drop them."

There are quite a few steps before I get to my panties. First, Dustin puts his lips to my neck, distracting me for a moment as pleasure surges through me. I wriggle until my purse falls off my shoulders. Dustin chuckles and grabs my hips, pressing my ass against his crotch.

He leans against me and whispers. "Good girl. Better get those off before I have to spank you."

I know he's joking – we paused our spanking when I confirmed my pregnancy – but there's a part of me that still flinches when Dustin threatens to palm my ass. I drop my leggings and my underwear quickly and hurriedly slip out of my shoes and socks too as I work my body free.

Dustin kisses me and hoists me directly over to the couch in our Penthouse's living room. I squeal as he stumbles over to the couch, but instead of throwing me onto the couch, Dustin bends me over the back and drops to his knees. Before I can protest, he parts my thighs and slips his tongue between my legs.

My cheeks grow hot. I'm totally not fresh after spending over nine hours in the sky. Dustin slurps at my lower lips and rubs his tongue over my clit before nibbling more at my lower lips. Holy shit.

"Stay still," he growls, spreading my thighs further apart with a tighter grasp to allow his tongue greater access to my pussy. Just his firm palms on my thighs would be enough to make me wet, but Dustin's long tongue happens to be flexible, and he rubs it over my slit until I emit an unwilling moan. I press my hips back and Dustin's hair tickles my butt cheeks as he slides his tongue all the way back, pressing it against my back door. I yelp in surprise as he touches it with his tongue.

Dustin chuckles and pulls away, kissing my ass cheeks. Impatient for a climax, I wiggle my butt and Dustin lands a gentle smack on my ass.

"Before I make you cum," he whispers. "I want to taste your ass. I'm going to use my finger. I'm going to be gentle. Do I have your permission, kitten?"

Dustin sinks his teeth into my ass cheek like he's biting into a peach. I know that's not the part of my ass he wants to taste.

"Yes. You have my permission."

He doesn't waste an instant. Dustin spreads my ass cheeks apart and presses his soaked tongue against my back door. I make out an ungodly sound somewhere between a yelp and a moan, which only provokes Dustin to grip my butt tighter and swirl his tongue in slow circles around my back door. He licks his lips and then drives his tongue over my pussy lips before returning his attention back to my ass.

"Cum for me, kitten," he murmurs, nibbling his way up my thighs and then rubbing his tongue over my clit for a few more moments. Dustin presses his thumb against my soaked back door and eats my pussy until my core tightens and I feel my body edging towards release.

He licks my clit faster and then eases his thumb into my ass as he wraps his lips around my clit and sucks hard. I explode when he slides his thumb in my ass past the first knuckle. I can't take the pressure in my ass and Dustin's tongue against my clit without cumming hard. I moan and ease my hips forward, my baby bumps pressing into the back of the couch until I adjust myself and prop my body up with my elbows so the gush of euphoria doesn't force me to fall over.

Dustin doesn't intend to let that happen. As my weight falls into my elbows, he stands behind me and wraps one arm around my hips as he works to free his hardness from his pants. Dustin's pants thud from the weight of his belt and wallet once he works them free.

I feel the soft heat from the head of Dustin's cock teasing at my entrance as he rests it there and sucks in a sharp breath.

"I can't slow down," he growls, using his grasp on my waist to pull my body against his. "Lift your leg."

I lift one of my legs to the back of the couch, opening my thighs for Dustin's access.

"I wish I could lick you again," he murmurs. "But right now, I need this…"

Dustin eases his hips forward. My pussy resists the first push from his cock. Dustin grips me tighter and then edges his hips forward again. This time, he gets the head of his cock between my thighs and I feel the first surge of pain from accommodating Dustin's freakish size.

A low, unwilling growl emits from his throat. "Fuck…"

"More…" I whimper.

Too big. That was the first thing I thought when I saw Dustin's freakishly large dick the first time. Now, I can't imagine anything else. I can't imagine giving up that deep sensation of fullness. Dustin rubs my tummy and my core tightens as his cock pushes deeper inside me.

"Easy," He murmurs. "Tell me if it hurts…"

"More…"

Dustin pushes forward again. He stretches me wide, but he still has inches left of his cock to deliver. I whimper and push back to meet his hips. Dustin's fingers sink into the curvy flesh of my thighs and he thrusts forward with a final deep push. I moan and climax as Dustin's cock fills me.

"Great," he says. "Now I'm fucking you in the living room… I think we have 12 rooms left."

12 rooms? Dustin can't possibly have sex twelve times tonight. He has a lot of stamina but… Apparently, he

wants to test my doubt. He pulls my body against his and moves his hips slowly, plunging his cock deep and then biting down on my neck as he withdraws. His bites aren't hard enough to break skin, but they feel wild and possessive. After a few more thrusts, I cum again and feel a warm gush between my thighs as I climax.

Dustin pulls out of me and turns my body to face him. As he kisses me, his palm runs over my bare ass and he squeezes my butt cheeks, pulling my body against his.

"You pick the next room, kitten. Kitchen or bathroom."

"Kitchen."

The choice is simple. Feeling Dustin inside me on our new kitchen counters feels hopelessly romantic and naughty beyond belief. I want the full happy ending. I want the romance with the tall scary guy with piercing blue eyes and a heart of gold. I don't just want to find my happiness in books anymore. I want to believe that I deserve the real thing.

"The real thing" juts away from Dustin's torso, still raging with his desire for me. I wrap my hand around it and Dustin tilts his head to the side like a happy but uncertain puppy.

"Before we go to the kitchen," I whisper, pulling him closer to me, dragging him by the dick a little. "Let me get on my knees for you. Please."

"No," Dustin growls. "I'll cum right in your mouth.

Kitchen, kitten. Please... just your touch makes me want to burst."

"I should return the favor."

He leans forward and grabs my cheeks with his hand. "No. You should go to the kitchen so I can fuck you properly. Now do what I say or I swear Raven, I really will spank you."

This time, I believe his threat. I release my tight grip around his cock and his shoulders relax.

"Yes, sir," I reply teasingly. "I'll present my cunt to you in the kitchen immediately."

"You don't know what that does to me," he says. "Now hurry. Or I'll drag you there like a caveman."

"Don't you dare, Mr. Rathbone."

"Run along then, Mrs. Rathbone. Or I swear, I'll do it."

I scamper to the kitchen without turning to look behind me. I can hear Dustin's firm footfall behind me. He barely waits for me to get past the threshold before he grabs me squealing and plops my bare ass on the counter. As I wince and wriggle from the cold marble, Dustin spreads my lower lips with his fingers and pushes two fingers inside me. I cry out. This feels good, but I'm impatient with the way those fingers tease me.

I want more than Dustin's fingers. I want his dick. Badly. He teases me until I push against his chest with frustration. Then he stops teasing and uses his hands to make me cum. As I climax, he slips his fingers out and eases his big cock into my pussy as I moan.

My fingers sink into his curls, and I pull his firm, muscular body closer to mine. His muscular hips spread my thighs, and he pins me to the counter with his cock as he starts slowly thrusting. Making love. Neither of us cares what position we're in as long as the love between us starts slow and sweet. We kiss and touch and nibble with the gentlest movement of our hips until we can't take it anymore.

When we desperately need to come, our desire changes us into animals and we thrash our bodies together in our kitchen until we cum simultaneously. Dustin's first orgasm shakes his body and his muscles tense, so I can see every defined detail of his chiseled body. His face turns bright red and his pupils dilate so widely that his gorgeous blue eyes look black.

We make love in every room of the house. It takes all night. By the time we reach the bedroom, Dustin and I are sore and sweaty, not to mention exhausted. We don't bother to shower or change when we land under the covers together. Our gross, naked bodies melt together and we fall asleep cuddling.

I feel eyes boring into me before I wake up. Humans — at least human women — have a sixth sense about when someone or something is watching us. I read somewhere that it's because the males of our species hunted us, and we need that extra sixth sense to stay woke when a man might look at us.

My eyes snap open and I expect them to be Dustin's gorgeous eyes. Instead, there's a hard, scaly face centimeters away from mine and the eyes belong to Ovie — Dustin's escape artist snake. I shriek.

"DUSTIN!"

He's not lying next to me in bed, which I expect because he still barely sleeps. His nightmares have definitely improved, but he only 'needs' four hours of sleep.

"DUSTIN!"

My next shriek actually sounds like more of a croak. I've never fully conquered my fear of Ovie. Watching that thing chow down on a mouse didn't improve the situation in the slightest. I hear Dustin's footsteps outside the bedroom and I holler his name again.

He thrusts the door open and tilts his head to the side. "Babe. Have you seen Ovie?"

"YES!"

"Oh shit. Hold on…"

"Dustin, that snake is going to eat our children."

"He won't. He doesn't eat people."

"He doesn't eat adult people. The snake could eat our kids. Our children, Dustin. Snake food."

"Is that one of your religious prophecies again?" Dustin grumbles.

I roll my eyes. I should have never confessed to him about Sydney's prophecy and how, honestly, she probably made the whole thing up. I never really talked about it with my mama. Dustin approaches the bed and allows Ovie to crawl up his arm. Mercifully, he puts Ovie back into his cage and then returns with a cup of herbal tea.

"Some mint tea for your troubles, wifey?"

"We've talked about how wifey is even worse than kitten, right?"

"But you're black, Raven. I need to be down for our kids. Call you my wifey. My lil' shawty."

I grimace. Dustin's attempts to be down for our kids don't involve him devolving into some cringey Eminem wanna-be.

"Please never call me lil' shawty in front of anyone, especially not Kya."

Dustin isn't ready for the lecture that would ensue, and he knows it.

"Fine," he says. "Take the tea. Let me rub your feet."

"When did you get so romantic?"

"Pretty much the day I saw you."

"Wait…" I tell him. "Use my jojoba oil."

"Your Jo-Jo oil?"

I sigh. Some things this white boy won't ever understand.

"Yes. That one."

"Gotcha, kitten. Now lie still, enjoy your tea… daddy's got you."

•

I have another hockey romance series which begins October 30th 2023.

The Laguna Grove rivals, McGraw College Minotaurs have their own dark bad boys and their own spicy stories…
Click here to order my next steamy/dark hockey romance books.

Click here for an update when the next book comes out:
bit.ly/textjamila

ABOUT JAMILA JASPER

The hotter and darker the romance, the better.

That's the Jamila Jasper promise.

If you enjoy sizzling multicultural romance stories that dare to *go there* you'll enjoy any Jamila Jasper title you pick up.

Open-minded readers who appreciate **shamelessly sexy romance novels** featuring black women of all shapes and sizes paired with smokin' hot white men are welcome.

Sign up for her e-mail list here to receive one of these FREE hot stories, exclusive offers and an update of Jamila's publication schedule:
bit.ly/jamilajasperromance

Get text message updates on new books:
https://slkt.io/gxzM

EXTREMELY IMPORTANT LINKS

ALL BOOKS BY JAMILA JASPER

https://linktr.ee/JamilaJasper

SIGN UP FOR EMAIL UPDATES

Bit.ly/jamilajasperromance

SOCIAL MEDIA LINKS

https://www.jamilajasperromance.com/

GET MERCH

https://www.redbubble.com/people/jamilajasper/shop

GET FREEBIE (VIA TEXT)

https://slkt.io/qMk8

READ SERIAL (NEW CHAPTERS WEEKLY)

www.patreon.com/jamilajasper

JAMILA JASPER

Diverse Romance For Black Women

MORE JAMILA JASPER ROMANCE

<u>Pick your poison…</u>

Delicious interracial romance novels for all tastes. Long novels, short stories, audiobooks and more.

Hit the link to experience my full catalog.

FULL CATALOG BY JAMILA JASPER:
https://linktr.ee/JamilaJasper

PATREON

13 SEASONS OF SERIAL CHAPTERS

NEW preview chapters published WEEKLY on my Patreon.

Read all 6 seasons of *Unfuckable* (Ben & Libby's story)…

UNFUCKABLE

For a small monthly fee, you get exclusive access to over 375 chapters of my first completed bwwm dark and spicy serial romance, as well as the spin-off serial...

DESPICABLE

The second serial, despicable has 300 chapters available for all Patreon subscribers to access instantly and... we officially have a **third completed spin-off bwwm romance series.**

And yes you get access to all of this at the $5/month tier with more benefits at more pricey tiers.

The third serial is about Clover + Thomas. Thomas has a shocking connection to a character in the second serial and Clover is an all-new African American female lead.

POWERLESS

This series has three *very long* "seasons" of chapters, the length of five full-length novels all-together.

You will probably have over three months of binge-reading before catching up to current content, making this one of the most 'bang for your buck' author Patreon subscriptions out there.

Don't take my word for it.
Check the post history:
www.patreon.com/jamilajasper

PATREON HAS MORE THAN THE ONGOING SERIAL...

INSTANT ACCESS

- NEW merchandise tiers with **t-shirts, totes, mugs,** stickers and MORE!

- **<u>FREE paperback</u>** with all new tiers
- **<u>FREE short story audiobooks</u>** and audiobook samples when they're ready
- #FirstDraftLeaks of Prologues and first chapters **weeks** before I hit publish
- Behind the scenes notes
- Polls and story contribution
- Comments & LIVELY community discussion with likeminded interracial romance readers.

LEARN MORE ABOUT SUPPORTING A DIVERSE ROMANCE AUTHOR

<u>www.patreon.com/jamilajasper</u>

THANK YOU KINDLY

Thank you to all my readers, new and old for your support with this new year.

I look forward to making 2023 an INCREDIBLE year for interracial romance novels. I want to thank you all for joining along on the journey.

www.patreon.com/jamilajasper

Thank you to my most supportive readers — my Patreon subscribers!:

Martha

Nikki Valentina

xjkpop

Valeria

BlkBae

SweetS

Msteeq

Rhonda

Darrah

Killa

Shavon

Misty

India

Kassandra

Imani

Nala

Chantell

Benvinda

Roger

Lexi B

Zapphire

Vbrooks

Tasha G

Kiera

Valencia

Stacy

YANITZA

Texansgurl76

Emma

Tinette

Jenny

Mariah

Nale

Tanisha

Trenita

Shelle

dulcemaria413

Shanice

Letarsha

Tania

Neeka

Julia

Linda

Lisa

Jiannie

Jillian

Tameka

Asia

Scarlette

Olwyn

R W

Fayefaefee

Brianna

Tiffany

Katie

Diamond

Kera

Tia

Love Reading

Dominique

Sheria

Jennifer

Georgette

Monique

Wendolyn

King Turtle22

Jessica

Nic M.

JustChill

DJC

Atira

TheeLastHokage

Yvonne

Chrissy

Janelle

Rian

LaRonda

LaRonda

Deanna

dlawson382

Jasmine

Haley

Belinda

Sercee

Yvonne

Jadelock

Farah

Tamiya

Quin

J.Payton

Geek Girl

Ashley

Rubi

Pilar

Sandra

Jurnee

Anni

Shannet

Joneesa

GlitzyHydra

Amanda

Barbara

Brianna

Jamica

Lyons

MARY ANN

Marketia

SarahD

LoverofHawaiiHearts

ceblue

Yolanda

MonaGirl Lewis

Dianna

Mary

amna

Nysha

fayola

Ty

Abria

Shyra

Andi-Mariee

Jamila

Naee's World

KEISHA

Jennett

Fredericka

Candece

Chante

Pholuv

Lydia A

Sabrina

JM

Jackie

Mo

Natrilly83
Ashaunte
Tolu
Margaret
Wendolyn
Lori
Dionne
ZLB
Kristina
Nicol
ELBERT
A. Harris
Jesi
Brenda
Desiree
Angela
Frances
LaShan
Only1ToniD
Debbie T.
Tiffanie
April L
shawnte
Kay
Lisema
Yvonne F
Natasha
Colleen
Julia
Amy
Jacklyn

Shyan R

Kiana B

Pearl

Javonda

Sheron

Maxine

Dash

Alicia

margaret

Love2Read

Juliette

Monica

Sandhya

MaryC

Trinity

Brittany

June

Ashleigh

Nene

Nene

Deborah

Nikki M

Dee

TyKira

Kimmey

Laytoya

Shel W

Arlene

Judith

Mary

Shanida

Rachel

Damzel

Ahnjala

Kenya

momo

BJ

Akeshia

Melissa

Tiffany

sherbear

Nini J

Curtresa

REGGIE A.

Ashley

Mia

Tink138110

Phia

Sharon

Charlotte

Assiatu C

Regina

Romanda

Catherine

Gaynor

BF

Perpetua

Tasha G

Henri Ann

sara

skkent

Rosalyn

Danielle
Deborah J
Kirsten
ANA
Taylor R.
Charlene
Louanna
Michelle
Tamika
Lauren
RoHyde
Natasha
Shekynah
Cassie
AnnaBooms
Keitheena
Nick R
Gennifer M
Rayna
Anton
Jaleda
Kimvodkna
JaTonn
Jazmine
Anoushka
Raynischa
Audrey
Valeria
Courtney
Donna
Patrisha

Jenetha

LaKisha J.

Ayana

Taylor

Christy

Monica

FreyaJo

GRACE

Kisha

Christine

Alexandra

Amber

Natasha

Stephanie

LaKisha

kristylove7

Cynthea

DENICE

Latoya

monifacd .

Doneishia

Mariah

Gerry

Yolanda T

Yolanda P

Susan D

Phyllis H

Alisa K

Daveena K

Desiree S

Kimberly B

Robin B

Gary S

Stephanie MG

Georgette A

Kathy

Marty

JanetDaniels

Megan

Shelle

Delores

Janet

Lydia

Phyllis

Freda

Charlott R

<u>Join the Patreon Community.</u>